3800 18 0056267 4

HIGH LIFE HIGHLAND

KT-417-414

PRAISE FOR THE GUILTY PARTY

'Dark, thrilling, impossible to predict'
ERIN KELLY

'Brilliant'
ANN CLEEVES

'Toxic friendship at its worst. Disturbing
and dark yet very compelling'
MEL SHERRATT

'A morally-complex, haunting thriller. The prose is
breath-taking. The plot, layered, tense and utterly
captivating. If you're in the market for something
sublime, you could not do better than this'
IMRAN MAHMOOD

'Gripping, haunting, unstoppable. A
ruthless and savage page turner'
ROSS ARMSTRONG

'A dark and immersive journey into the heart
of a toxic friendship group and the lies they tell
themselves and each other to survive. I loved it'
HARRIET TYCE

'A psychological *tour de force* with a superb plot from one of the UK's most gifted crime writers'
KATE RHODES

'An intriguing, deftly plotted novel of unravelling friendships and dark secrets'
LIZ NUGENT

'Honest, dark and searching. I couldn't put it down'
ALISON JOSEPH

'Compelling, twisty, thought-provoking, and utterly unputdownable'
ROZ WATKINS

'Mel McGrath expertly peels back the layers of her characters' moral self-justification to expose the ugly truth. A scorching, clever thriller'
TAMMY COHEN

Mel McGrath is an Essex girl, co-founder of Killer Women, and an award-winning writer of fiction and non-fiction.

As MJ McGrath she writes the acclaimed Edie Kiglatuk series of Arctic mysteries, which have been optioned for TV, were twice longlisted for the CWA Gold Dagger, and were *Times* and *Financial Times* thrillers of the year. As Melanie McGrath she wrote the critically acclaimed, bestselling memoir *Silvertown*. As Mel McGrath she is the author of the bestselling psychological thriller *Give Me the Child*. *The Guilty Party* is her latest novel.

The Guilty Party

Mel McGrath

HIGH LIFE	
HIGHLAND LIBRARIES	
38001800562674	
BERTRAMS	05/03/2019
THR	£12.99
AF	

ONE PLACE. MANY STORIES

This novel is entirely a work of fiction. The names, characters and incidents portrayed in it are the work of the author's imagination. Any resemblance to actual persons, living or dead, events or localities is entirely coincidental.

HQ
An imprint of HarperCollins*Publishers* Ltd
1 London Bridge Street
London SE1 9GF

This edition 2019

1
First published in Great Britain by
HQ, an imprint of HarperCollins*Publishers* Ltd 2019

Copyright © Mel McGrath 2019

Mel McGrath asserts the moral right to be
identified as the author of this work.
A catalogue record for this book is
available from the British Library.

ISBN HB: 978-0-00-8326166
TPB: 978-0-00-821707-5

MIX
Paper from
responsible sources
FSC™ C007454

This book is produced from independently certified FSC™ paper
to ensure responsible forest management.

For more information visit: www.harpercollins.co.uk/green

This book is set in 11.4/16.5 pt. Sabon

Printed and bound in Great Britain by
CPI Group (UK) Ltd, Croydon, CR0 4YY

All rights reserved. No part of this publication may be reproduced, stored in a retrieval system, or transmitted, in any form or by any means, electronic, mechanical, photocopying, recording or otherwise, without the prior permission of the publishers.

This book is sold subject to the condition that it shall not, by way of trade or otherwise, be lent, re-sold, hired out or otherwise circulated without the publisher's prior consent in any form of binding or cover other than that in which it is published and without a similar condition including this condition being imposed on the subsequent purchaser.

For my friends – I promise that none of these characters are based on you.

There is no greater sorrow than to know another's secret when you cannot help them.

ANTON CHEKHOV, UNCLE VANYA

I

Cassie

I'm going to take you back to the summer's evening near the end of my friendship with Anna, Bo and Dex.

Until that day, the eve of my thirty-second birthday, we had been indivisible; our bond the kind that lasts a lifetime. Afterwards, when everything began to fall apart, I came to understand that the ties between us had always carried the seeds of rottenness and destruction, and that the life we shared was anything but normal. Somewhere in the deep recesses of my mind I think I had probably known this for years, but it took what happened late that night in August for me to begin to be able to put the pieces together. Why had I failed to acknowledge the truth for so long? Was it loneliness, or was I in love with an idea of friendship that I could not bear to let go? Perhaps I was simply a coward? One day, it might become clearer to me. Perhaps it will become clear to you, once I have taken you back there, to that time and that place. And when I am done with the story, when everything has been explained and the secrets are finally out, I will ask you what you would have done. Because that's what I really want to know.

What would you have done?

Picture this scene: a Sunday morning in the early hours at a music festival in Wapping, East London. Most of the ticket holders have already left, and the organisers are clearing up now – stewards checking the mobile toilets, litter pickers working their grab hooks in the floodlights. Anna, Bo, Dex and I are lying side-by-side on the grass near the main stage, our limbs stiffening from all the dancing, staring at the marble eye of a supermoon and drinking in this late hour of our youth. None of us speaks but we don't have to. We are wondering how many more hazy early mornings we will spend alone together. How much more dancing will there be? And how soon will it be before nights like these are gone forever?

At last, Bo says, 'Maybe we should go on to a club or back to yours, Dex. You're nearest.'

Dex says this won't work; Gav is back tonight and he'll kick off about the noise.

We're all sitting up now, dusting the night from our clothes. In the distance I spot a security guard heading our way. 'I vote we go to Bo's. What is it, ten minutes in an Uber?'

Anna has spotted the guard too and jumps onto her feet, rubbing the goosebumps from her arms.

'I've got literally zero booze,' Bo says. 'Plus the cleaner didn't come this week so there's, like, a bazillion pizza boxes everywhere.'

With one eye on the guard, Anna says, 'How's about we all just go home then?'

And that's exactly what we should have done.

Home. A long night-tube ride to Tottenham and the shitty flat I share with four semi-strangers. The place with the peeling veneer flooring, the mouldy fridge cheese and the toothbrushes lined up on a bathroom shelf rimmed with limescale.

'Will you guys see out my birthday with one last beer?'

Because it is my birthday, and it's almost warm, and the supermoon is casting its weird, otherworldly light, and if we walk a few metres to the south the Thames will open up to us and there, overlooking the wonder that is London, there will be a chance for me to forget the bad thing I have done, at least until tomorrow.

At that moment the security guard approaches and asks us to leave the festival grounds.

'Won't the pubs be closed?' asks Anna, as we begin to make our way towards the exit. She wants to go home to her lovely husband and her beautiful baby, and to her perfect house and her dazzling life.

But it's my birthday, and it's almost warm, and if Anna calls it a day, there's a good chance Bo and Dex will too and I will be alone.

'There's a corner shop just down the road. I'm buying.'

Anna hesitates for a moment, then relenting, says, 'Maybe one quick beer, then.'

In my mind I've played this moment over and over,

sensing, as if I were now looking down on the scene as an observer, the note of desperation in my offer, the urgent desire to block out the drab thump of my guilty conscience. These are things I failed to understand back then. There is so much I didn't see. And now that I do, it's too late.

Anna accompanies me and we agree to meet the boys by Wapping Old Stairs, where the alleyway gives onto the river walk, so we can drink our beers against the backdrop of the water. At the shop, I'm careful not to show the cashier or Anna the contents of my bag.

Moments later, we're back out on the street, and I'm carrying a four pack but, when Anna and I reach the appointed spot, Bo and Dex aren't there. Thinking they must have walked some short distance along the river path we call and, when there's no answer, head off after them.

On the walkway, the black chop of the river slaps against the brickwork, but there's no sign of Bo or Dex.

'Where did the boys go?' asks Anna, turning her head and peering along the walkway.

'They'll turn up,' I say, watching the supermoon sliding slowly through a yellow cloud.

'It's a bit creepy here,' Anna says.

'This is where we said we'd meet, so. . .'

We send texts, we call. When there's no response we sit on the steps beside the water, drink our beers and swap stories of the evening, doing our best to seem unconcerned, neither wanting to be the first to sound the alarm. After all, we've been losing each other on and off all night. Patchy signals, batteries run down, battery packs mislaid, meeting points misunderstood. I tell Anna the boys have probably gone for a piss somewhere. Maybe they've bumped into someone we know. Bo is always so casual about these things and Dex takes his cues from Bo. All the same, in some dark corner of my mind a tick-tick of disquiet is beginning to build.

It's growing cold now and the red hairs on Anna's arms are tiny soldiers standing to attention.

'Shall we call it a day?' she says, giving me one of her fragile smiles.

I sling an arm over her shoulder. 'Do you want to?'

'Not really, but you know, we've lost the boys and . . . husbands, babies.'

And so we stand up and brushing ourselves down, turn back down the alley towards Wapping High Street, and that's when it happens. A yelp followed by a shout and the sound of racing feet. Anna's body tenses. A few feet ahead of us a dozen men burst round the corner into Wapping High Street and come hurtling towards us, some facing front, others sliding crabwise, one eye on whatever's behind them, clutching bottles, sticks, a piece of drainpipe and bristling with hostility. A blade catches the light of a street lamp. We're surrounded now by a press of drunk and angry men and women. From somewhere close blue lights begin to flash.

'We need to get out of here,' hisses Anna, her skinny hand gripping my arm.

They say a person's destiny is all just a matter of timing. A single second can change the course of a life. It can make your wildest dreams come true or leave you with questions for which there will never be any answers. What if I had not done what I did earlier that night? And what if, instead of using the excuse of another beer to test the loyalty of my friends and reassure myself that, in spite of what had happened earlier that night, I couldn't be all bad, I had been less selfish and done what the others wanted and gone home? Would this have changed anything?

'Come on,' I say, taking Anna's hand and with that we jostle our way across the human tide, heading for the north side of the high street but we're hardly half way across the road when we find ourselves separated by a press of people surging towards the tube. Anna reaches out an arm but is swept forwards away from me. I do my best to follow, ducking and pushing through the throng but it's no good. The momentum of the crowd pushes me outwards towards the far side of the road. The last I see of Anna she is making a phone sign with her hand, then I am alone, hemmed in on one side by a group of staggering drunks and on the other by a blank wall far too high to attempt to scale.

Moments later, the crowd gives a great heave, a space opens up ahead and I dive into it, ducking under arms and sliding between backs and bellies and a few moments later find myself out of the crush and at the gates of St John's churchyard, light-headed, bruised and with my right hand aching from where I've clutched at my bag, but otherwise unhurt. I feel for my phone and, checking to make sure no one's looking, use the phone torch to check inside the bag. In my head I am making a bargain with God. Let me get out of here and I will try harder to believe in you. Also, I will find a way to make right what I have done. Not now, not right away, but soon. Now I just want to get home.

The light falters and in its place a low battery message glows. God's not listening and there's nothing from the others. I tap out a group text, *where r u?*, and set myself to the task of getting out.

Taking the path through the churchyard, feeling my way past gravestones long since orphaned from their plots, I head along a thin, uneven stone path snaking between outbuildings at the back of the church. From the street are coming the sounds of disorder. Somewhere out of view a mischief moon is shining, but here the ground is beyond the reach of all but an echo of its borrowed light and it's as quiet as the grave.

The instant my heart begins to slow there's a quickening in the air behind me and in that nanosecond rises a sickening sense that I'm not alone. I dare not turn but I cannot run. My belly spasms with an empty heave then I am frozen. Does someone know what I've got? Have they come to claim it? What should I do, fight for it or let it go?

A voice cuts through the dark.

'Cassie, darling, is that you?'

There's a sudden, intense flare of relief. Spinning on my heels, I wait for Anna to catch me up. 'Oh I'm so glad.'

She flings an arm around my shoulders and for a moment we hug until the buckle of my bag digs into my belly and I pull away. What a shitty birthday this has turned out to be. If they knew what I'd done some people would say it's kismet or karma and if this is the extent of it I've got off lightly. They'd be right.

'Have you seen the others?' I ask Anna.

'Bo was with me for a bit. He and Dex got caught up in the crowd which was why they didn't make it to the Old Stairs, then they got separated. No idea where Dex is now. He might have texted me back, but my phone's croaked.'

'I got nothing from him either.'

'You think we can get out that way?' She points into the murk. 'Hope so.'

We pick our way down the pathway into the thick black air beside the outbuildings, me in front and Anna following on. As we're approaching the alleyway between the buildings my eye is drawn to something moving in the shadows. A fox or a cat maybe? No, no, too big for that. Way, way too big.

I've stopped walking now and Anna is standing right behind me, breathing down my neck. Has she sensed it too? I turn to see her pointing not to the alley but to the railings on the far side of the outbuildings.

'Anna?'

'Thank God!' She begins waving. 'The boys have found us – look, over there.' In the dim light two figures, their forms indistinct, are breaking from the crowd and appear to be making their way towards us.

'Are you sure it's them?'

'Yes, I can tell by way they're moving. That's Dex in front and Bo's just behind him.'

I watch them for a moment until a group of revellers passes by and the two men are lost from view. From the alley there comes a sudden cry. Spinning round I can now see, silhouetted against the dim light of a distant street lamp, a man and a woman. The man is standing and the woman is bent over with her hands pressed up against the wall, her head bowed, as if she's struggling to stay upright. I glance at Anna but she's still looking the other way. Has she seen this? I pull on her arm and she wheels towards me.

'Over there, in that alley.' It takes a moment for Anna to register, a few seconds when there is just a crumpled kind of bemusement on her face and then alarm. The man has one arm around the woman's waist and he's holding her hair. The woman is upright now but barely, her head bowed as if she's about to throw up.

Anna and I exchange anxious looks.

Every act of violence creates an orbit of chaotic energy around itself, a force beyond language or the ordinary realm of the senses. A gathering of dark matter. The animal self can detect it before anything is seen or heard or smelled or touched. This is what Anna and I are sensing now. There is something wayward happening in that alley and its dark presence is heading out to meet us.

With one hand the man is pressing the woman's face into the wall while, with the other, he is scrabbling at her clothes. She is as floppy as a rag doll. He has her skirt lifted now, the fabric bunched up around her waist at the back. Her left arm comes out and windmills briefly in the air in protest. Her hand catches the scarf around her neck and there's a flash of yellow and blue pom-poms before the man makes a grab for her elbow and forces the arm behind her back. The woman stumbles but as she goes down he hauls her up by her hair. Her cry is like the sound of an old record played at half speed.

Something is screaming in my head. But I'm pushing it away. Another voice inside me is saying, this is not what I think it is, this is not what I don't want it to be, this is not real.

The man has let go of the woman's hair. He's pressing her face into the wall with his left hand while his right hand fumbles at his trousers. His knee is in the small of the woman's back pinning her to the wall. The woman is reaching around with her arm trying and failing to push him away but her movements are like a crash test dummy at the moment of impact.

'Oh God,' Anna says, grabbing my arm and squeezing hard, her voice high-pitched and tremulous.

In my mind a furious wave is rising, flecked with swirling white foam, and in the alley the man's pelvis is grinding, grinding, slamming the woman into the wall. The world has shrunk into a single terrible moment, an even horizon of infinite gravity and weight, from which there is no running away. Anna and I are no longer casual observers. We have just become witnesses.

I feel myself take a step forward. My legs know what I should be doing. My body is acting as my conscience. The step becomes a spring and Anna too is lunging forward and for a moment I think she's on the same mission as me until her hand lands on my shoulder and I feel a yanking on the strap of my bag and in that instant, Anna comes to an abrupt stop, sending the bag flying into the air. It lands a foot or two away and breaks open, its contents scattering. The shock soon gives way to a rising panic about what might have spilled and I'm down on my knees, rooting around in the murk, scraping tissues and lip balm, my travel card and phone, cash and everything else back inside the bag, checking over my shoulder to make sure Anna hasn't looked too closely at the spilled contents.

As I rise she's grabbing my wrist and squeezing the spot where my new tattoo sits. I try to shake her off but she's hissing at me now, her body poised to pull me back again. 'Don't be so bloody stupid! You don't know what you're getting into.'

'He's hurting her! Someone needs to intervene. At least let's call the police.'

My hand makes contact with my bag, peels open the zip and fumbles around in the mess. And in that moment in my mind a wave crests and rushes to the shore and the foam pulls back exposing a small bright pebble of clarity. What would the police say if they found what I am carrying? What would Anna say?

In my mind an ugly calm descends. My hand withdraws

and pulls the zip tight. They say that it's in moments of crisis that we reveal most about ourselves.

'My battery's dead. You'll have to call from yours.'

I'd like to say I'd forgotten that Anna's phone was out of juice but I hadn't. In any case, Anna isn't listening. Something else has caught her attention. On the far side a phone torch shines, a light at the end of a dark tunnel, and in its beam is Dex, as frozen as a waxwork. Behind him, in the gloom, lurks a shadowy figure that can only be Bo. If anyone is going to put a stop to what is going on in the alley it'll be Bo.

Won't it?

'Please,' murmurs Anna. 'Please, boys, no heroics.'

Dex continues to stand on the other side of the alley, immobile, his gaze fixed on me and Anna. It's at that moment that I become conscious of Anna shaking her head and Dex acknowledging her with a single nod. For a fraction of a second everything seems frozen. Even the man, ramming himself into the woman in the alley. And in that moment of stillness, an instant when nothing moves.

We all know what we are seeing here but in those few seconds and without exchanging a word, we make the fateful, collective decision to close our eyes and turn our backs to it. No one will intervene and no one will tell. The police will not be called. The woman will be left to her fate. From now on, we will do our best to pretend that something else was happening at this time on this night in this alley behind this church in Wapping. We'll make excuses. We'll tell each other that the woman brought it on herself. Privately, we'll convince ourselves that this can't be a betrayal because you can't betray a person you don't know. We will twist the truth to our own ends and if all else fails, we will deny it.

We'll do nothing. But doing nothing doesn't make you innocent.

The light at the end of the tunnel snaps off and in a blink Dex and the shadowy figure of Bo have disappeared into the darkness. I look at Anna. She looks back at me, gives a tiny nod, then turns and begins to hurry away up the path towards the church. And all of a sudden I find myself running, past the alley where only the woman remains, slumped against the wall, past the wheelie bins, along the side of the church, between tombstones decked in yellow moonlight and out, finally, into the street.

2

Cassie

As the train is pulling into Weymouth a text comes through. *So soz, darling, held up, take cab*, followed by the address and postcode of the holiday cottage. Not the best of welcomes, but never mind. We're at the start of a lovely extended weekend, just the four of us, and that's such a rare event these days, life and careers being what they are, and husbands and babies being what they are. Four whole days in the company of your best friends. Your only real friends.

At the station, a fellow passenger helps me lift my case from the carriage onto the platform. It was cold and drizzly when I left London and it's more or less the same now, only colder, and naturally, me being me, I'm wearing the wrong jumper for it, but never mind. I'll find something warmer in the case when I reach the cottage. The bag is heavy with new clothes, new shoes, the results of a rare online spending spree. This weekend I'm intending to dress to impress. If anyone asks where I got the money (and they will) I'll say I got promoted at the school, something more of a hope than a reality.

The driver slings my bag into the boot of the taxi while I let myself inside. A taxi is fine.

'You been to the island before?' the taxi driver says, when I show him the text containing the address.

'No. Is it nice?'

'If prisons and quarries are nice,' he responds, drily.

'We're celebrating my friend Bo's birthday. He used to come here with his dad to collect fossils. It's his shout.' Jonathan Bowman was a City lawyer with a passion for palaeontology and a rocky heart that gave out at fifty-six. None of us thought the fact that Bo went on to study the subject at uni was anything but the prince looking for the king's approval. I have wondered more than once whether this trip is an act of reconciliation, a reckoning of the past as well as a means of reinventing it. Not that Bo, who has never been one for introspection, would ever put it that way.

'If you ask me, you'd be better off in Weymouth. We got a TGI Fridays,' the taxi driver says, pulling from the station drop-off into the traffic.

As the taxi makes its way through the scrappy splendour of central Weymouth into nondescript suburbs I'm caught up in the anticipation of it all. Four days. No partners or babies or distractions. It'll be just like old times. After all that happened at the Wapping Festival, this is what we need.

The road narrows onto Chesil Spit. To our right stretches the long, thin finger of Chesil Beach, empty now save for a few gulls, to the left is a huddle of industrial-looking buildings set on an expanse of what looks like wasteland. The driver explains this was the old naval base where the 2012 Olympic water sports were staged. Then, all of a sudden, we are on the Isle of Portland.

'Why do they call it an island?'

The taxi driver's eyes flit to the rear-view mirror. 'I've never asked.'

We sail past an old boozer, an ad outside reading, 'Wanted: New Customers', over a mini-roundabout and left up a steep hill on the top of which perches what looks like an ancient fort.

'The Citadel,' volunteers the driver, observing my gaze. 'It was originally a prison for convicts waiting to be transported to Australia. It's a detention centre for refugees now. Nothing's changed.' He lets out a grim laugh. 'There's another prison in the middle of the island. Young offenders mostly, that one. I get a lot of business from that prison. Mums visiting, that kind of thing. There's a bus from the mainland but it doesn't drop off or pick up at visiting hours. Crazy, innit, but that's Portland. Nothing here makes much sense.'

Above the roof line, beside a ragged buff, a fistful of raptors swoops and hovers in a beautiful, sinister choreography. The taxi driver says he has no idea what they are. Hawks? Kestrels?

'They do that when they're hunting.'

He turns off the main road onto a tiny unpaved lane. We climb steeply through low, wind-burned shrubs in silence, wrapped in our own worlds. Halfway up the hill the driver makes a sharp right into a driveway surrounded by wind-breaking hedges and suddenly, as if rising from the murk, a large cottage of ancient brick with a mossy slate roof appears and a voice on the GPS announces that we have reached our destination.

The driver pulls up behind a silver BMW and a midnight blue Audi coupé and I use the time it takes for him to go round to the boot to fetch my bag to take in the scene. The air is clean and carries a tang of seaweed and moss and even now, before sunset, it's cold and raw in the way London never is. The cottage itself is Georgian or maybe early Victorian, built for a time long gone when keeping out the elements was more important than bringing in the light. A creeper whose leaves are already turning curls around tiny, squinting windows untroubled by the sun and gives the place a forlorn and slightly malevolent air. It's beautiful in the way that dying and melancholy things are beautiful.

'Right then,' says the driver, depositing my bag on the gravel drive. He mentions the fare, a sum that only a month or so ago would have sent me into a spin but now feels perfectly manageable. I reach for my bag and pull out my purse. How lovely to be able to be so casual about money. This must be how the others feel all the time.

At that moment the front door swings open and Anna appears and comes towards me, arms outstretched. 'Darling. Look at you!' she says, flashing her wide, breezy, Julia Roberts smile and wrapping me in a hug before pulling away to pluck at the collar of my cherry-red blouse. 'Such a good colour on you. But then you've always been so brilliant at picking out the charity shop bargains.'

Anna herself looks radiant. Anna is always radiant. And thin. And secretly unhappy. She checks my bag. 'Such a practical bag. I've brought all the wrong things. Of course. I'm so sorry we couldn't pick you up. Bo's new car.' She waves in the direction of the Audi. 'Some enginey widget went wrong and we had to sit in the garage until the mechanic had fixed it. Bo's being a bit boring about it, tbh, but it's his birthday weekend so we all have to find something nice to say.'

Beside us, the taxi driver hovers for his money. A mariner's lamp flickers on in the porch and Bo appears, dressed in smart casuals draped expensively over a treadmill-lean body.

As I open my purse Anna reaches out a staying hand.

'Oh, don't worry about that. Bo will sort it out.' Anna turns her head and flashes Bo a smile. 'You'll bring in Cassie's bag and deal with the fare, won't you, darling?'

'Of course.' Bo slings an arm around my shoulder and drops a kiss on my head. 'Welcome to Fossil Cottage, Casspot.'

'Top wheels.'

Bo eye-rolls. 'I know you couldn't care less, but sweet of you to play along. I'm trying not to go on about her but first flush of love and all that. Once we've had a few bevs, and I'm wanking on about the multi-collision brake assist function, which I guarantee you I will be, please feel free to tell me to shut the fuck up.'

'You never bore us, Bo darling, does he, Cassie?' Anna says, looking to me for confirmation.

'There's always a first time.'

Bo laughs and tips me a wink. Anna and I move across the mossy gravel drive towards the front porch leaving Bo to sort out the taxi driver and my bag.

'Isn't this heavenly?' Anna says, meaning the cottage. 'As soon as I saw it on the website I thought: yes. It's got a kind of *Rebecca* meets *Wuthering Heights* with a *Paranormal Activity* vibe, don't you think? Wait till you see inside. You're going to love it. We've given you the bedroom at the top of the house.'

'The mad woman in the attic spot.'

Anna's left eye flickers and for a moment she searches my face. 'Oh I see, yes. Funny you!' We're almost at the front porch now. 'So listen, Dex is in the kitchen sorting out supper. We're having roast chicken.'

'My favourite.'

Later, Anna will push whatever Dex cooks around on a plate before hiding it under her cutlery. But for now, she steps jauntily around a large stone carving of what appears to be a cockerel with the tail of a fish.

'Some Portland thing called a Mer-chicken, Bo says. But maybe he was joking. It's not always obvious with Bo, is it? Don't worry, it won't bite.' Her voice softens to a whisper. 'Gav's here, though, and he might. He gave Dex a lift and they must have had a row on the way because he's in a terrible grump. Thank heaven he's not staying, but he wanted to say hello to you before driving on to Exeter to have dinner with his sister.' She holds the door and waves me through a hallway lined with worn stone flags smelling of new paint in a Farrow and Ball drab.

'Seems ages since we last did something like this,' Anna says, directing me to a row of Shaker style coat pegs.

'Wapping Festival was only a month ago.' From the corner of my eye I see Anna stiffen.

'I meant the last time we were together for a whole weekend. Bestival, wasn't it? Do you remember that Bo threw a strop because that glamping yurt cost him a fortune and it was bloody freezing.'

As I recall it was Anna who threw the strop, but Anna has a habit of reinventing things.

'I remember the rain and that amazing fluorescent candy floss.'

'Oh yes, yum,' says Anna.

We enter the hallway and move into a large kitchen done out boho country style, where Gav is sitting in a bentwood chair at an enormous old pine kitchen table, dressed in the full upper middle class fifty-something Londoner's idea of country garb, cords and an Aran with a jaunty silk neckerchief tucked beneath to signal both his class and sexual preference, and fiddling with his phone. An expensive-looking wax jacket hangs over the chair. Behind him Dex is smearing butter over a large prepared chicken. A whisky bottle sits on the table and the room smells warm and peaty but there's a palpable tension in the air.

'No bloody signal!' Gav looks up, sees me and manages a smile. 'Oh, hello there, dear Cassie. Give this old man a hug and he'll be on his way.'

Gav has always been a huge, beary barrel of a man but the weight loss in the six months since I last saw him is shocking and not altogether flattering. It makes him seem much older and a bit clapped out.

Dex turns and holding two buttery hands in the air, whoops a greeting, then Bo appears carrying a rolled-up newspaper.

'I've put your bag in the hallway, Casspot. The driver said you left this?' He slaps a copy of the *Evening Standard* on the table.

'Not mine, but never mind.'

'Why don't I show you to your room?' Dex says. The chicken has gone in the oven and he's now washing his hands in the kitchen sink.

We clamber up a steep flight of stone steps with a grab rope on one side onto the first-floor landing off which come three bedrooms and a bathroom. Above each room hangs a fossil, or, more likely, a reproduction of a fossil.

'Anna allocated the rooms. She thought it would be

funny to give everyone the room with the fossil that was most like them, so that one's Bo's.' Dex points to a panelled door at the end of the corridor above which sits what looks like a large elongated snail. 'Guess.'

'I don't know. Leaves a trail of slime behind him?'

Dex's eyes crease with mirth. 'That's what I said too. Wrong though. Apparently it's called a Portland Screw.'

'Boom tish.'

'You have to admit it's good though. Bo once told me that sex was the only contact sport where he'd played all the known positions.'

'Funny man. What's yours?'

'Oh, my room is named after some kind of fossil oyster called a Devil's Toenail,' Dex says, gesturing at a closed door beside the bathroom. 'Anna thought that was *hilaire*. Her room is the one at the end. That thing with all the arms is called a Brittle Star.' He turns and smiles. 'No one can accuse Anna of not being able to take the piss out of herself.'

And with that we proceed up another, even narrower and more steeply inclined staircase, onto a small landing.

'Yours is the Urchin room. Tiny, but so are you. You're the only one with a direct view over Chesil Beach and you've got a shower to yourself so we thought you wouldn't mind.' Dex opens the door with a flourish. 'Ta da.'

The room is just large enough to hold a double mattress and a few stylish cushions. A stool doubles up as a bedside table. Through a small window comes the thick smell of brine and the sound of the waves on the shingle. The lights of Fortuneswell wink.

'It's brilliant.'

'Oh good, well, I'll let you settle in.' Dex turns to walk away but hesitates by the door, waiting for me to address the elephant in the room. Though there are two, really: Gav's weight loss and what happened a month ago at the festival.

'Is Gav OK?'

'He's in a sulk, is all. He's got it into his head that someone took some money from the house. It's bullshit. He's just forgotten where he left it.'

'I meant his weight.'

Dex is hovering with one foot outside the door. He doesn't like talking about difficult stuff. Never has. When we split up, all those years ago, he took me out for a drink in a very noisy bar, waited until Michael Jackson was working his way through the first chorus of 'Billie Jean' on the PA system, and, evidently imagining his moment had come, blurted, 'I seem to have fallen in love with a man,' and that was that. Four years as a couple. Game over.

Back then he screwed his eyes tight so as not to witness my distress and he's doing the same now. He says, 'Gav's got pancreatic cancer. It's pretty advanced. We got confirmation a couple of weeks ago and a couple of days later he was having his first chemo. That's why he's going to see his sister, break the news. He's bloody angry about it.'

'Is it . . .'

'Terminal?'

'I wasn't going to say that.'

'But you were thinking it, weren't you?' There's an accusatory note in his voice. 'Yes, probably.'

When I make a move towards him he backs off a little, unable to be comforted.

'I'm sorry.' I really am. Even though he stole Dex from me, I don't wish anything nearly as final as death on Gav. A little bad luck, maybe, but this, no. Way too much.

'To be honest, I just want to be able to forget about real life for a couple of days and try to enjoy the break. Have you seen much of the island yet? Not the most obvious spot for a birthday weekend, but at least it's not dull.' He softens the corners of his mouth. 'I should go down and see Gav off, get back to the cooking.'

I wait for him to disappear before drawing the curtains and taking a quick shower, then sit for a moment trying to absorb the news about Gav. If there was a time to bring up what happened in Wapping, this isn't it. Then putting on my game face, I make my way to the ground floor.

At some point, the owners of the cottage have knocked down a few walls to create a semi open-plan living room cum kitchen. Anna has the oven door open and is peering at the chicken, Bo is setting a fire in the grate in the living room. A bottle of red stands aerating on the kitchen table beside Dex who is sitting at the table with his chin in his one hand, looking pensive. Gav appears to have left.

'Oh, darling, did you like your room?' Anna says, swivelling to look at me.

'Is Gav gone?'

'Only just. You'll catch him if you're quick,' she adds, with a tilt of the head and a press of the lips to let me know that she too has heard the news.

I run outside, crunching across the gravel and waving madly. Gav is sitting in the BMW adjusting the heating and looking very old and very, very alone. The driver's side window whines open and before I've opened my mouth he cuts me off with, 'No outpourings, please. It is what it is.'

'Can I at least say I'm sorry?' He pauses, as if considering this. To my surprise, because Gav is nothing if not old school, his eyes go filmy. 'What you can do is be good to Dex. I'm scared I won't be around for him.'

'Done.'

'Another thing. That festival business, with the woman?' His rheumy eyes fix on mine. 'I think I should tell you that he is in a lot of trouble about what happened. He thinks he isn't, but he is.'

I feel myself slump back. What trouble could he possibly be in?

'I see he hasn't spoken to you,' Gav says, drily, registering the shock on my face. 'Well, since you're probably closer to Dex than anyone other than me I should probably tell you: the police came round.'

I nod calmly, but my mind is racing. There was that scrap Dex got into at the festival . . . Anna said it started over some drunk accusing him of looking at his girlfriend, but it didn't amount to anything. Surely the police wouldn't come round for that?

'Don't tell him I let the cat out of the bag, please, or mention it to the others. He'd kill me. Solemn promise?'

'Yup.'

'In the scheme of things, really . . .'

'I understand.'

Gav blinks a thank you and the car window begins to whir to the vertical. He waves and turns the steering wheel and the BMW crunches across the gravel and disappears from view.

3

Anna

7 a.m., Sunday 14 August, Royal London Hospital

When Dex finally emerges from the cubicle in Minors, Anna has been calming herself with some mindful belly breathing exercises for over half an hour and is able to greet him with what she hopes is her normal face.

Since the events of earlier – she'll say events because it makes what they saw seem less real – she's been a bit of a mess. Can't get her mind to engage. Something inside her head is making a sound like a slipped gearbox. The whole evening feels like an odd dream, although she is wide awake and as sober as a judge now. She'll wake up tomorrow hung-over and wonder if any of it really happened.

Dex is still drunk. She can tell by the way he's walking towards her. That's good too. The more everyone's mind is scrambled the easier it will be for all of them to get through this. Dex is unlikely to remember many of the details. Bo might but he's less easily shaken than the others. Cassie will do whatever Dex does. Anyway, the worst has been averted. She rises from the plastic chair in the waiting area and spots on the seat beside her a small still wet nugget of gum. Shaking off her disgust, she sets her mouth into a smile and waits, arms outstretched, for Dex to approach.

'Dex, darling, ouch, oh poor you.' A bandage is wound over the right fist, a plaster on the right cheek, right eye as burst as a stewed plum. She leans up and plants a kiss on his lips. He gives her his forlorn look. A bit little boy lost.

'You should see the other guy,' he says, playing hanging tough. He means the guy at the festival, of course. Some arsehole over by the beer tent, apparently. *You looking at my girlfriend?* As if. Anna had noticed his war wounds as soon as Dex had got back to the main stage earlier but, honestly, it hadn't looked particularly bad. Now it's been a few hours and the injury has had time to swell and fester.

'Is Bo still in there?' she asks.

'I guess so. He got called just before me, but maybe he's had to have an x-ray or something.'

'He's not badly hurt, is he?' Not long after what happened in the alley Anna had received a message from Dex to say that Bo, too, had got into a skirmish – this time with a couple of guys, something to do with a spilt beer, and they were going to A&E to get him sorted.

'He'll live. Where's Cass? I thought she'd be with you.' Dex checks his phone and runs a hand over bedraggled hair.

'We got separated in the churchyard. My phone's croaked. She's probably back home by now though. What a horrid birthday celebration it's turned out to be, poor darling.'

Dex cocks his head, presses his lips together and nods at the truth of this. He's so easily placated, so much less demanding than Bo. She watches him frown then peer at her neck.

'That looks like a nasty bruise.'

Anna taps the dark spot then dismisses it with a wave of her left hand. 'Oh, it's nothing, darling, I got shoved in that scrum. To be honest I'm more pissed off about my jumpsuit.' She points to the tears in the fabric, pre-empting any awkward questions. 'Speaking of, what happened in the churchyard?'

Dex closes his eyes, trying to summon a memory, opens them again and blinks. 'Oh, you mean that couple?'

'Is that what they were?'

'What I saw, a couple of randos having a quickie.' He seems anxious to change the subject. Good, thinks Anna. In that case, he'll be cooperative. 'I thought that arsehole was about to come at me so I decided to take off.'

This is not how Anna remembers it. What Anna recalls is that Dex switched off his phone light and ran away into the night, leaving the woman in the alleyway to her fate. Lowering her voice, Anna says, 'I honestly don't think we should talk about it any more, darling. Why get involved? God, it's a madhouse in here. Let's find somewhere else to sit.' She picks up the Diet Coke she left as a placeholder and holds it out to Dex. There's nothing she wants more than to put this whole awful night to bed. 'You want some?'

'Thanks.'

While Dex drains the can, Anna scouts for a more genial spot to wait, not easy in a London A&E during the early hours of a Sunday morning. The place is a heaving mosh pit of drunks and wasters, most, by the looks of them, walking wounded from the fight that kicked off after the festival. A name is called and one of the anxious parents stands up and offers a hand to his son, leaving a couple of plastic chairs empty near the triage station. Anna points and lets Dex lead.

A nurse glides by, smiling, followed by two policemen. All three disappear through swing doors into another part of the hospital. Anna jams her hands in her lap and watches them go with mounting relief. They'll have other things on their minds. 'Want another Coke, darling?'

'Not really.'

The guy opposite is doing his best to remove an Egg McMuffin from its paper bag with one hand. A sickening, sulphurous smell drifts over. Anna flaps her hand and wrinkles her nose. The Egg McMuffin guy gets up and obligingly moves off. A moment later the swing doors part and the two coppers reappear. Anna sits on her hands while they go past. A nurse walks by. A man's name is called. The Egg McMuffin guy sinks into a more distant chair.

'When did you get here?' Anna says. She needs to be careful about the timeline. Doesn't want to get caught out.

Dex checks his watch. 'Ages ago. Not sure, to be honest. They kept me waiting in the cubicle for what seemed like forever. Man, I'm wrecked.'

At that moment a figure emerges from behind the swing doors, eyes unfocused, a bit staggery, evidently still high, a couple of nasty-looking abrasions on his face and a puffy nose. Anna feels herself stiffen then soften then stiffen and then, putting her feelings aside, rises up and goes towards him, with Dex following on behind.

'That looks sore.' In the circumstances, it hurts her to have to take him in her arms and give him a hug but it's necessary. Men have to be managed. His body is electric and uncoordinated, like a cheap firework display. He doesn't notice the bruise on her neck.

'I'm fine,' he says, shrugging her off. His pupils are a single grain of lumpfish roe floating on a tissue of blood. What the hell has he taken this time? Whatever it is, the nurse has discharged him so it's clearly not life-threatening, thank God. 'Nurse said some bastard must have gone at me with their house keys. I don't know about you lot, but I need a fry-up.'

'You need to go home, like now,' Anna says. She throws him a steady look which he returns, very briefly, the only focus he can manage right now. He's understood her, though. He's picked up something serious in the tone. 'Make sure he gets to bed, Dex, won't you? I have to get back for Ralphie,' Anna says.

Slowly, they lead Bo through the corridor towards the exit. As they pass the lifts, the doors open and the two coppers appear from within, solemn-faced, as if they've just come from dealing with some hard business.

Anna looks away. Thank God they're about to be rid of the stale air, the smell of vomit and egg and antiseptic, the tang of fear and adrenaline. What an unspeakably difficult night. She's within whispering distance of being able to put it all behind her. This night, at least. There might be repercussions, though, God knows. But she'll think about that later. She's exhausted, at breaking point. If only she could just run home to her parents. If only she had the kind of parents you could run home to. Hers would only make everything worse. Mummy would find a way to make it all about her and Daddy would dump her off on her stepmother.

'Ordering the Uber right now,' Dex says, pulling his phone from his pocket.

Anna leans against the retaining wall of the municipal flower bed beside the entrance and waits with them, over-whelmed by the effort of seeming so normal when she's feeling as if she might at any moment crack open and the separate pieces of her heart fly out into what remains of the night.

'Anna, gorgeous girl, you're shaking!'

She brushes this off with a smile. Why does it always have to be Dex who notices these things? 'Just tired.'

The cab arrives and takes the problem back to the flat with the river view from where he came. And oh, the relief! The instant the vehicle is out of sight her legs go from under her and she has to sit back against the flower bed and recompose herself.

She takes a deep breath and holds it until her face feels as if it might explode then lets it out in one, in the hope that it might take all the guilt and the trauma of the night with it. Adjusting her jumpsuit and smoothing her hair she goes back through the hospital swing doors and picks up the taxi phone.

A voice asks, 'Where to?'

Home, she thinks. Back to Ralphie.

4

Cassie

6.05 p.m., Thursday 29 September, Dorset

Within minutes of my arrival at the cottage, we have settled back into our habitual routines. Dex, the entertainer, is telling one of his bad jokes; Anna, the doer, is rifling through cupboards looking for box games and, even though there's no signal, Bo, the bystander, is scrolling idly through his phone. And I am sitting at the kitchen table observing all this, beside me a bottle of wine, more than half empty now, and the discarded copy of the *Standard*, reminding me of all those years, before I gave up on myself, when I would grab a copy at the tube on my way home from teaching and look forward to sitting down with a glass of wine and unwinding with the crossword. And now? Why not?

'Anyone got a pen?'

'There's one in that pot there, by the sink,' Anna says, as if it's something she has always known. Of the four of us, Anna has always been the most observant and the tidiest, the pickiest eater, the most careful driver, the girl in control, the subject of male admiration and female envy. It was Anna who introduced me to Dex. She was in my seminar group but it was months before I plucked up the courage so much as to smile at her. Anna was both posh and cool, which was rare at Oxford, where the cool set and the posh set didn't often intersect. She had a smartphone then, in 2006, which was the hippest thing I'd ever seen. I would overhear her talking about people she knew who had parts in Harry Potter films, people who went snowboarding in Aspen and went to Glastonbury on 'access all area' passes. She wore tiny shorts and minis with Uggs and she had all this hair which she wore long with a fringe half obscuring her eyes. In Oxford, where it rains all the time, I never once saw her look anything but perfectly groomed. And of course she lived out of college, in a house in Jericho, which was where all the cool students had rooms and her housemates were all DJs and part-time games designers.

To a girl like me, who'd grown up on an estate in a dreary commuter belt town at the end of the Metropolitan Line, with a mother who drank and served family sized packs of Wotsits for tea and a father who pretended to go to his job at the council every day for six months after he'd been sacked, Anna seemed to have come from another planet. From the moment I first saw her in my seminar group I was half in love with her. I still am.

As for what Anna saw in me? A certain kind of naïve intelligence perhaps. A willingness to please. Early on I had given up on understanding people, who were beyond me.

Instead I had made myself a quick study of the material business of the world. By the time I was ten I knew the names of thirty-seven species of migratory birds and could name all the capitals of the world. Facts were the barricades behind which I retreated from Mum's alcoholism and Dad's weirdness. People-pleasing was the Technicolor coat I wore to disguise the drabness of my surroundings. Soon I became good at being able to absorb, even to take on, the self-serving lies of others, and pretend they were true. I knew my dad wasn't really going to work every morning and I knew my mother was keeping vodka miniatures buried in the cat's kibble long after she swore she'd given up. I never confronted them because I knew it wouldn't change anything and would probably make all of us even unhappier. Perhaps it's this that Anna sensed in me. She knew I would never challenge her. So long as she and I were friends, Anna would always be the Group's number one girl.

'You're not going to do crosswords all weekend, are you, darling?' she asks me now, one eyebrow raised.

'Nope.' I flip the paper over to the front page to find the relevant page number on the printed ticker and I'm flicking through when my eye is drawn to a headline in the Metro pages.

The body has its own visceral intelligence. It reacts before the mind has time to catch up. Daffy Duck has run off a cliff and is paddling in the air. His mind can't compute, which explains the expression of stupid bewilderment on his face, but his body knows exactly what's about to happen.

It happened to me when two policewomen appeared at my door with news that my mum had been found dead beside an empty two-litre vodka bottle. It happened when I watched the man in the alley grab the woman's hair. It's happening now.

Police appeal for witnesses in festival woman's death

As I read on it's as if tiny particles of dark matter begin to collect in the air like soot rising from a coal fire. How could we have missed this? How could we not have known?

Police are launching an appeal for witnesses in the death of 27-year-old Marika Lapska, a Lithuanian national, resident in London. Lapska worked as a food delivery bicycle courier. Her body was discovered in the Thames hours after a music festival in Wapping. She was wearing a festival band around her wrist. Police are anxious to speak to anyone who may have known Lapska or seen her on the night of Saturday 13 August.

There's the usual Crimestoppers number and below it, almost impossible to look at, is a grainy, heart-stopping CCTV still of a round-faced woman with sharp features and bold, enquiring eyes. Is this her, the woman we all saw in the alley? I scan the cheekbones, the eyes, the full, soft lips, check the shape of the hairline, the placement of the ears, but nothing rings any bells – and there is no particular arrangement of human features, after all, which says, *I have been raped*. Is this the face? So difficult to tell. There's no clear picture in my mind, hardly surprising since whoever was attacking her was pushing her face against the wall. But what if I *did* see her face and have somehow blanked it from my memory? Aren't eye witnesses supposed to be notoriously unreliable? What if the figure in the alley wasn't her? What if the woman we saw walked away from that obscene event and brushed herself down and is living her life somewhere in the capital?

Stealing another glance at the picture now, focusing on the woman's clothes, is there anything there I remember? I take my time and do a bit of peering. It's then it happens. A sudden illumination, like a camera going off in a dark room. A mind flash in canary yellow and sky blue, the colours of the scarf the woman in the picture is wearing.

I remember that scarf. Every detail remains as clear to me as it was on the night itself, illuminated briefly in Dex's camera phone. A jaunty canary yellow with sky blue pom-poms. I remember the incongruity of it. The holiday colours, those perky pom-poms which seemed somehow innocent. There's no question that this was the same woman. How desperately I'd like to shut the pages of the paper and pretend not to have seen her. But it's too late. Marika Lapska has spoken to me. She's calling out and it would be inhuman to ignore her now.

'Guys . . .' The tremble in my voice startles them. Three pairs of eyes shoot up and settle on me. Dex stops whatever he's in the midst of saying, his mouth still open. Bo frowns. Anna spins on her toes to face me. There's a moment's silence during which an army of thoughts marches through my mind. How did she end up in the river? Did her attacker take her there? Did he push her – or did she launch herself into the water? Did she try to swim or give herself up to death? Aside from the man who raped her were we the last people to see her alive? Isn't it a crime to leave the scene of a crime? That makes us criminals, doesn't it?

Is this why Dex is in trouble?

'Let's see that picture.' Dex lurches over and sweeps up the paper.

'I don't know,' he says. 'I got a good look at her face when I switched on my phone light. That definitely wasn't her.'

'I promise you, the woman in the alley was wearing that scarf, I mean, the exact same one.'

Dex takes another look. 'It's a scarf, Cass. There's probably a zillion of them in, like, Accessorize.'

'Don't you think we should go to the police, anyway, just in case?'

'I didn't see a damn thing,' Bo says. Dex, who still has the paper, drops it on the table and takes a seat.

'Mate, were you even there?' asks Dex.

'Of course he was,' Anna says, pulling out a chair and sitting beside Dex. 'He was standing right behind you.'

'Oh,' Dex says, sounding mildly surprised.

'I might as well not have been, though, because I didn't see shit,' Bo says from his perch on the sofa.

'Dex, Anna and I did see, though, and we really should tell the cops,' I say.

'But, darling, what did we see exactly? Because what I saw could easily just have been a pissed knee-trembler. And she was definitely alive last time I saw.' Anna's face is a smooth white mask.

'I really don't think this was the same woman, Cassie,' repeats Dex.

Could I really be the only one who saw Marika Lapska raped in that alley on the night of 13 August? What if no one is lying? What if I didn't see what I think I saw? What if my eyes are deceiving me? But no. I remember so clearly the scarf illuminated in the light of Dex's phone. The colour of the pattern, as yellow as the moon that night. The bright, sunny blueness of the pom-poms. And what if Dex is right and there are a zillion of those scarves, what are the chances that the woman in the alley and the drowned woman are one and the same? Very high, I'd say. A virtual certainty.

'I know I saw this woman being attacked. It could have been the same guy who killed her. People, she died.'

'Casspot, do we even need to do this now? It's my birthday weekend,' says Bo.

'Why don't you just call the cops yourself if you're that convinced?' Dex says. 'No one's stopping you.'

'Cassie, I forbid you to do that. We'd inevitably get

dragged in,' Anna says, giving Dex an urgent, accusatory look.

'God, no. I've got enough on my plate,' says Bo. Anna is staring intently at Dex.

'Really?'

'Yes, really.'

'Casspot, you're being tiresome,' Bo adds more harshly than he probably intends. 'And I can tell you now, I have absolutely no intention of going to the police. Because I didn't see shit. As I keep saying.'

'And I didn't see anything that could be remotely helpful either,' says Anna, settling herself into the sofa. 'We were all rather pissed. Including you, Cassie.'

Dex has moved over to the French windows leading out to the garden now and he's holding up the wine glasses. 'Come into the garden with me, Cass, while Anna works her miracles with the veg.'

It's cold outside. A blanket of midnight blue from which the odd star shines.

'Isn't this amazing? We should make the most of it.' He stands and surveys the scene with the lights of Fortuneswell below us and beyond them, Chesil Beach and the wide midnight blue selvedge of the sea. 'There was a doc on the TV the other day about kids with alcoholic parents. It was just on, you know? It was talking about, you know, how the kids often . . . about how they develop these saviour complexes because they couldn't save their parents. The doc said they often grow up unsure about what's real.'

'Fuck's sake, Dex. I know it was her . . . and it's sort of low to bring my mum into it, don't you think?'

'You really don't know it was her. I had the best view and I hardly saw anything.'

'You saw a woman being raped. We all did.' Dex removes a rollie from his pocket, lights it and takes a deep inhale. The thick scent of grass drifts over and out towards the sea.

'You know it's an offence to leave the scene of a crime, right?'

'I could just go to the police on my own?'

'C'mon, Cass, you know as well as I do that Anna's right. They'd want to know who you were with. Or there'd be CCTV or something. One way or another we'd get dragged into it. That woman's just some rando. We live in a city of eight million randos. We can't fix everyone.'

'She probably came to London looking for a better life. Don't we owe her at least a bit of concern?'

'Look, either she made a really bad choice or she just got really unlucky. It could have happened to anyone.'

'I could call Crimestoppers and leave an anonymous tip-off.'

This is where you tell me that you're already dragged into it, Dex. Into something, anyway. This is where you come clean.

Dex sucks on his rollie. 'Cass, I love you but you're missing the point. I'm begging you, stay under the radar. Think about that promotion you're after. What if they decide to prosecute you for leaving the scene of a crime?

You think you're going to get promoted if you end up with a criminal record? You're not going to be able to work in a school at all. That's it. End of career. Finito.'

He smiles and, reaching out, grasps my chin between the index finger of his right hand and the thumb, a gesture from the old days, whenever I got tearful or scared.

'There's nothing to be gained here, except some misplaced conscience salving. You want to do something virtuous give fifty quid to your favourite charity. You won't get arrested and you'll probably be doing more good.'

'I'm not trying to be a do-gooder. I'm trying to do the right thing.'

'Well, don't.'

It's cold now though the rain has stopped at least. A moth flaps around Dex's head and, as he bats it away, flutters against the light.

'Why did the police come and see you?'

He turns, the light now illuminating his left cheek, leaving half his face in the shadows. 'Did Gav tell you that?'

'He seemed to think you were in a lot of trouble.'

Dex shakes his head. 'Gav's all over the place at the moment. He's got the wrong end of the stick. You remember that scrap I got into with the numpty at the festival about whether or not I was looking at his girlfriend? The cops were just trying to find out what started the rioting, you know, covering all bases. It was nothing.'

He takes my wine glass and puts it down on the concrete and with one arm around my shoulder he presses me to him. 'I'm sorry, Cass, but think about what me and Gav have got ahead of us. We really, really don't need this. For the next four days I just want to pretend I'm young and free again. Is that so much to ask? Tell you what, if you're still upset about that woman at the end of our trip, we'll revisit it, OK?'

'OK.'

'Good.' He plants an unexpected kiss on my lips.

And so it's done. The decision made. There will be no more mention of Marika Lapska or the events at the Wapping Festival. For the next four days the official Group version will be that nothing ever happened.

5

Bo

The arm around his neck pulling him back smells familiar. He twists his head round and meets Dex's face.

'Mate, drop it.'

'What?' His body is peeling. He feels weird and wired. He spins back to look at the bloke who, just a few seconds ago, was about to slug him. He hears Dex say, 'Sorry, mate. My friend's a bit, you know . . . he's not trying to disrespect you.'

What the fuck? thinks Bo. He bloody does mean dis-respect, he means a fistful of it. He watches the bloke's body language soften. Stupid bastard wants out of the scrap, looking for any excuse. He's so tight now, though, everything he's seen tonight, the adrenalin. Bloody great neither of them has a knife or a gun. He could easily have slipped a blade between that guy's ribs, thought no more about it, the way he is now. How wired his body feels. His legs slacken, cease their forward momentum, the muscles melting into one another. He's rooted to the spot. He'll be fucked if he's going to give way but it looks like he might not have to come forward. It's all those hours in the gym, Bo's thinking. Not the job title or the river view apartment or the strings of women. That fucker knows nothing about any of that.

'Get out of here, mate, just go,' he says.

The bloke hesitates. Bo knows exactly what the fucker's thinking. He's totting up the square meterage of muscle. Bo plus Dex equals . . . what? The stupid, stupid shit. The bloke's eyes sweep the small gathered crowd. Ha! Ask the audience, phone a friend, thinks Bo. I fucking dare you.

For an instant it could go either way, then Shitface fills his lungs and blinks and it's all over. Bo watches him turn and walk away with a bit of a swagger, wait till he's out of the fist zone, then spit onto the paving. Yeah, whatever.

'What the fuck?' Dex's voice is in his ear. He's let go of Bo now. Funny, Bo thinks, first time I've knowingly been hugged by a gay. He doesn't mind it. Doesn't care who or what or how people want to fuck. He laughs to himself. Ha, he's hardly got a leg to stand on in the sex department, given what . . . given everything, but he's not a fucking hypocrite. Not like Dex was for all those years.

The small crowd has dissipated now. Nothing to see here. Bo and Dex are alone in the little turning. Dex loves all this, Bo thinks, the rookeries, the remains of cobbled mews that neither the Luftwaffe nor the town planners managed to destroy, all those tiny pathways stinking of urine that snake between the thoroughfares of the old

East End and the City. He's always been drawn to old stuff, whereas old stuff doesn't interest Bo at all. Ancient stuff, like fossils, fine, otherwise new. Why he loves his apartment so much. A brand-new tower standing between what were once crumbling warehouses and are now bits of retro-fakery. Like someone punched through the river bank straight into the twenty-first century.

'We should go to A&E, get you looked at,' Dex says.

'I'm all right.' The bits and pieces of his torso are beginning to fuse back together. He feels suddenly tired, exhausted in fact. 'Think I'll just go home.'

'Mate, you're coming with me.' Dex is at his side now and sounding insistent. He wonders if Dex knows his secret. Thinks not. Dex is the sort to have said something. It's actually rather wonderful to be looked after, especially by a man. So long as Dex doesn't try to interlink arms or pat him or anything gay. He feels protected. Loved, even.

As they walk down the street together, Bo is remembering that time when a stranger decked him outside the house. It must have been when they were living in Chelsea. Had he taken the dog out for a walk around the square? Anyway, the stranger – looking back he thinks maybe a wino or a guy with some mental health issue who had maybe climbed the railings – he recalls running into the house and his father being there, so it must have been a weekend, and his father bundling him back out of the front door ranting about no son of his and saying, 'Get out there and don't come back till you've showed him a fucking lesson,' and Bo going back into the square and seeing the guy who'd punched him, collapsed on the bench with piss running down his trousers and his father clapping him on the back when he returned to the house, saying, 'A man who comes running home without seeing to his business is a bloody coward.'

The adrenaline is beginning to wear off and be replaced by a horrible throbbing on his right side. Is that where the punch landed? Must be.

They are walking north now away from the river and towards the Mile End Road. Dex is saying something about losing each other earlier in the churchyard and seeing some random woman getting beaten up, but to be honest, Bo can't really focus on anything except the pain in his right side and the reoccurrence of the much deeper emotional pain of his childhood. The first he doesn't really care about. The second he wants done with.

'Hey,' he says, 'you look like all kinds of shit yourself, mate. What's with the eye?' Dex has clearly been in some minor war himself and he's hoping to deflect the discussion back to safer ground.

'That massive a-hole wanting to know why I was looking at his girlfriend. Remember, at the festival? I told you.'

They're walking past a bakery now and the waft of scorching dough reaches Bo's nostrils and makes him think, briefly, of the pizza delivery girl from earlier.

'Some women are just trouble,' he says.

'Whoa. Where did that come from?' There's a pause,

which is what Bo has been dreading. He imagines the cops, going to court, all that shit, but to his surprise, Dex says, 'I'm going to text the girls and let them know where we're going, though if they've got any sense they will have gone home.'

'Good man,' Bo says, holding up his right palm for a high five, forgetting the state of Dex's hand.

They've passed Watney Market and are heading up the side of the Holiday Inn now. It's quiet here. The mess down in Wapping hasn't reached this far north.

Dex's phone pings. 'Cass is home. She and Anna got separated but she says Anna's phone was running out of battery and she hasn't heard from her.'

'Oh?' Bo says, not liking the sound of that.

Another ping. 'Hang on,' Dex says, manoeuvring the phone into his unbruised left hand. 'That's Anna now. Says she'll meet us at the hospital.'

'Tell her not to bother if she's already on her way home.' On balance, Bo would rather just sort this out with Dex. He doesn't want it to become a whole performance and he absolutely does not wish to be questioned about what happened in the churchyard. It's a massive relief that Dex hasn't yet mentioned it and he hopes he won't. They've all been through enough this evening. They are at the entrance to the Royal London's A&E department when Dex's phone next pings.

'Anna says she's in Ali's getting a fry-up.'

'Really? Anna? A fry-up?'

Bo doesn't remember Anna having any food issues when they were first dating all those years ago, though he probably wouldn't have noticed in any case. On the contrary, she was curvy back then. All that borderline anorexia stuff must have started after they split up. He recalls that she managed to conquer it for a while, just before her accident, then it came back with a vengeance. Bo presumed she'd got to grips with it again when that thing happened between them – she wasn't looking particularly skinny that night – and during her pregnancy with Ralphie, but in the last year or so even Bo had noticed that she'd lost weight again. He didn't really get women. He figured, being gay, Dex probably understood them better. Anything too deep about the female psyche pretty much freaked him out. He just wasn't all that interested in what was going on in their minds. He was fundamentally an algorithm bloke. Code, formulae, all that stuff. There is an honesty to numbers. They're clean. An internal laugh bubbles up, despite the pain, which he does his best to suppress and he realises he's been thinking how ironic that is, for a guy who'd made his money reinventing the dating app. The laugh, though silent, causes the pain in his ribs to surge.

'She'll be along in a bit. She says don't leave A&E without her.'

They've just walked through the swing doors into a heave of mostly blokes with what look like minor injuries; casualties of the fighting, Bo supposes. He wonders if there's a private A&E he can go to, avoid the queues, but if there is, the likelihood of its being here in the East End is pretty low. He thinks about packing it in and just going home, then thinks it might be useful to have himself on camera in the A&E.

They join the line at the triage desk.

'Fancy a coffee?' says Dex. In one corner of the waiting room is a bank of vending machines. Bo looks over and spots a camera on the ceiling above the machines. Could be useful. Certainly won't hurt.

'You stay in line,' he says. 'I'll go.'

6

Cassie

Bo is uncorking an expensive-looking bottle of wine.

'A Chevalier-Montrachet. Before you say anything, I already know you think I'm a tosser and this weekend I mean to make you all beneficiaries of my tosserdom.' This is how Group evenings usually start, and end for that matter. With wine and Bo and Bo's money. Anna, who is popping potatoes in the oven, slaps her hands together, and comes over to receive her glass.

'Here's to tossers,' Dex says. The wine is creamy and complicated and gone in an instant.

'God, that's dee-lish,' Anna says, accepting Bo's top-up. 'I can't tell you how nice it is to be here. You know how much I adore Ralphie . . .'

Making a show of not listening, Bo sticks his fingers in his ears and begins loudly singing, *la la la.* 'No babies, diseases or unfortunate events.'

Anna, who has already polished off her second glass, fakes a smile.

'Let's eat,' says Bo.

At the table is Anna's home-made pâté which is, of course, delicious, because, though Anna herself rarely eats, she makes it her business to be an amazing cook. Even when we were students and all we cooked was beans on toast, Anna would always come up with some delectable little variation on the theme, a grating of cheese, a splash of Lea and Perrins, a sprinkle of mustard powder, a spoonful of treacle and a splash of lemon and then sit and watch us eat it.

'So, mate, what's the plan?' Dex asks, tucking into his third slice of pâté. 'There's a farmer's market at the weekend, apparently.'

'Fossils. Wine. Walks. A small addition to the Big Black Book. Otherwise, there is no plan,' Bo says.

Anna spreads a cracker and lays it delicately on her plate. 'You're going on a date?'

'Already arranged,' Bo says, knocking back his second glass. He's swiped right on a woman living in one of the villages in the south of the island. 'Because why not? Let's just say I'm field testing my app's performance in rural areas.'

Anna leans in, her eyes bright, and momentarily rests her head on Dex's shoulder. 'What about you, darling?'

'I haven't really thought about it,' says Dex.

Bo has helped himself to seconds, and with his mouth full says, 'Between getting trashed and bouts of casual sex, I'm intending to go on some lovely walks with my friends.

Only if you want, though. It's all really chill. Tomorrow morning we could go over to the Weares. There are feral goats everywhere and the fossiling is good if you get the right day. There's a climbing outfit down that way too, if anyone fancies it. You climb up this rock face and onto the top by the prison. It's kind of cool.'

'Oh God, all that lycra,' says Dex, camply.

The pâté finished, Anna brings over the chicken. Neither Bo nor I have much talent in the kitchen, Bo because he always eats out and me because there's always someone else's washing up in the sink at the flat in Tottenham and because, until a month ago, I was always broke. The supposedly legendary entrepreneurial millennial spirit somehow passed me by. Ambition too. Hence temporary teaching assistant. Great work when there is any but, like any line of work these days that doesn't involve tech, finance or roasting artisan coffee, terrible pay.

Bo has now opened a third bottle.

'By the way, Casspot, you're looking very hot. Is that a new outfit or have you done something to your hair?'

'Both.'

'Oh?' Anna's eyebrows rise.

Dex leans over from the other side of the table and plants a kiss on my hair. 'You got that promotion! Why didn't you say?'

'Let's drink to promotions,' Bo says, raising his glass.

The glasses clink prettily and for a moment silence falls and is then broken by the strangled screech of some nocturnal creature.

Anna puts down her glass. 'What the hell was that?'

'The cry of the Mer-Chicken,' jokes Bo.

'We're about to eat its mate and it's very, very angry,' says Dex.

'Whoever heard of a Mer-Chicken anyway?' Anna says.

'Everyone on Portland?' says Bo.

'It sounded like a vixen to me,' I say.

'Mate, if you're talking about that thing in the porch it's a crap stone mermaid with eighties hair someone bought on sale in the local garden centre,' says Dex. 'Wooo, I'm scared.'

'Obviously that's not the real one,' Bo says.

'Oh, and could that be because there is no real one?' Dex eye-rolls.

'Portlanders say it's a harbinger of death,' Bo goes on.

'Don't be creepy, darling,' says Anna, addressing herself to Bo and, wielding the carving knife and fork, in her practical way, adds, 'The only chicken in this house is the one sitting on the table getting cold. Now, leg or breast?'

Later, after another few glasses of wine, we are sitting over plates of Normandy apple tart Dex bought from the French bakery in Butler's Wharf when I hear myself say, 'Maybe we're rather creepy?'

There is a stillness around the table. If you really want to know the truth, the Big Black Book has given me a queasy feeling for years. After what happened at the festival, I don't know any more. Somewhere along the line did we lose our moral compass?

'Oh dear, Cassie's in one of her dark moods.' Dex wipes a paper napkin across his lips.

'Where did that come from all of a sudden?' says Bo.

'I don't know . . . just all the in-jokes, never bringing new people into the Group, the Big Black Book.'

Let me tell you a little about the Big Black Book. It feels as though we summoned it into being a lifetime ago. All these years later it still seems like the product of a spell. But it came out of one ordinary evening, when we were celebrating Anna's birthday in Pizza Express. I was the girl who ordered the Veneziana back then, not because I particularly liked it (raisins on a pizza, God no), but because they donated 50p to charity if you did. I see that now for what it was – a particularly self-defeating form of virtue signalling, a product of the feeling of inadequacy which shadowed me then. I still had only the skimpiest notion of why Anna, Bo and even Dex seemed to want to hang out with me. Now I know that they saw me as living in a parallel moral universe, one that was no better or worse than theirs, only different and, in their view, as charmingly quaint as a piece of the expensively retro furniture with which they decorated their newly purchased bank-of-mum-and-dad luxury apartments. Anna, who viewed anything edible as reason to engage in moral combat, ordered a salad niçoise with no dressing or dough balls. Naturally, the boys always ordered whatever they wanted, never imagining that anyone would be stupid enough to do otherwise.

Bo had stumped up for a bottle of cava – this was when

he was still a struggling IT entrepreneur – and we were raising a glass when Anna said, 'For my birthday, I'd like everyone to tell us all a secret. Don't you think it would be fun for us to know something about each other that nobody else does?'

We decided it would.

We met the following evening at Bo's. As I recall, Dex told his secret first. At age fifteen he'd lost his virginity to his PE teacher called Jamie. It happened one night in the Sainsbury's car park behind the school. In exchange for his secrecy, Jamie gave Dex a pass out of PE for the rest of the term. At the time Dex revealed his secret, he and I were still a couple, and no one thought to ask whether Jamie was a man or a woman. In retrospect this was, of course, a mistake.

Bo admitted to dognapping the family lurcher, Grace, in whom his parents took more interest than they did in their children. He caught a train home from boarding school, picked up Grace and, without his parents' knowledge, took her on the train first to London then to Leeds where, claiming to have found her wandering the street, he dropped her off at the nearest shelter. His parents spent months trying to track the dog down but never found her. His father withdrew from the world and his mother fell apart. A year or so after Grace's disappearance the new owners got in touch with Bo to thank him for bringing the dog into their lives. They'd named her Joy. It still tickled Bo to think about it.

Anna admitted to sleeping with a reality TV star. She and Bo were in the off phase of their on-off romance at the time. I could tell you the star's name but everyone's forgotten him now. Back then, though, he regularly made the front pages of the tabloids.

'Picture or it didn't happen,' Dex said.

Anna whipped out her smartphone, itself a small miracle in those days, tapped a few times on the screen and there he was, in the buff, lying on the bed in a posh hotel room, Anna's bag just visible on the table beside him.

'We need to know everything and we need to know it now,' Dex said. (Again, I should have known.)

Anna had loaded the image onto her MySpace page though the rest of us hadn't seen it there. One of her followers had asked her to grade the date out of ten. Flirting (9), Kissing (3 – he had smoker's breath), Other Foreplay (6), Overall (7).

We all noticed Bo had gone very quiet.

'That's not really a secret, is it?' Dex said.

'It would be if we all did it and only showed each other – oh my god, that's genius. We should keep a joint Black Book!' Anna said.

'Dex and I are, like, monogamous,' I said.

'Well, then Bo and I can do it.'

And that was how the Big Black Book was born, as an instrument by which Anna and Bo could take unspoken sexual revenge on one another, though it was never a book, really, but rather a secret Facebook group and, latterly, after

Bo decided that Facebook was insecure, an encrypted site on the Cloud. It should have stopped there but when Dex and I split and Dex began an open relationship with Gav, there was a crazy period when all four of us were uploading pictures of our dates in the buff, captured whilst they were asleep or looking the other way. It became a game, though looking back I can see it was a kind of warfare conducted by other means, as everything involving Anna always was.

We kept the Book secret as our lives morphed and we moved to different corners of the capital. We were working all hours, Anna in PR, Dex in a law firm then at a gallery, Bo in software design and me in teacher training, and the Book became the thing in our present we all had in common. In the backs of our minds we all feared that, without the secret of the Book to keep us together, we'd wind up as cybermates: four friends who were once closer than family, sending each other smileys on high days and holidays and gradually, inexorably, losing touch with each other's real lives.

As it was, the four of us would sometimes meet for Sunday brunch and talk about the week's encounters: the guy who wanted his ankles stroked, the woman who showed up with her friend. Soon it became a reckoning of the weird and the inadequate and the bizarre, a sort of Domesday Book in which our sexual experiences were recorded and ticked off. We became the holders of each other's secrets and by that means we survived as friends. None of us ever stopped to think about the invasion of other people's privacy or whether by what we were doing – capturing the images of lovers when they were at their most vulnerable – we were in some small way stealing some private essence of their innermost selves and repurposing it for the purposes of gladiatorial combat.

'It would only be creepy if other people were doing it, but because it's us, it's not,' says Anna now.

'Us? You haven't done it for years, Anna,' Dex says.

There's a moment's silence, punctured by Anna who, in a tinkly, brittle voice, says, 'As you all know, I'm happily, happily married.'

Everyone around the table holds their breath. It's as if we're all suspended in time. Then, all of a sudden, Bo lets out a bitter little laugh.

7

Anna

1.30 a.m., Sunday 14 August, Wapping

Anna is standing to one side of the main stage at the front, swaying to the music, glad, on balance, despite all that unpleasantness earlier, that she'd come.

She hadn't wanted to, not really, but had forced herself out for Cassie's sake. Plus it would have looked bad if she'd cancelled at the last moment, even if, as she'd done before, she'd lied and used Ralphie as an excuse. But it has turned out to be really quite a relief to have a night away from Isaac. What a bloody bore husbands could be. Bo did warn her. He said, marriage is for bores, don't do it, Anna. And yet, it was because of him that she had. Daddy had warned her too. She remembers him saying, 'Is that Isaac fellow really the best you can do? He's a solicitor, for God's sake.' He's a terrible snob, but it's always the ones who have the least right to be who turn out to be the worst. Daddy just wanted her to marry someone who was either very, very rich or from a family who sat at the top of the Establishment. Preferably both.

Anna takes a sip of beer and runs the bottle along the scars on her forearms, smiling at the memory of Daddy telling her to keep her limbs covered so prospective beaus wouldn't see them and assume she was a fruitcake. Which was exactly what she was. Mostly thanks to Daddy's grim ministrations. Mummy wanted her to marry Bo, who had flirted and charmed his way into her affections and because he'd been to Harrow. She had always sensed that her mother resented lovely, kind, sensible Isaac, who was immune to her flirtations. What would they think if they knew who their grandson's father really was? Not that Anna would ever tell them about Ralphie even though her mother, she thought, would probably be thrilled and a little envious. Her father? Who knew? In some odd way she thought he might turn protective, two decades too late.

She wouldn't want to give either of them the satisfaction. In any case, men generally don't seem put off by the scars. There are three, just over there, really obviously checking her out. All younger. All fit.

She turns herself slightly so as to present a side-on view of her long, slender legs and tiny waist. The lovely sharpness of her collar bone. Absolutely no one would know she'd had a baby. Stomach like a runway. They're very insistent, her admirers. It must be something to do with the aftermath of sex. Even Bo and Dex. Like dogs scenting a bitch on heat. They're not even conscious of it. How could they be? They've no idea what she's been up to. Which only makes it all the more delicious.

As for the other thing with Oliver, that will calm down and sort itself. There may well be a rapprochement. And if there isn't, there are plenty more fish. Ha, maybe she could build a secret profile on Bo's new app? But no, that wouldn't be wise. Maybe one day, when Bo has had sex with everyone in London, he'll boomerang back.

Speaking of, here he is, making his way through the crowd with three Coronas aloft. Which must mean . . .

She waits until he's near before asking, 'You didn't find him?' Even though they've been losing and finding one another all night, it makes Anna anxious when a member of the Group goes off on their own, particularly when it's one of the boys. It's been fifteen minutes since Dex disappeared without saying where he was going.

'Nope.' Bo passes out the beers and takes a long swig of his own, doesn't meet her eye. She knows exactly what this means. He hasn't taken the time to look. A whirl of irritation, like a little spinning top, starts up inside, but she knows it won't last. It never does when the whipping cord is Bo.

'Maybe we should just go,' she says, taking a sip from her beer. She checks the time on her phone. She'll stay on if the boys want to though she's rather hoping they won't. She's never really liked festivals anyway, too touchy-feely, far too woo-woo and it's just occurred to her that at this point, she's got everything she wants from the evening. The company of Dex and Bo (particularly Bo), a session leafing through the Big Black Book, which set off her imagination and led to some great sex, albeit with an upsetting finale, and a ton of male attention. Plus celebrating Cassie's birthday, naturally. She could hop in an Uber and be at the house in half an hour. Isaac will be asleep, so it'd be a lovely undisturbed rest of night in the bed in the spare room or she could slide in with Ralphie. The prospect suddenly seems incredibly appealing.

'It's not even two yet,' says Cassie.

'Don't be boring, Anna,' Bo says, shooting side eyes.

Anna takes a step back, stumbles, really. A thin thread of alarm worms its way up through her belly and into her chest. She wouldn't be able to bear it if Bo thought motherhood and marriage had made her boring. Christ, if only he knew! Not just about Ralphie, obviously, but about Oliver too.

'Obviously, I didn't mean go home,' she says, smiling. A very sour taste collects in her mouth. Why does she still give Luke Bowen the power to hurt her? Why does she allow it? She watches Bo drain his beer almost in one. They started drinking around nine and are all quite pissed, but Bo takes the biscuit. Part of a recent pattern. Well, the last couple of years anyway. The pressure of work, all that, he says, but you have to wonder about the timing.

She begins to rock in time to the beat of the indie band on stage, whose music she actually hates, to show Mr Bojangles that she's still switched on, still sexy, still knows how to have a good time.

'I vote to stay. Just in case that dickwad has got himself

into some sort of trouble,' Bo says, wiping the back of his hand across his mouth.

Dear Bo. He's always been under the illusion that the Group is a democracy. Dex knows it's not, so does Cassie. But Bo? No idea. Anna does her best to stifle a laugh of relief. Bo's forgotten his little jibe, if that is what it was. He never holds grudges, never remembers much these days, though that might be the drink. She wonders if he could be taking pills or anything else on top of the booze?

'Where do you think he can have got to?' Cassie shouts above the music.

No one answers. The indie band plays a half-hearted encore and wraps up its set. Moments later some old nineties numbers, perennials from the Britpop era, thump from the sound system while the next band gets set up. This is stuff her parents might have listened to if they hadn't been opera bores. Does Anna actually remember those nineties tunes or have they gradually become earworms over the years? Most likely the latter since, for reasons she's never cared to investigate, she doesn't choose to recall a great deal from her childhood. It's funny how rich girls are always the saddest. Rich girls like her, anyway, the sort who aren't the right kind of rich (father a corporate lawyer, how boring) never precisely the most acceptable form of thin (not tall enough, not classy), seldom just OK. The thought occurs to her then that her life began in Cool Britannia and spat her out in Brexit Britain. This probably means something, though she's too juiced to think about what exactly.

Beside her Bo and Cassie are making silly hip-hop hands to some old House tune. Cassie sticks out a hand and drags her into the circle. To Cassie's horsing around Anna allows herself a decorous bounce which is fine because it shows off her fabulous hair. One of the few advantages of being someone like Cassie is you get to look ridiculous and no one cares. Anna doesn't have that freedom because looking absurd isn't hot. She envies Cassie her carelessness. Her authenticity.

'Two guesses.' Bo is making arcing moves with his arm in time to the beat. He wants one of them to name the track, a game he likes to play, a kind of off-the-cuff version of charades. Bo only ever plays games he knows he can win. Like Anna herself, except that Bo doesn't realise it. There's a lot Bo doesn't realise.

A blonde woman drops her ciggie and adds herself to Bo's harem. Very tight abs and a crop top designed to show them off. Face not great, though, so that's fine. This always happens when the Group goes out dancing. Anna doesn't like it. She prefers it when Bo goes on a hook-up and comes back to report it. The blonde woman has managed to manoeuvre her way through Anna's force field and is standing right in front of Bo, mirroring his moves. Anna looks around to see if there are any men looking her way then smiles and pretends to be into it, though she actually feels as if some tiny insect has just bored a hole in her.

My body is full of secrets, she thinks, that's why I'm so fat. Moments later she is pulled from this mental rabbit hole by the blonde woman screaming her name ('Lisa!') above the music and holding out her arm to Bo's for a fist bomb.

'Boom!'

Bo breaks into his most dazzling smile and fist bombs back. Beside him, Anna sees Cassie very discreetly rolling her eyes so only Anna can see. This is why Anna loves Cassie. One of the reasons.

For the next ten minutes, until he gets tired of his little game, Bo spins and shadow boxes with his new friend, glancing every so often at Anna. Each time she feels her groin pulse and her heart almost shake with rage. This too is part of the game. It's his way of teasing and punishing her at the same time. All that stuff they've said over the years about back-up plans. How if they were both single by thirty they'd get married. Well, it didn't work out that way, did it? And whose fault is that? So Anna has her own secrets now. A life not even Bo knows about. Fuck Bo for giving her no alternative.

8

Cassie

I follow Anna out into the little garden at the back. It's cold now and whatever was screeching earlier has stopped. Through a gap in the hedge I can just see illuminated by moonlight the foam from the surf as it crashes along Chesil Beach. On one side of the garden is a raised area on which sits a plastic table and chairs. Anna clambers up and takes a seat and, pulling out a joint and a lighter from her pocket, lights it. Drawing the smoke deeply into her lungs, she pats the seat beside her.

'Sorry,' I say.

Anna inhales and closes her eyes but does not respond. The surf hisses against the pebbles as it pulls away.

'No, *I'm* sorry. Really. It's all a bit shit at the moment. Except for your promotion and Bo's birthday, obviously,' says Anna.

For a moment her brow furrows and I wonder if she's going to cry. Instead, taking a deep breath to steady herself and letting a smile perch on her lips, in a weary voice, she goes on, 'Take no notice of me, I'm just horribly hormonal. They don't tell you when you have a baby that your hormones will never be the same again. There's a lot of things they don't tell you.' She lets this hang in the air for a while.

Now is the time to say something.

We're quiet for a moment while Anna, conscious that I have something to say, waits for me to say it. And after a quick silent rehearsal, I do.

'Gav seems to think Dex might be in some kind of trouble, but he's made me promise not to talk about it.'

Anna swings round and gives me a worried look. 'What kind of trouble?'

'He didn't say exactly. Something that happened at the Wapping Festival.'

A cloud crosses Anna's face then her eyes widen and her expression softens. 'Oh, it'll be to do with the fighting Dex got caught up in. I don't think it's anything serious.'

'Gav seemed to think it was.'

Anna sits with this a moment before dismissing it with a wave of her hand. 'You know how he exaggerates everything. And anyway, he's not really thinking straight. Poor Dex.' Observing the look on my face, she goes on, 'He's been thinking of leaving Gav for years. He hasn't done it because he likes the money and now he's trapped, at least until Gav dies.' She passes me the joint then, looking away, towards the moon, holds up a finger and begins moving it to and fro as if trying to wipe out the stars. 'He never told you, did he? I suppose he couldn't bring himself to, in the circumstances. I think he loves Gav but they lead separate lives.' Her eyes cut to me. 'You can't have him back, you know, once Gav goes. It would never work.'

At the dark edges of the sky, where the moonlight does not penetrate, there are stars visible, intense pinpoints of light bringing proof of life, messages that are old and redundant before we can even read them. Every one of those stars is dead now, little more than a collection of debris or a black hole.

Anna's hands are in her lap, the fingers of her right hand idly twirling the ring around her left ring finger. 'You're so much more real than any of us, Cassie. So much less complicated.' She looks up. 'Maybe you think I'm being condescending but I'm really not. When you say things, you mean them. You have no idea how rare that is in the world I come from. I feel safe when I'm with you.' She signals for the joint, takes a deep inhale and blows out rings across the sky. 'I suppose that's what also makes you such a bad liar.'

'Which means?'

'I know where you got the money to buy those clothes you're wearing and it wasn't a promotion, was it?' She drops the joint and extinguishes it under her foot. 'The thing is, everyone's got a secret they think no one else knows, but most of the time someone else does. I saw what was in your bag that night in Wapping. When it fell open. Funny that Gav loses a wad of cash from his hallway and a wad of cash turns up in your bag.'

'I didn't take Gav's money.'

'Well, then, maybe all the more reason for not drawing the attention of the cops,' says Anna, and, hugging her chest, in a breezy tone adds, 'It's suddenly got awfully cold. Shall we go in?'

While we've been gone, Bo has filled our glasses, Dex has brought out a plate of wonderful cheeses and a box of silky, expensive chocolates and with night staring in from the French windows and the flickering shadows of candles on the thick, enveloping walls of Fossil Cottage it is almost possible to believe, even now, that everything is normal. But our world is anything but normal. Even the word will not hold, as it runs along tracks made wet with wine, heading towards an as yet unnamed catastrophe. The not-normalness. I know then that by going back to what I'd seen, to what we all witnessed, will be to risk not only being cast out but something more, some permanent injury which will be impossible ever to put right. If I could I would stop the train and head off the crash but I do not know how. A family like ours, tied not by blood or birth but by love and secrets, is so much more delicately but also more complicatedly bound, the contract between kin willingly entered into and habitually renewed, but at the same time so exquisitely fragile, so will-o'-the-wispish, that it might at any moment crack and splinter like dropped glass. It's hard to lose your blood family. I know that to be the case. Something of them remains inside you. But your family of choice can be taken from you in a blink. If that happened to me, what – after the years of emotional investment, of love and shared history – would be left? A going nowhere job and a dingy room in a rented flat overlooking a bus station.

Dex brings out the Scrabble board and for the next hour or two we make our way through another bottle or two of wine and attempt to fill the board with words, too drunk by now to play with any skill.

Game finished, cheese and chocolates polished off, Bo says, 'So, who's for a nightcap? There's some ridiculously pricey cognac somewhere,' and without waiting for an answer pulls back his chair and makes his way unsteadily towards the kitchen. Then just as suddenly he stops in his tracks and turning to face us with a grin, he says, 'That bloody word, it's finally come to me!' He'd stumbled during our earlier game and lost points. 'Revenant!'

'Is that a word?' Anna says.

'Don't you remember, there was a film out a while ago, Leonardo di Caprio doing battle with a man in a bear costume,' Bo says.

'I missed that one. What a shame.'

'Anyway, it means a dead soul who comes back into the world of the living bringing a message. Damn, if only I'd remembered! It would have been millions of points. More than enough to win.'

'But mate, you didn't. Remember or win,' says Dex.

Anna lets out an extravagant yawn. 'It's time for my bed.' And with a flirtatious little wave, she gets up and wafts towards the staircase.

I bump into her a few minutes later in the upstairs hallway. I'm coming out of the loo, and she's waiting to go in.

'Goodnight, darling,' she says, kissing me on the cheek. Everything else goes unsaid. Now I know Anna knows my secret. And I, in turn, know hers. If one of us spills, we both go down. That makes us quits.

A little while later, when one of the candles gutters on the kitchen table, and Dex licks his thumb and stubs out the flame, I read it as a sign to remain in the dark. *Stay in the shadows. Don't try to find out what you don't want to know.*

But still, the feeling of shock and betrayal doesn't go away. All night in the Urchin room, turning in the bed, the owls outside the window hooting, *You did nothing. You did nothing.*

At some point, when it's still dark outside, I get up and take a shower, soothed by the warm water, the steamy atmosphere inside the cubicle through which I can neither see out nor be seen. I've become such an expert at cover-up and pretence I'm no longer sure what's me and what's a version of me. Am I Cassie 1.0 or Cassie 2.3? Who is left to ask? I am the sole child of dead parents. My only friends in real life are the other members of the Group. I don't really speak to my flatmates and the only relationship I've ever had was with Dex. I sometimes wonder if I have made myself up from fragments of other people's online avatars. I only ever feel like a proper person when I'm with the

Group as we were a few hours ago now, sitting round the table, drinking Bo's posh wine. It's then that I'm able to persuade myself that I could really be someone, an actual person and not just a collection of borrowed algorithms and virtual characteristics. Perhaps that makes me sound more complicated than I really am. What I really am is pretty simple, like Anna said. I am unsure. I am both the keeper of secrets and secretly a lost soul.

If the world knew what I had seen, I wondered as the water poured down, what would it ask of me? What would Marika Lapska ask? Would she come out of the world of the dead to speak to me? Would she say that, because I saw what was happening and did not intervene, I owe her? Would she consider me responsible? Do I owe her? If so, what and how much? Enough to risk my career, my friendships, even my liberty?

I am unsure of all of this. The only thing I am sure of now is that for the next four days I am going to be the Cassie who has friends who are real and funny and who give every sign of wanting to be with me. I am going to be the Cassie who belongs.

9

Bo

As Bo walks by the burger bar he spots Dex standing at a three-quarter turn away from him, in the patch of ground between the food trucks and the chill-out tent.

Ah, so that's where the old tosser went. Bo lifts an arm to wave then stills himself, aware, suddenly, that his friend is staring intently at something, or someone. He can't get a clear view of what Dex is glaring at, but his stance seems wired, almost predatory. Could Dex be on the pull? Oh, now, this is interesting. An opportunity to see his friend in the wild.

Naturally, Bo's had gay men making the moves on him for years, the way he looks, but Dex has never once tried it on. Mind you, though, Bo isn't really Dex's type. He already knows from Dex's entries in the Big Black Book that he likes tough-looking guys with shaven heads and aggression rippling not far under the surface. The polar-opposite of Gav, in fact. Poor bastard, trapped by domesticity. Though at least he gets to play away, so he has

77

it easier than Anna. Though women like that domestic shit, don't they? Funny, it all seems to have happened while his eye was off the ball, his friends settling down, becoming that tiny bit more boring. He doesn't envy any of it. Why would he? Look what life has laid at his door. A fabulous river-view apartment, a great set of wheels, friends who love him, stimulating, highly paid work, all the booze and drugs he could ever want, the best bloody pizzas in London courtesy of the Big Fat Pizza company (hats off to Dex for that recommendation), and access to a city full of women at the swipe of a screen. Wey-Aye, Man. Literally living the dream.

He's jolted out of his reverie by movement. Dex is heading towards something or someone. Actually it's more like a pounce. Like a cat, almost. Bloody hell, he hasn't seen Dex move like that since they were both teenagers trying out for varsity football.

What's this? A girl is standing by the chill-out tent with her back to them and Dex is tapping her on the shoulder. Thin girl, petite, dark hair, red dress. Hot, so far as you can tell from looking at the back. Hot, if you like that sort of thing. Which, as it happens, Bo does. But Dex? What possible business could Dex have with her? Plus she seems shaky on her pegs.

She's turning round now. Dex has moved to one side and turned somewhat too, so his face is now partially visible. Whoa, Bo thinks, finally getting a purchase on that facial expression, stay well clear. It takes a lot to make Dex angry but that's exactly how he looks at this moment with his eyes flaring and his mouth opening into a shout. Something odd about this. An unstable energy. For an instant he considers intervening to calm the situation. But that would mean getting involved in whatever shit Dex has got himself into. Bo positions himself behind a sign to avoid being spotted and peers at the scene.

The wiser part of him thinks he should just leave now. Better all round to be able to say truthfully that he didn't see anything. Yes, that's what he'll do, he thinks. Walk away and go and get a burger. Maybe buy the girls a burger. Make himself popular. So far as he can recall none of them has eaten since they arrived several hours ago. And there were those lines he snorted, earlier, before the pizza. And the Viagra to get him in the mood. And the jellies maybe? Shit, he can't actually remember. Plus he never actually ate that pizza, did he? In any case, all the food and drugs seem to have worn off now. Yeah, he thinks, trying to convince himself, I am actually hungry. He makes a move towards the bar and in that instant remembers: Dex spotted him as he was leaving the portaloos. Couldn't have been more than a minute or two ago. More than that, they'd exchanged words. Bloody hell, what am I doing to my brain that I didn't even remember that till now? He lets out a weird little laugh. What was that about? Anyway, he does actually recall Dex looking intense even then. Maybe even angry. Bo had watched him go and wondered what was going on.

Dex isn't a man to lose his temper easily. In fact, Bo can't remember the last time he saw Dex crack. Maybe when Dex's dad refused to come to his wedding to Gav? But even then it wasn't rage as such, just more like a kind of growl. But there's some weird shit going down here.

Bo turns back to Dex. He's already forgotten about pretending to be hungry. He watches, rapt, as his friend reaches out a hand and grips the girl's upper arm in an attempt to spin her round. Bo has never seen a performance like it. Has anyone else noticed? He turns his head this way and that. Nope. It's dark after all. Darkish anyway, despite all the lights. Why has Dex taken such a firm grip on her arm? Is he trying to help her? No, no, he's definitely not trying to help her. In fact he's tugging on her and she's shaking her head and doing all she can to back away from him.

As she does so, Bo catches a glimpse of her cheek and the shape of her nose and a hint of the outline of her lips. Shit. Is it? No, how can that possibly be? The woman has turned a hundred and eighty degrees now and at this new angle her face is more fully visible. He blinks, takes a moment to compose himself, then blinks again. The sight before him remains. Can it really be the pizza delivery girl from earlier? It looks remarkably like her. What was her name? Bo searches his memory and comes up with nothing.

If it's not her then it's a dead ringer. He peers more closely, his mouth open with shock. He'd bet any money it's her. What the hell's she doing here? And what business does Dex have with her? Hang on, don't they use the same takeaway pizza company? He wishes his head weren't so fuzzy and thumps his knuckles against his forehead in the vain hope of forcing himself to think more clearly. *Think, you stupid bastard.* He hears his father's voice saying, 'Number one, number one.' Why is that bloody worthless turdmonger still taking up Bo's head?

Before him an increasingly hectic scene is playing out. Dex is shaking the woman now. What on earth is happening? Could she have sold him some dud grass? A few pills? No, hang on, Dex isn't a pill head. Grass is more his speed. Bo smiles internally, amused by his pun. Speed. Ha ha. But the momentary hilarity is soon superseded by a rising wave of panic.

Didn't the pizza woman say she was going on shift? He checks his watch. That was hours ago. Maybe she just came off. Was she wearing that red dress earlier? Bo thinks not. What can she have done to arouse such rage in Dex? Nicked something from him? Pretty girls think they can get away with stuff like that.

Bo is transfixed now. Dex is suddenly right in the woman's face, one hand on her shoulder, doing his best to yank off her bag strap. To be honest, this looks really bad. Some random pissed cockwomble aggressing a woman at a festie. What the fuck is Dex up to? If he doesn't back off right now, Bo will have to go over and sort it.

But no, shit, of course, he can't do that because it's her, and she might recognise him, put two and two together and then – boom! And even if she doesn't, supposing some have-a-go hero pitches in? Dex isn't in any fit state to fight back. Bo would have no choice but to intervene then.

So far no one has got involved, though Bo can see that others have noticed what's going on. Not surprising in the circumstances, because Dex has grabbed the girl's bag now, breaking one of the straps, and is peering inside. With his left hand he's holding the bag while the right scoops around. The girl is literally crying, her hands in a tight knot.

Bo is working out his next move when a bloke built like a Viking steps from the chill-out tent. Bo watches as the Viking's eyes flit from the girl to Dex and back again, sees the guy's prey instinct kick in and feels himself freeze. This isn't going to end well for Dex. A pressure ridge builds up at the back of Bo's skull. Fight or flight? He has no idea. His head is such a jangle of clips and samples and dubbed-over noise. Any case, it's not good. It is the very opposite of good, whatever the fuck that might be. He thinks for a moment but nothing comes. Words are the absolute least of all his worries right now. Oh crap. The Viking has swivelled on his heels and he's striding over to Dex and the girl. What follows is a moment of intense conversation, if you can call it that. Dex is waving his hands and the woman is shouting and the Viking's body language suggests he isn't having any of it. This thing is ready to blow.

Bo's fighting spirit, if that's what it was, has suddenly drained out of him, the pressure in the skull replaced by a whorl of bees and a dry swelling in his throat. That guy is an Alp. Bo watches him move in and give Dex a shove,

82

thinking, strike that, this guy isn't any old Alp, he's the Matterhorn, he's Mont Fucking Blanc. He watches as if in slow-mo as Dex stumbles backwards but then gets his bearings and begins to come at the big bloke with a raised fist. The situation is beyond finessing. No way is Bo going to take on some Nordic gorilla just because his friend has decided to be a shite monkey. Did Dex seen him? Bo doesn't think so. He could just slip away and no one will be any the wiser. Sorry, mate, but you know, you did bring this on yourself. Plausible deniability. Been doing a lot of that lately. Not great but a whole lot better than the alternative. Angling his body away from Dex, he lowers his head, digs his hands in his pockets and strolls casually away, taking the roundabout route back to the girls, shaking his head and muttering to himself. *For fucketty fuck's fucking fuck-sake*.

10

Cassie

6.50 a.m., Friday 30 September, Isle of Portland

Dawn breaks and I am awake in bed, unable to drift back off to sleep for the unsettling feeling of being watched. Who knew the countryside could be so disturbing? The night has been a racket of howling and hooting. Mostly hooting, from some bloody owl in the trees right outside my room.

Twit twoo.

What did you do?

Is that what the owl would say if it could speak? Owls are supposed to be wise. The owl might say, doing nothing doesn't make you innocent. But what does an owl know? An owl is just a bird. Shut up. Leave me in peace

A new, blue light pushes in from behind threadbare curtains and makes its way past my hangover to the more sentient parts of my brain. Yes, I remember now, this weekend is supposed to be fun. Sorry, Marika Lapska. Dex says I can't mention your name again till after the fun is all over and done. Well, then.

I rinse off the night's rime in the shower, pull on new

underwear, new clothes. Fix my hair. Head still fuzzy from last night. As I leave the room I'm thinking about some strong coffee but the moment I reach the top floor landing a strong sense of being observed overcomes me. Above the door the fossil urchin sits immobile, as if watching. How odd to feel overlooked by something so inanimate, so very long dead.

Revenant. Bo's word. I don't believe in afterlives or hauntings. You have your time on earth and then you are gone. This is how nature works.

I need that coffee.

The house is as still as a cliff. In the kitchen the mess from last night's bacchanal is scattered over the countertop. The living room's worse. There's a smell of sour wine and stale grass everywhere. Plates and cheese rind. I pick up a mug and some escaped crisps skitter across the floor. This is too much. I'll do it once I've come to. For now, though, there's nothing for it but to retreat back to the kitchen.

A glass containing a few dregs of some nondescript brew stands on the draining board. Without bothering to empty it first, I fill it to the brim from the tap, drink and repeat. After a bit I'm feeling human enough to locate an espresso pot in the cupboard above the kettle, fill it with ground coffee and put it on the stove to brew while I get to work clearing up, stacking the dishwasher with plates and hand washing the glasses. Judging by the mess something not-human has been at the chicken carcass. I don't like to think too hard about what. The remains can go outside.

I take it to the French doors and hurl it as far from the house as I can. The foxes can have it, or the Mer-Chickens or giant dogs or whatever other freaks of nature apparently lurk on this island. A fine rain is falling though splashes of blue visible through the clouds. I pluck my phone from the pocket of my trackies to check the weather, remember there's no phone signal, go back inside and scope about for a Wi-Fi router or a house book and finding neither, remember the coffee which is both strong and bitter.

Marika. I happen to know that the name derives from the Hebrew for bitterness, though it can also mean star of the sea. The fossil hanging above Anna's door could be a Marika. Brittle star. Bitter star.

How I know this I'm not sure. I'm good at collecting obscure facts and better still at hanging on to them. Maybe someone told me. The night creatures singing and screaming and carrying on in the garden.

In the week or two after the festival I thought about Marika a lot, though, of course, I didn't know her name then. I thought about going to the police and asking to give a statement but something stopped me. If I had to guess what, I'd say cowardice. Instead, I comforted myself with stories. What if I inadvertently brought something into the light which Marika herself would rather remain buried? What if the scene in the alley wasn't what I thought it was? What if the young woman woke up the next morning completely oblivious to the night before? I might be invading her privacy to say anything. I might be putting her at risk.

What would be served by my stirring things up? It might only re-traumatise her. What had happened was gone and done. The time to get involved was there and then.

Timing is all, Anna said.

'Anna?' A voice is calling her name. I turn my head towards the sound and see a tall smiling man of about my age hovering by the back door. I like what I see.

'I'm Will, the delivery guy?' He transfers the bag to his left hand and comes forward with his right hand out.

'Cassie, Anna's friend. The others aren't up yet. Bit of a late night.'

I take the hand in mine and he squeezes it without shaking, which seems oddly intimate. The palm is warm and work-hardened. He has brought farm milk, bacon, eggs and home-made bread for breakfast, prearranged by Anna, of course.

'I just made coffee if you fancied some?'

Will seems pleased to be asked and nods a yes. Maybe he doesn't get asked this very often, though with his looks, that's difficult to believe. I get up to close the door to the stairs, praying Anna doesn't hear the sound of his voice and come down because if that happens it's all over. I'll be Dolly to Anna's Jolene.

'Maybe you could recommend some proper fun things to do in the area? Not just lighthouses and museums. We're here till Sunday.'

'Sure, if you like.' He pulls out a chair and folds himself into it like a cat, a smile playing on his lips to tell me that he's got my drift and isn't averse to the idea of fun things to do. I've never had trouble coming on to men, not because I think of myself as particularly attractive, but because I'm unashamed of my desire. And why not? I'm on holiday, after all.

The pot gives up two treacly espressos. Normally I'd add hot milk, and a lot of it, but there was none until Will brought it. Besides which, I want to appear sophisticated. Which, OK, is sad, but which of us doesn't want to impress?

'Sugar?'

Will smiles and shakes his head. 'Mind if I add milk?'

There, see.

'Of course not. Want me to heat it? I can put it in the microwave.' I'm suddenly conscious of using my people-pleasing voice and have to clear my throat to get it to go away. Not sexy.

'It's fine,' says Will. Of course. He smiles. He does not bare his teeth. 'Sorry, I didn't catch your name.'

'Cassie. Well, Cassandra really. My parents had a thing about Greek myths.'

'Not familiar, I'm afraid.'

'She's the daughter of King Priam and Queen Hecuba, the one Apollo fancied, so he gave her the gift of prophecy but when she refused him he cursed her by making no one believe any of her prophecies. It's a bit bleak, to be honest. Why I prefer Cassie or Cass even.'

Here endeth the sermon.

'OK, then, Cassie,' Will says. 'So, fun things to do.'

Christ.

We chat for a while about pubs and cliff walks and local lore. I might mention I'm single. Will says he left the area only briefly to study biosciences in London but decided instead to return to the island. For the last few years he's worked bar at The Mermaid pub in Fortuneswell, odd-jobbed for second homers and rental agencies and hired himself out as a fossilers' guide. He's familiar with every cove and turn and twist in the shingle from Portland across to Poole in the east and beyond Lyme in the west. And with all the currents and undertows.

'Nothing interesting's ever on the surface,' he says.

We finish our coffee and Will glances at his watch. He's got another couple of deliveries to do further up the hill.

'Are you driving?' I'm thinking on my feet now. 'I don't suppose you could give me a lift? Anna told me there's a mobile signal up there.' Naturally, I'm not interested in the signal. Not that kind of signal anyway.

Will has a Land Rover, one of the old ones that makes a racket, scattering birds from the hedgerows. At the crest of the hill he brings the vehicle to a halt and heaves on the handbrake, then leaning across me to open the door so that his body is almost pressed against mine he points to a small copse, still lovely in its early autumn livery.

'If you walk through the quarry towards the prison, you'll come to a car park on the other side of that wood. An amazing view of the beach and the sea.' He draws himself back into the driver's seat. 'You'll find me at the

Mermaid. If you want. If I'm not there, Trev, the owner, usually knows where I am.' We both know what's going on now. The fact that it's not been said out loud only makes it more delicious.

I tumble from the car in my best casual manner, trying to swing my hair like Anna but Will doesn't seem to notice. He pulls off the handbrake, checks me in the rear-view mirror and waves. Then he's gone.

The drizzle has cleared. Up here the air is cold and oddly still. A peregrine sails by making its plaintive wail, followed by a handful of quarrelling ravens. I cross the car park towards a muddy footpath between hedgerows. Further on, the path becomes stone and eases down inside the bowels of the quarry, a hell-pit of skinned earth, strewn boulders and violently exposed rock carved into strange and sinister shapes. At the quarry's lowest point the ground turns soft and shaley. From here another path, damp and sprung underfoot like a dance floor, disappears into dark woods. I move through the trees for a while until the path warms with light and I find myself at the edge of the wood beside the car park once more, as Will said I would. Here the air smells densely of washed leaves. From where I am now I can see the trees surrounding Fossil Cottage and a scree path leading down from the cliff running roughly parallel to the road. Beyond that is the yellow sweep of Chesil Beach and the grey mass of the sea. If I had been on my own I might have wandered aimlessly along the cliff path for hours. As it is, I want to get back to the others.

I'm about to make my way to the scree path when the tinny sound of 'Greensleeves' starts up from the far end of the car park and echoes across the cliffs. Turning towards the sound I spot an ice cream van, part obscured by trees. The owner waves. I wave back and as I do, the back of a familiar metallic silver BMW parked behind the van catches my eye.

Gav is sprawled in the front seat, which has been flipped almost horizontal, with his mouth open, breath lightly misting the window, still fast asleep. I go back round to the front of the ice cream van and ask for a couple of teas then take them back to the Beamer, rest them on the roof and knock on Gav's window. An eye opens, then another. Gav looks about then shakes his head free of sleep. It takes him a second or two to register me.

'I've brought tea.'

The corners of Gav's mouth curl upwards. The door lock pops open and I slip inside, a tea in each hand. The interior smells like a drunk tank.

'Hiya.' I don't have the heart to tell Gav how truly shit he looks. Instead I let him come to and drink his tea without asking any questions. As he tips the cup to catch the final drop, something seems to give. His body shakes and he begins to let out a series of extravagant sobs. Unsure what to do, and, frankly, a little alarmed, I put an arm around his shoulder and wait until he has collected himself, after which, in a voice freighted with misery, he says, 'I'm dying, did he tell you that? The cancer's everywhere.' He runs a hand along his body as you would if you were showing off a new outfit but in Gav's case the new outfit is fatal.

'I'm so sorry.' What else is there? In any case, Gav's not listening. He's rattling on now about how Dex needs him, how he's in trouble, how he can't be trusted to look after himself. After a while, I interrupt.

'Is all this about the missing money? Or what happened at the festival?'

As suddenly as they started, the sobs dry up and he stares wide-eyed at me for a moment as if he's trying to size me up, to determine what I do or don't know.

'I'll get some more tea.' When I come back Gav is up and by the looks of the hasty rearrangement of his trousers, has taken a leak before getting back in the car.

'I feel ridiculous. I bet I look ridiculous.' He brushes himself down.

'You always look bloody brilliant.' I lean over and brush a bit of cack off his shoulder.

'Was it a lot of money?'

Gav's face scrunches and there's a grimace on his lips. He sets his Styrofoam cup in the cup holder and turns to look at me. He seems perplexed, as if one of us hasn't yet caught up but he's not sure which.

'The cleaner,' I prompt.

'Oh that. No. Well, yes. A few grand. A client paid me cash for a painting, off the books. But I'm more worried about the other thing.'

The fight then. Of course, I wasn't there when it

happened. I was with Anna beside the main stage. When Dex came back shaking his knuckles he seemed to think it was a small thing, one of those freak events, a drunk looking for somewhere to park his fist and finding Dex's face. Dex retaliating. Dex didn't start it, he said, and I believed him. In all the years we've been friends, I've never known Dex be the first to throw a punch. He and Gav very seldom even have a disagreement. Neither of them is the type. The other guy must have filed pre-emptive charges just in case Dex went to the police himself, or maybe he was a chancer hoping for a payoff.

'The fight?'

Gav frowns and rubs his head as if he's trying to chivvy a thought to the surface where he can catch it. A new energy comes into his eyes.

'No. I mean the woman at the festival.'

In a tone of mild curiosity, though my throat is throbbing with anticipation, I go on, 'What did he tell you exactly?' An old stalling trick I've often found useful – answer a question with another question, give nothing away until you are sure of the terrain. It pays to move slowly.

'The same as he told you and the police, I imagine.'

He continued. 'You know he didn't have anything to do with it, right? She was off her face, pestering him for money. It was just unfortunate that they were caught on CCTV. They must have found a festival wristband on her body and checked the security feed. She never even told him her name.'

On her body? The blood quickens. Could this be about Marika Lapska? If it is then Dex must have known about Marika before yesterday, known she was dead and that the police were treating the death as suspicious, which is odd because he gave a very good impression of being as surprised as the rest of us.

The facts are beginning to resemble Scrabble tiles. If I can only get them in the right order they might make sense. What did Dex not do?

'Obviously he didn't do anything wrong,' I say to be supportive, though I'm still not sure what, exactly, we are dealing with here.

Gav begins to drum his fingers on the steering wheel. 'That's why I didn't want to leave last night. I don't really care about the money. I mean I do, but, you know, given what Dex is having to cope with right now . . . I got halfway to Exeter then I thought, I should turn around and make things right, so I drove all the way back here. I planned to have a drink or two to calm down.' He grimaces and flicks his head to an empty bottle of Bell's on the back seat.

From the ice cream van 'Greensleeves' starts up but there's only us, the van driver and the circling peregrines and the noisy ravens to hear it. I'm quiet now, waiting for Gav to make his move. Wiping a hand over his weary, baggy face, he says,

'Did he tell you I gave him an alibi? I told the cops he was home by two. Which isn't strictly true. But you were with him the whole night, weren't you?'

94

'Yes, yes, of course.' Also not strictly true. What am I doing? What am I *saying*? What am I committing myself to?

Why is Dex keeping secrets from us?

'That's good. I'm sure you won't need to come to the rescue. They haven't even been back since they first questioned him. If they were going to charge him they would have done it by now, wouldn't they?' Soothed by his own compelling logic, Gav stops drumming and his mouth sets in a weak smile.

'Would he be pissed off to see me if I came back to the cottage with you?'

'I don't know but . . .' But he would be. But none of us wants Gav around. It's becoming increasingly obvious that the next few days will be the time for making new secrets and repairing the cracks in the old ones. Just us four.

'Gav, the woman who died . . .'

Gav frowns. The drumming starts up again, this time to the rhythm of 'Greensleeves'. He's not aware of doing it, but the effect is faintly comical, a middle-aged man with death on his mind bashing out a rhythm to an ice cream van's cheery jingle.

'Did I say she died? Perhaps I did. The police dragged her out of the water. No ID, nothing. I don't know how police identified her. I suppose they have ways of doing that. Of course, Dex is very upset, not that he'd let you see—'

A phone beeps. Gav fumbles in his jacket pocket and glances at the screen. 'My sister. She wants to know where I am. I'd better give her a call.' Something in his mood has changed. He's facing forward once more. Patting my thigh to signal an end to our conversation, he says, 'Don't say a word to Dex about this, will you? He'll think I'm fussing, which . . .' He tails off. The smile resettles on his face. 'You know,' he says, looking up at me with the eyes of a supplicant, 'you've always been my favourite, Cassie. Sometimes, I wonder if Dex might have been better off staying with you. He loves you, you know that, don't you?'

11

Dex

1.15 a.m., Sunday 14 August, Wapping

Dex is making his way back towards the main bar thinking how much Gav would have hated tonight. The noise, the music, the general chaos.

For years now, Dex has obligingly kept up the pretence of being highbrow to please his husband. Modernist opera, Godawful experimental dance, all the stuff Gav seems genuinely to like and Dex secretly considers to be a crock of shit. Still, most couples rely on at least one of them pretending. Doesn't mean he doesn't love Gav.

He peers in to the bar tent and sees the long queue for service. He's remembering there's another bar over by the chill-out tent, though that probably won't be any better, then remembers his VIP pass but can't recall any more where the VIP tent is. At some point, he supposes, he's going to have to start drinking less. But that point is definitely not tonight. It's probably just easier to stand in line here. As he's waiting his phone buzzes with a call. He is pulling his phone from his pocket when he becomes aware of a guy in the queue a few metres ahead of him. Cute, spring-action body, nice buzz cut and beard combo. Giving him the eye. A couple of years ago he would probably have returned the come-on, left the line and allowed himself to be led somewhere more private. Back then he was more anxious to make up for lost time. These days he's pickier about the set-up. Plus, didn't he already have sex earlier that evening? He thinks back. It's as if his mind is a packet of mixed nuts and amidst all the cashews and the peanuts he's trying to locate a single hazelnut. Oh yeah. The French guy. Shit, he thinks, I must be really wasted not to remember that. Pulling the phone from his pocket, he checks the screen, thinks about shutting it down then realises it's too late. Since it didn't go to voicemail immediately, Gav will know it's switched on and powered up.

What's up now? Either Gav is pissed and feeling insecure again or he's just had a horrendous time with his sister in Exeter and is keen to vent. Whichever, Dex really doesn't want to deal with it. He struggles to relate to Gav when he's being needy. Besides which, it's too noisy for a phone conversation here and he doesn't want to leave his place in the queue. He slips his phone back into his pocket and becomes aware that the cute guy hasn't stopped looking at him. His eyes flit toward his admirer who returns the look, raises a finger in the air and swipes right. Dex's groin twinges. Why not have some fun while he can? He winks at his admirer then remembers why he's at the festival in the first place. Cassie's birthday. Everyone expecting him to buy a round. The guy is just a guy but – Gav would hate him saying this – the Group is his life.

He returns to staring ahead, doing his best to blank his admirer, but the guy is remarkably persistent. From the corner of his eye Dex can seeing him smiling and winking. But no. With what he hopes is a regretful smile, he turns to face the guy and with his finger in the air swipes left. The guy raises his middle finger in an unmistakable gesture and in that moment the phone buzzes again. This time, Dex decides, it's a well-timed distraction, the perfect excuse to leave the queue and the now hostile ex-admirer behind.

'Hey, babe, 's'up?' he says, finding a relatively quiet spot round the back of the beer tent.

'Babe?' Gav doesn't sound panicked or even drunk. It's not a happy voice though. Definitely not that.

'You back home?' Dex asks, checking the time on his phone, and thinks, *shit*, Gav's just going to bed and he's found something of Fabien's in their bedroom. Please God, don't let it be a condom. Anything else, Dex reckons, can be finessed, but there's really no smoothing over a rubber bag of someone else's junk juice when the rule – pretty much the only rule he's expected to follow – is that he doesn't bring other guys into their home.

'Did you take the money in the console table drawer?'

'What? No!' With a jolt to the brain he remembers he *has* actually dipped in to the roll in the drawer. Maybe a grand or two's worth, but not all of it. Not even half. A small loan. Anyway, whatever. They're married. It's all their money, isn't it? He stops in his tracks, takes a deep breath and tries to think through the fog in his brain.

'Why, is it gone?' he says, stalling for time. Dex fishes in his shirt pocket for a cigarette and failing to find one, jams his hand in his pocket.

'Yeah, the whole lot.'

'Everything?' Doesn't he remember seeing what remained of the cash roll in the drawer when he went for the keys to let in the pizza delivery woman? And why is Gav checking now?

'Anyone been in the house while I've been away?'

'No,' he lies. A possible get-out clause comes to his mind, which he feels bad about but not bad enough to stop himself. 'Well, obviously, there's Sandra.'

No response. Evidently Gav doesn't believe the cleaner is the thief. Obviously Dex doesn't believe it. Sandra has been with them for years and in all that time has shown herself to be completely trustworthy. Something terrible would have had to have happened for her to have resorted to thieving and if it had, Dex and Gav would have been the first to have found out about it. So who did take the money? Dex's mind works back to the encounter with Fabien. He recalls coming down the stairs and going to answer the door, then remembering that he'd locked it and asking the pizza delivery woman to wait. He went back to the console table, opened the drawer and took out the house key. He distinctly remembers the slight, dark woman in the porch. After that it's less clear. He's pretty sure Fabien called him about finding a towel in the bathroom. Did he ask the pizza delivery woman to wait a moment for her money while he went upstairs and dealt with his date? Did he close the console table drawer? He can't recall. What he does remember is the irritation he felt at the sound of Fabien's voice. In any case, he must have turned his back for a moment or two. Long enough for the pizza delivery woman to have taken the cash? Or had Fabien grabbed it on his way down from the bathroom? Didn't Dex open the drawer again when he let Fabien out of the house? Or was the door still unlocked from the pizza delivery? What if he just tells Gav he got a takeaway pizza? But no, because then Gav will want to investigate the delivery woman and it'll come out that he actually bought two pizzas. And anyway, Gav might check on the CCTV and see the pizzas being delivered. Worse still, he might see Fabien's departure. Dex is kicking himself for not having access to the CCTV camera. That's always been Gav's department.

He feels himself stumble a little and his head begins to swim. He's too drunk to be having this conversation right now.

'Let's sort it in the morning, sweetheart,' he says.

There's a pause. Gav's not going to be deflected that easily.

'If you took it, you need to tell me right now, Dex.'

Gav's hectoring, faintly parental tone really gets up Dex's nose. He's using it more and more even though Dex has told him how much he dislikes it. He only skimmed a few hundred pounds off the roll here and there because he assumed Gav had forgotten it. He's become very flaky over the past few months.

'How long has it been since you checked it?' he ventures. He knows Gav can't have looked at the money in a while because, if he had, he would have noticed that it wasn't all there.

'I haven't spent it, if that's what you're suggesting,' Gav says, irritably.

Some music starts up nearby. Dex doesn't want to be in this situation, being snapped at on the phone in the middle of the night when he should be enjoying himself.

His finger hovers over his phone screen.

'Sorry, hon, it's just too noisy here, talk tomorrow,' he says, tapping the red phone icon and dropping the phone back in his pocket.

A wave of relief crashes over him. He takes a deep breath and tries to get his vibe back on, but it doesn't quite work. Damn, Gav has spoiled his night. What I need right now is a jaegerbomb, or a jelly shot, take the edge off, he thinks. He looks about, spots a bar tent and makes his way towards it, diving around groups of extravagantly costumed revellers and sparkly girls in couples. He wonders why he takes part in hook-up culture, really. It's actually not about the sex. He's always had a low libido. Could it be that he's still rebelling against his dad? Shit, that would be sad, but not beyond the realms of possibility. He had hoped he was out on the other side of all of that now. God knows he'd tried to conform. That whole period with Cassie, playing the happy straight guy, telling himself that the circle jerks and mutual masturbation seshes at boarding school were just growing up stuff. If only his parents hadn't been such bigots he could have avoided all of that. Saved him – and Cassie – a lot of heartache. He thinks about them with hatred, the way they tried to shoehorn him into living exactly the same dreary, conventional, brain-dead life in the suburbs that they themselves were leading. He thinks, who does that to their kid? No wonder he doesn't see them any more. No wonder he rebelled.

A drunk guy crashes into him and slaloms away. Something about it sets him off. He suddenly feels quite murderous. Mate, calm down, he says to himself. Get yourself a shot, feel better, go back to the others, dance, have fun. He's approaching the bar tent when he sees her. At first he's not sure. She's wearing a red outfit now. Before, she was in cycle gear. But the closer he gets, the surer he becomes that the figure standing unsteadily beside the chill-out tent, smoking a cigarette, is the pizza delivery girl.

12

Cassie

8.00 a.m., Friday 30 September, Isle of Portland

Tapping the words 'Marika' and 'Lapska' and then the
word 'Thames' into Google brings up links to two articles
in the *Standard* and a small mention in the *Southwark
Sentinel*. The first article is dated 17 August, two days
after Marika Lapska's body was dragged out of the river.
There's nothing in it I don't already know. At that stage
the police would not be drawn as to whether this was a
suspected suicide or the result of foul play. They say they're
making further enquiries. It must be these enquiries which
led to the call for witnesses in the second article. There's
no mention in either piece of evidence of rape or sexual
assault or of drugs or alcohol. The piece in the *Southwark
Sentinel* fleshes out the bones a little. It notes that you
were twenty-four years old, Marika, and that you lived on
the North Peckham Estate. It says you arrived in London
from Lithuania three years ago. Lithuania. I've ever been
there or know very much about, though from somewhere
in the great heap of geekery in my mind I'm able to pick

out Vilnius as the capital. My fingers peck at letters on the screen. Lithuania. The Wikipedia entry starts:

> Officially the Republic of Lithuania (Lithuanian: Lietuvos Respublika) is a country in the Baltic region of northern-eastern Europe. One of the three Baltic states, it is situated along the south-eastern shore of the Baltic Sea, to the east of Sweden and Denmark. It is bordered by Latvia to the north, Belarus to the east and south, Poland to the south, and Kaliningrad Oblast (a Russian exclave) to the south-west. Lithuania has an estimated population of 2.8 million people, and its capital and largest city is Vilnius. Lithuanians are a Baltic people. The official language, Lithuanian, along with Latvian, is one of only two living languages in the Baltic branch of the Indo-European language family.

The article in the *Sentinel* goes on to note that for the last year you worked for a food delivery company – it doesn't specify which one – and that your family back home have been informed of your death. I can barely bring myself to imagine how that conversation went. Parents do not expect their healthy twenty-four-year-old daughters to die.

But none of that tells me anything about how you lived. Did you come to London drawn to adventure or the prospect of a better life? In the three years you were in the city did you get what you wanted? What did you want, I wonder? Either way, you paid a huge price for the move.

Tapping the name into Google only brings up those three short articles. No social media accounts or tagged photographs in your name. Is that in itself a clue?

I read somewhere that a body turns up every week in the Thames and if every one of the drowned appeared in the news there would be stories all the time. All the same, it hardly seems possible that a young woman can exit this twenty-first-century world without leaving any virtual ghost of her former self. Yet it seems that's what happened to you, Marika Lapska.

None of us slept well last night. I heard doors open and close and the sound of the loo flushing at all hours. The owl kept me awake too. And the rush of the sea on the shingle. And the spirit of restlessness in the cottage. But mostly the owl. Even with earplugs jammed deep into my ears I was unable to shut it out completely. On and on it went.

If I tapped owl into Google right now, I'd no doubt be told that the owl is associated with wisdom and with death. I already know that. *Twit twoo, what did you do?*

Let's just establish what we did or didn't do, shall we, owl? Then perhaps you won't have to keep asking. We did nothing to help you. Nada, zip, nowt.

Are we clear now, owl?

Because another thing I already know is that the owl is you, Marika. Maybe not literally, or even spiritually. Maybe not in the sense that you inhabit the owl or that you and the owl are one. But in some other way which doesn't require definition.

Revenant. That's Bo's word.

So why don't you tell us what happened? Tell us what was going on in the alley that night? Were you drugged then raped by someone you knew or by a stranger? It's usually someone the woman knows, isn't it? Someone she trusts or someone she does not trust but cannot get away from. We could have got you away from him, Marika, couldn't we? If we'd tried. Did you see us, looking on, doing nothing? Was the shame of having your rape witnessed very terrible? Do you hate us for it? Do you blame us as much as you blame your attacker? What happened after we ran away, leaving you slumped in the alley, Marika? Did you come to yourself and stumble from the churchyard to the river's edge? Did you throw yourself into the water? Or did your attacker put you there?

Let me tell you something, Marika. I don't expect forgiveness but it might help you to understand. The window in my room in the flat I share (and which, I'm guessing, isn't so different from the flat you probably shared), gives out over Tottenham bus station. I can spend hours, sometimes whole weekends, staring out of that window, witnessing the pull and drift of lives I know nothing about. In the couple of years I've lived there, I've seen acts of extraordinary kindness – an elderly woman giving money to a junkie, a man stopping a bus with his hand to allow a handicapped person to board, a teen holding back a stranger's hair while she is sick. And I've seen acts of terrible brutality. A teen stabbing another, a gang setting on a drag queen, a homeless guy beating his dog. In the city a stranger is always looking. And at Tottenham bus station that stranger is very often me.

Maybe that's why I've never once intervened, never spoken up or called out, never phoned the police or posted anything on social media. Never done anything, in fact. I've watched my own life go by as if through that window too. I'm someone who doesn't intervene. Someone passive. A person psychologists would call the ultimate bystander. In general I drift from one thing to another. I let things happen. I do not fight for anything and I do not fight against anything. I'm just someone who floats along in the current and tries not to feel much. It's easier that way. It's also probably why I have reached the age I am without making many friends or much money or any real progress in life. I'm a keeper of secrets, an introvert, or, as a therapist once informed me, I have the classic profile of a child of alcoholic parents. A gift for tying myself up in knots in order to ignore their hidden surfaces. Expert at turning a blind eye.

The one time I might have intervened, in the churchyard, what I'd done earlier that evening meant I couldn't get involved. Couldn't call the police. Couldn't do anything.

Or perhaps not couldn't, exactly. More like *chose not to.*

As I lay sleepless in bed at the top of the house, I felt the presence of the Group below me but, far from being comforting, their restless energy felt like a hand pressing on my heart. I've been ignoring what I saw in the churchyard for weeks and most of me wants it to stay that way, but the *Standard* article has made that a whole lot harder. Until I read it just now, there were only a few observations and a few facts about what happened that night. Now there are the same number of observations but many more facts. I have always gathered facts, and among the facts now apparent is your name, Marika Lapska. Another fact is that Dex was captured on CCTV at the festival talking to a woman who was most probably you earlier the same evening. Which is why police have questioned Dex about the incident. But the most important new fact is that you died that night in as yet unknown circumstances and that your body was pulled out of the Thames. Did you drown, Marika? What does that feel like? I wonder. Is there only panic or also pain? What happens to the brain in the instant the water first enters the lungs? How do the lungs fill? Gradually or in one great rush? Does the chest compress, the diaphragm billow and protest? What do the eyes see as they dim back into the darkness?

I don't want to think that Dex might have had anything to do with your death. He certainly had nothing to do with your rape because while it was happening, at the far end of the alley, I saw his face lit up and terrible. In any case, I've promised Gav I won't say anything and I tell myself, because it's easy to tell myself this, that a promise to my friend trumps any responsibility I might have to you, Marika, or to the truth. Besides which, I know all the reasons now for not coming forward. And they are also facts.

I am going to stop talking to you now, Marika, and make my way back down the footpath to Fossil Cottage and let myself in by the back door. There's no need to follow me. I'm sure I'll be hearing from you again tonight.

In the porch I pull off my outdoor boots in the porch and try to forget my meeting with Gav and what I learned about Marika and the way that she is haunting me.

What you don't know can't hurt you.

In the kitchen Anna is slicing bread. A smell of bacon wafts from the grill and behind it, I detect the dank, spicy aroma of coffee.

'Oh hello, darling, how's the hangover? I thought you might have gone back to bed.' Anna tries a few probing questions about Will and, getting nowhere, gives up.

'Others awake?' I ask.

'Bo's gone for a run to clear his head. Dex is still in bed, obviously. I'm doing the bacon butties.' She begins spreading butter on toast. The kettle wheezes then clicks off. 'Be a sweetheart and make some more coffee, will you?'

Bo appears from the back porch, breathing heavily. His eyes land on the sandwiches and boom, he's at the table pushing a greasy triangle of meat and carbs into his mouth.

'Don't wait to be asked. Oh darling, how clever, you didn't,' Anna says, one eyebrow raised.

Many years ago, it must have been Trinity term of our

first year because I can still picture the sun beaming through the leaves of the great oak in Christchurch meadows, not long after I joined the group, Bo staged a buttie eat-off in his rooms. Being a Scholar, Bo had two, a study and off that a small bedroom. We cooked the bacon by hanging it over the antiquated two-bar electric fire in the study. As the bacon sizzled then began to burn we had to wrap the smoke alarm in foil to stop it giving away our antics. Anna, of course, didn't eat, and despite my best efforts I was no match for Dex or Bo who were, like most nineteen-year-old men, at the human dustbin stage. Dex ate more but Bo claimed victory on a technicality and Dex, who was always, even then, attracted to the path of least resistance, conceded. I understood then that Bo would never enter any competition unless he was already confident of winning. And if he couldn't win by fair means, foul ones would do just fine.

Dex was always lazier and less ambitious and, perhaps, more laid back. It's what I loved about him when we first got together. It made him a slow, sensual lover. I loved making love to him. It's still painful to be reminded of that sometimes. Like now, when, drawn from his bed by the smell of bacon and coffee, he appears in the doorway in his boxers, drowsy as a bumble bee, yawning and stretching that lovely, familiar body and giving no sign at all of a man who has anything to worry or feel guilty about. Dex never did do guilt. I admire that about him too. Life washes over Dex and he always manages to come out clean.

'Hello, darling, you look like you could use a coffee,' Anna says.

Dex slaps over in bare feet, arms pinned to his sides in a chest stretch.

'Who's that bloke I saw you flirting with from my bedroom window?' he says to me.

'Was I flirting?'

'You were practically dry humping. Not that I blame you. We are talking hot. The bloke, I mean. Obviously, *you* are smokin'. I've got a boner just thinking about you.'

'Ha ha.' It's been a long time since Dex felt anything move on my account.

'Speaking of.' He's thumbing his phone, too hung-over to remember there's no signal. 'While Mr Bojangles here pounds some Portland pussy and Cassie is drilling the milkman . . .'

Mouth too full to talk, Bo flips Dex the bird.

Dex puts down his phone and reaches for the bacon butties before, thinking better of it, he throws his arms around my neck and plants a kiss on my head. Then, as suddenly, pushes back his chair, stands and begins belting out a rendition of 'Mr Bojangles', windmilling his arms and tapping out the rhythm with his feet, one half Bob Dylan, the other Robbie Williams. Moments later, he flumps down into the chair beside me and, like a cat in sunshine, stretches out, his mouth gaping into a luxuriant yawn.

'We . . .' he points to each of us in turn '. . . are going to have bloody good fun today.'

13

Cassie

I'm watching Dex throwing himself around to the band on the main stage.

Lovely, funny, lazy Dex. He hasn't changed his dance style in more than a decade. The same slide of the right leg and odd left hip gyration so familiar from the early days when all four of us would sneak into the Botanical Gardens together at night, drink vodka, share a joint and make Lady Gaga shapes to the soundless tunes in our heads. Is that where Dex is now? Perhaps we're all stuck in a time warp, to some degree or another. I take myself back to the time just after graduation, when we were all living in that horrible, damp house off the Iffley Road and not in any hurry to begin our lives in the real world. How free and effortless everything seemed! How wonderfully intense and yet, somehow, uncomplicated.

If only it had stayed that way, but, of course, the real world arrived and, in one way or another, we moved out to meet it. As I recall, I was the last to go, clinging on to my former life as long as I could by taking tutoring jobs for hothoused kids from private schools and in the evenings helping undergrads rewrite their essays in exchange for cash. And although some part of me knew the instant I walked out of the exam school at the end of finals that this part of my life was over, I struggled to accept it. We all did. This is why some part of who we are has remained fixed in that moment. It's the reason their friendship has survived the drift away from Oxford to London, the break-up of our respective relationships and the formation of Dex and Anna's marriages. This is why the Group remains at the heart of our lives, a back channel to the days when everything seemed to shimmer with hope and possibility.

Isn't that what all long-standing friendships are about?

The song ends and with it the distraction and in its dying fall the soreness where earlier the tattooist left his mark and at some more diffuse and tangible place, the pricking of my conscience starts up again. I still have no idea what possessed me to do what I did but supposing I could find the woman I wronged, attempting to explain the act would only get me into more trouble because there's simply no reason for my having behaved the way I did. I can't even claim that I was overtaken by a moment of madness. It was all very calm and rational and that's what's so troubling about it. I was offered a choice between right and wrong and I chose wrong and now I'm stuck with it.

'Hey,' Dex says, muzzing my hair. 'What's with the long face?'

'Nothing. Ink's a bit sore. Painkiller wearing off.'

He cups my chin in his hand and bops my nose as he used to do when we were together. Old habits.

'You need another drink, Cass. Mother Nature's best analgesic.'

I've already drunk too much but the ink thrums and the conscience continues to prick. 'Maybe a beer?'

On stage the band begins another song. A little way away Bo is impressing his moves on two dark-haired women a good decade younger than him. Anna has her back to Bo and she's started dancing and doing the flippy thing she does with her hair. Briefly catches my glance, chin dips towards Bo and eye rolls. Observing this, Dex waits until Anna's looking away before cracking a knowing smile. Anna and Bo, Bo and Anna. No longer dancing together but still doing the dance.

'Emergency vodka jelly shots all round. You stay here with the others. I'll get them, it's my turn.'

Dex waves a hand to attract the attention of the others, swings his wrist in a drinking gesture and shouts. Anna and Bo give a thumbs up.

I watch Dex shouldering his way through the crowd, pull my bag in close and wonder when my ex became someone I keep secrets from.

14

Cassie

Morning, Friday 30 September, Isle of Portland

We're following Bo up a steep scree-lined path to the quarry about fifteen minutes' walk from Fossil Cottage. What began as a blustery morning has calmed. In the low bushes on the cliffs bees buzz and in the mackerel sky the peregrines sound their warnings. Ravens chatter. Bo wants to show us the bestiary of creatures carved out from discarded blocks of Portland stone which he remembers from the days he spent here with his dad.

'For years I used to dream about this place,' Bo says. 'I'd wake up blubbing and covered in sweat. No one ever came to see if I was OK. I still do dream about it sometimes.'

Scattered about the scrub is a macabre petrified zoo of nightmares, odd unsettling combinations of goats and fish and Mer-Chickens, and dogs with unicorn heads.

'Oh God, I feel I'm trapped in someone else's bad acid trip,' Dex says, sweeping his head around to take it all in. 'Whoever made all this has some scary shit going on in their head.'

'Remind me not to come up here in the dark,' Anna says, shivering.

'Mate,' begins Dex, 'not being funny, but can we leave now?'

And so we follow Bo back to the main path, through a stile leading onto a slope of low brush and heathers. There are goats here, Bo says, which were released a few years ago to keep the vegetation down and have since gone feral. Hence the fencing. We emerge from the brush and walk on to another stile and down a steep track giving onto the beach at West Weare. On the cliff behind us looms the grey expanse of the prison and young offender institute. To the north lies the port from where the convict ships left for Australia.

'I think this might be the weirdest place I've ever been apart from Newcastle on a Saturday night in winter.'

'What's weird about Newcastle?' Bo wants to know.

'Have you *been* to the Toon on a Saturday night in winter? It's freezing and the streets are full of packs of young men and women out hunting and everyone is, like, dressed to the nines and at the same time almost naked.'

'Oh, this is much weirder than that,' Bo says.

'How is that even possible?' asks Anna.

Bo just smiles and says, 'You'll see.'

Heading downhill we pick our way through gorse and bracken towards the beach in the hope of finding fossils. This being late September, the earlier calm didn't last long and a chill wind is now blowing off the sea and onto the

Underhill. In among the rocks a few hardy shrubs poke their heads experimentally from the shelter of the grass, their branches waving plastic wrappers and the occasional dog poo bag. We separate and begin to comb the beach. In the quiet by the shoreline, Marika begins to resurface in my mind. Perhaps it's the proximity to the water. Eventually Anna moves closer and shifts the pebbles with her foot.

'Find anything yet?'

'Nope. You?'

She doesn't answer but stands for a moment in silence, looking out to sea.

'So what did Gav want?' Her face is turned to mine now and she's smiling.

'What, last night?'

Anna presses her lips into a line and waggles a finger in the air. 'Now, now, Cassie, don't be coy. I saw his car in the lane this morning then you trotted in a few minutes later.'

'Oh that. He asked me not to say anything. I think he was feeling embarrassed about being so grumpy so he drove all the way back from Exeter to come and apologise but I persuaded him out of it. You know what Gav's like. Bit of a drama queen.'

Anna hovers for a moment then flashing a smile, says, 'Well, I'm glad. We all want this weekend to be about just the four of us, alone, together.'

We carry on for a while, sweeping the beach for fossils. Eventually Anna loses interest and begins to meander through the rock pools. Dex takes to a nearby rocky ledge and sparks up a smoke.

'Bloody lightweights,' mutters Bo, without any real feeling.

At the mouth of the path which leads off from the beach and winds its way along the west side of the Fleet, Bo and I stop to admire the view from the water, across the Fleet to Chesil Beach and with Weymouth in the distance to the east.

'What happens now?' asks Dex, strolling over.

'We carry on looking for fossils,' says Bo.

'But we haven't found any.'

Bo digs into his pocket and pulls out a triangular-shaped rock. 'Shark's tooth.'

Dex's eyebrows slide up his face. 'How fitting.'

Just then Anna appears, holding out a small, bullet-shaped object. 'I found this, but I don't know if it's a fossil or just some old car part.'

Bo smiles. 'It's stone. A bit of a giveaway.' Turning the thing over in his hand, he says, 'If you actually want to know, it's a belemnite. I used to have a ton of these in my room at college.' He's looking at Anna as though she should remember that.

Anna waits a beat before replying, 'I was never looking at your rocks, darling.' It's always tricky, this Anna/Bo thing, even after all this time. Dex and I have got to the point of pretending not to notice.

'They're squid bits,' Bo says.

'What, like cocks?' Dex says, pursing his lips and giving a little shimmy.

'Fossilised phragmocone. Squid don't have cocks.'

'Of course they do. All blokes have cocks. Even squid blokes. I should know.'

Bo shakes his head in mock wonder. 'How did anyone ever mistake you for straight? No offence, Cassie.'

'Oh, Cassie doesn't mind, do you, darling?' Anna jumps in.

'Would it matter if I did?'

'Not really,' Bo says. *Ho ho ho.* 'Another half hour then lunch?'

Anna and Dex synchronise an eye roll then turn and head off together, hand in hand, laughing at some shared joke, leaving me and Bo standing beside the rocks.

'For someone whose husband is about to kick the bucket, he's remarkably cheery this morning,' Bo says, darkly.

'We're doing our best to get away from all the shit this weekend, aren't we?'

Bo turns his head and throws me a quizzical look, then, realising he's not interested in pursuing the question, resumes his habitual poker face. We start along the beach again, Anna and Dex by the water's edge and me and Bo up at the beachhead, where the pebbles meet the mud at the base of the cliffs.

'Do you miss all this?' I say to Bo.

He looks at me as if I'm a little mad. 'What, fossiling? The palaeo thing? Not really. You know me, Casspot, I don't give much thought to stuff like that. Anyway, algorithms aren't all that unlike fossils, really.'

'How so?'

'In the sense that they're just an expression of natural laws. They've been there as long as nature itself.'

'I don't get the analogy.'

'Really? You're usually such a brainiac. I guess all I mean is that an algorithm is an inherent part of nature, just like fossils are an inherent part of the rock strata. It's like us in a way. We're all just component parts of a bigger thing.'

'You mean, like God or something?'

'More like the Group. People used to think fossils were the remnants of animals that didn't make it onto Noah's ark. They didn't even start to question that theory until the beginning of the nineteenth century.'

'It's weird that it took so long.'

Bo shrugs. 'People choose not to ask the right questions when they don't want to have to deal with the answers. The larger point I'm trying to make is that fossils aren't just foreign bodies embedded in rock. They're actually part of the rock itself.' He stands tall, checks to see where the others are and swinging his rucksack across his shoulders, takes out a half of Bell's and hands it over.

'Hair of the dog. Don't tell Anna. She keeps nagging me about the booze.' I take a sip and hand back the bottle, the remains of which Bo pours down his throat all at once, as if he were putting out a fire. 'But it's my bloody birthday and we're bloody well going to have a bloody great weekend.'

By one o'clock we are all done and gathered together on the beach to inspect our haul.

'Whoever first described these thought they looked like

ram's horns, so they named them after the ancient Egyptian ram's headed God Amun, Lord of Good Counsel,' Bo says, fingering Anna's incomplete fragments of ammonite.

'It's funny. After all these centuries, Zoroastrians still place their dead on a raised platform, because they think Amun can't reach them there. The Dokhma, they call it. The Tower of Silence.'

'Why don't they think the dead deserve good counsel?' says Anna, squinting into the bright marine light.

'I guess because, if they got it, they might choose not to remain dead.'

'Ooh, scary,' says Dex, revealing a handful of stone clams, which are, according to Bo, ossedes, spineless molluscs, and something vaguely spiral shaped which Bo identifies as coprolite, better known as a fossilised turd.

'If we are what we've found, I'm a shark and you're some spineless things and a pile of crap.'

'It might be your birthday but you're still a dick.'

'You love dicks . . .' Bo says. 'Which reminds me, I'm peckerish. Lunch, anyone?'

We order crab sandwiches and beer at a café on the beach one along. Anna pops outside to call home and speak to Ralphie and his babysitter while the rest of us, who have no one at home to call, thumb our phones or gaze out as if purposively over Chesil Beach.

'Storm forecast tonight so there should be some good fossiling tomorrow,' Bo says.

Dex's phone bleeps. 'Gav.' He gets up and goes outside to return the call and I'm reminded uncomfortably of this morning's conversation and of Marika. Our unforgivable turning away.

At the table opposite me Bo continues to gaze at his phone. He's pushed up the sleeves of his jumper, a starfish on one forearm, a homepage logo on the wrist of the other. The homepage is new.

'Checking your matches?'

'Nah, I got one lined up, remember? Just work stuff.'

'Mind if I interrupt?'

He looks up, his curiosity roused by the hint of serious-ness in my tone. As a rule Bo and I don't do earnest or sincere. Neither of us is built for heartfelt one-to-ones. Our friendship is basically fifteen years of ho ho ha ha bantz.

'That woman's been on my mind, the one we saw in the churchyard.'

Bo's eyes flick back to his phone before settling back on me. He wants to return to the virtual world, the world where there are no real events and no real consequences.

'Casspot, please. We agreed we weren't even going to talk about that.' He leans towards me until I can see every raised red dot of the shaving rash on his neck. 'Whatever was going on in that alley, I'm, like, cool just to let it go.' He pulls back, resumes a relaxed position, eyes on his phone. Outside, Anna is sitting on the wall talking behind a cupped hand. Dex is standing a way off, one hand in his pocket, pacing.

The food arrives and with it, Anna and Dex. We eat and chat inconsequentially about London mostly and the impossibility of finding the time to get together except around one another's birthdays and how it hasn't always been like that. Remember that last summer in Oxford, just before Bo made the move to London and broke the spell? We'd all graduated by then, still loosely two couples, drifting happily in and out of jobs we knew were dead ends but so much time bloomed ahead of us it didn't matter. Anna was waitressing at Brown's while writing songs and spending all her free nights in the pub music scene. Bo was working in a bike shop and developing his first big software project. Dex had finished the internship that his dad had set up for him in the law firm and come back to Oxford to work in the café at the Ashmolean Museum, and I was working on my MA and trying to decide what I wanted to do with my life. We were lost, but that felt good, a way of escaping the well-worn paths we saw others slipping into. Instead we cultivated rebel attitude with the freedom of the young not to have to define what we were rebelling against. The days seemed short and the nights endless. After work, we'd take beer and wrapped chips out to Port Meadow or cycle up to the Trout at Wolvercote and sit drinking on the riverbank with our feet afloat in the cool water. It was the run up to the financial crash, the moment before the Fall, but, we were ignorant of all of that and so we were in Paradise.

Anna and I order coffee. Before it arrives I go outside

for a smoke, an old and very bad habit I've returned to, on and off, since that night in Wapping. I sit on the wall and idly scroll through matches on my dating app, but every one is a left swipe, so I put my phone away and endeavour to return to the present, to this lovely weekend in Dorset with my friends, but it's hopeless. My brain remains stuck in a groove at the bottom of which is Marika and the churchyard and thoughts of drowning. Why can't I just leave it like the others seem to have done? Why don't they seem to care?

It's suddenly got much colder out here. I stand and turn to go back inside and as I do, my eye lands on a small, dazzling object on the beach. When I move to avoid it, the sparkle appears to move too, so, heading towards the object, my phone still in my hand and expecting a wrapper or a pull-ring, I find instead a small ammonite, so shiny and so perfect in its definition that it looks brand new.

Returning to the wall where I was sitting smoking only a moment ago, I lay the fossil on my palm.

'You're lucky,' says a woman's voice. Belonging to a uniformed copper, taller than me and with dazzling conker-coloured hair. 'It's not common to find them in settled weather, and at the end of the season too.'

'Is it real?' It seems perfect, so untroubled by time I wonder if I haven't picked up an imitation of a fossil, a discarded piece of jewellery perhaps, or a pint-sized paperweight.

'Iron pyrite. Fool's gold, they call it. They're more common further west.'

We both stare at the object in my hand, in awe that such a small thing, a simple, mute, virtually brainless creature, alive in less than a blink in evolutionary time, should be transformed into something so perfect and so permanent. 'I'm Julie, by the way.' She points to her police badge. 'PC Blythe, Port Police.'

'You grew up here?'

She smiles. 'Is it that obvious?' We move on to a more general conversation about the island. I feign attention, but I am shocked to find myself longing to confide in Julie about the woman, drawn to her calm, authoritative presence as surely as if I were sailing into port after months at sea.

'Can't be much crime around here.'

'We get our share of the usual drugs, antisocial stuff, domestics, an occasional escape from one of the prisons. Every now and then some kid goes missing, but they always turn up.'

Shouldn't I be afraid of Julie finding out what we did, or what we didn't do that night in the churchyard at Wapping? Then why are the words already gathering themselves like a lifeboat about to put out to save a drowning soul?

Julie nods at the ammonite glittering on the palm of my left hand. 'I always think they're like messengers, you know, from history, or from another time. The things they'd tell us if only we understood the message. It's an old custom around here to put one of those under your pillow at night. People say it makes you dream about your future.'

'Funny, someone else told me that.'

We're looking directly into one another's eyes now. Can she see the dark clouds rushing across my face? My mouth opens and at that moment Bo bursts through the door. 'Your coffee's getting cold, Casspot.'

'Okey doke, well, fine words butter no parsnips, as my old dad used to say. I've got criminals to catch.' Julie holds out a hand. The fingers, which are more elegant than mine, brush against my fingertips and the moment for truth vanishes.

Bo says, 'What you got?'

'An ammonite, in fool's gold. And no, you can't have it for your birthday because I'm keeping it.'

He laughs, holding the door open in that way men do when they are laying claim to their size relative to yours, consciously or otherwise, with his hand clasped against the door above head height, giving me no option but to duck back inside the café. As we approach the table Anna finishes a mouthful of food and wipes her lips with a napkin.

'What were you doing out there all this time?'

I open my palm and let the ammonite fall onto the table. Dex picks it up and begins to turn it over in his hands.

'Is that what you were talking to that policewoman about?' Anna asks. There's something dark and raw in her tone, like a winter wind.

'Among other things.' I recount what Julie said about the old fort built by prisoners and the holiday park where you can get lovely Dorset cheeses, and the collection of old photographs and memorabilia in the prison museum up on the top of the hill.

'And she mentioned the stables, the ones Will said something about.'

Anna's eyebrows rise and a crispness reappears on her face. 'Oh, I'd love to go for a ride on the beach, wouldn't you, darling? Maybe we could do that when the men go fishing.'

A thought arrives. 'Oh, yes, and she says there's this old Portland custom where men who behave badly towards women can be stoned off the island.'

Dex eyes Bo. 'Mate, that's us on notice.'

We chuckle because we expect that of each other but, as I look around at the Group, I wonder which of us is laughing inside.

15

Anna

12.30 a.m., Sunday 14 August, Wapping

As she said it she felt bad using Ralphie as an excuse, but the feeling has long since passed and now, sitting in the Uber as it makes its way east from St Katharine Dock back to Wapping, it amuses her to think about what the others would say if they knew the truth. Not only about the affair, but about what came before it.

The desperation, after the accident, to run as hard as she could, and at any cost, towards life. The surprise pregnancy while she was still convalescing (her periods had stopped long before, hence the surprise), then the business of keeping Ralphie's paternity a secret, even after Cassie had already guessed it. Watching herself balloon while the people who were supposed to love her flat out lied about how gorgeous she looked and how blooming. And then her marriage to Isaac, which everyone but Isaac himself understood as a settling, and since then, the daily struggle to avoid slipping up and letting on.

She crosses her legs, admiring the stretch of the skin to

shininess over the knees, recalling the time it took just to be able to look at Ralphie without resenting the fact that it was he who had caused her to grow fat. The shame of her hostility towards her baby son like carrying something necrotic and gangrenous inside you. Thank God she was able to lose her baby weight, and then quite a bit more after Bo visited her a month or so after the birth and chucked her under what he described as her 'sweet little food chin'. She was so hurt she nearly broke. Thank God she didn't. He had always said even when they were together that he couldn't guarantee not to run if ever she got pregnant. Even now, nearly a year on, she reimagines the scene and what could have happened if she'd told Bo that he was in part responsible for the chin and, indeed, the baby. That would have been the last she'd have seen of him, most likely – the most important person in her life. Ralphie not excepted.

She catches herself in the rear-view mirror. People always say a baby looks like its father, at least in the first few months. In Ralphie's case they were not wrong. Anna can't see anything of herself in him. To her he's all Luke 'Bo' Bowen. Once Ralphie gets a bit older it will probably become obvious. Anna wonders if Isaac will notice. Her sense is that if he ever finds out he'll decide not to say anything and to carry on as before. In return, Anna will continue to pretend to love and be faithful to him. A devil's bargain, the kind couples make all the time. When the penny does eventually drop, Anna feels well able to handle it. If Bo finds out, on the other hand, say if Cassie ever blurts it, Anna would run the risk of losing him. It makes her sick just to think about that.

She shifts on the upholstered seat, in an attempt to chase the thought away, and in doing so releases a tang of vomit which rises to meet the stench of cheap vanilla air freshener. Great, so she's sitting in someone's lightly disguised Saturday night barf which has been poorly wiped. Though in a way it's a relief because both vom and air freshener serve to mask the unmistakable odour of sex. She feels the delicate tissue of flesh between her legs strain just a little. It makes her sad, the way it ended with Ollie, but also angry. Anna is used to being the dumper not the dumpee. Though there was Bo. The first and by a long way the worst. Has she brought this on herself, the unsettling sense of being trapped in the wrong life? Doesn't everyone feel that at some point in their lives? Having Ralphie didn't help, but she can hardly blame it on the baby. The pretence started a long time before.

It's not easy being beautiful. The manufactured air of mystery expected of women who look like Anna, the constant toggling between simpering sex kitten and ice queen which seems to be required. This is the only way in which she envies Cassie. There's no pressure on Cassie to be anything at all. No one cares. Cassie gets to be Cassie.

The taxi comes to a halt just outside the festival gates. Anna checks her hair very briefly in the rear-view mirror, fans away the flush on her neck. It's after 12.30 now. The touts are all gone. A few taxi drivers wander about in front of the entrance hoping to pick up some business from any early leavers either too drunk to work their Uber software or too impatient to wait. A lone copper chats with two security guys in hi-vis vests. Everyone looks cold and washed out and eager for the night to end.

Thanking the driver (always so bloody polite) she gets out of the cab, leaving the back door open until she's had a moment to check herself once more in the car side mirror. She's wiping a little stray glitter from her cheek when something or someone thickens the air behind her. A man? The next Ollie perhaps. A pulse begins in her left temple but she doesn't turn her head because it pays to be cool. Men expect it, the way she looks. She's moving to close the car door when an arm reaches out and a hand clutches the doorframe. Her eyes flit to the hand of a small-boned woman. The arm thin and wiry-looking, even dressed in a cheap leather jacket. Around the wrist is an entrance band from the festival. In her peripheral vision she notes the driver check the rear-view mirror. A wobbly, accented voice says, 'Please! I need taxi.'

Anna's head spins. She draws herself up to full height, turns in what she hopes is a regal manner. Behind her stands a petite brunette in heels, shifting her weight from side to side. East European, Anna thinks, and very drunk or maybe on something. Not my circus, not my monkeys. Leaving the cab door open, Anna steps aside to let the woman get by, but instead of getting in, the woman sinks her face into her hands and clutching the imitation leather bag around her shoulder, wails, 'I have no money, please. No credit card, nothing. Someone steal.' The woman is sobbing and thrusting her open bag in Anna's face now in a way that's quite frightening. The way her date with Ollie ended, Anna really doesn't need this.

'I can't help you!'

She's grabbing Anna's arm now. 'Please, I'm scared.' Anna feels herself give just a little.

The woman seems frail and vulnerable. Someone's taken advantage of the state she's in. Maybe . . . And she would have found her a tenner if at that moment the woman's fingernails hadn't embedded in Anna's skin like tiny knives. In an instant, she feels herself harden and grow brittle. No one made this woman take whatever high she's taken. This is not on Anna. How bloody dare this total stranger impose herself.

'I just broke up with my boyfriend!' Anna hears herself say. Somewhere inside she's laughing at herself. I sound like a love-sick eighteen-year-old! She pushes the woman's hand away, but instead of letting go altogether, the woman transfers her attentions to the fabric at the shoulder of Anna's jumpsuit, taking hold of it so tightly that Anna is afraid to move lest it tear. All her previous sympathy has completely drained away now, leaving only outrage at the intrusion. She lifts a hand and slaps the woman's arm hard enough to leave a red welt. Shocked, the woman lets go of Anna's shoulder but instead of fleeing or even retaliating, she stands fixed to the spot, bewildered, not knowing what to do next.

'You hurt me,' the woman says finally.

'What?! You *assaulted* me. I'm sorry but your bag isn't my problem. You need to tell the police.' This makes Anna feel better, much less like a bitch.

But the woman doesn't appear at all grateful for the change in Anna's tone and instead of moving away, she shakes her head, her lips trembling as if she's about to burst into tears.

'Police won't believe.'

This really is too much. A long whine. Slamming the door of the cab, Anna signals the driver to be on his way. He's watched all of this in the rear-view mirror. Now he hesitates for an instant, then shrugging and shaking his head, pulls back out into the road.

The last Anna sees of the woman, she appears to have slumped to the ground. The policeman has gone now and the security guard is very deliberately looking the other way. A tall man in a hoodie, who looks as out of as the woman, watches as she tries to pull herself to her feet.

That's not going to end well, thinks Anna.

16

Cassie

We decided to make Friday afternoon down time and after lunch the four of us went our separate ways. Bo took the car to his date, Anna was at the cottage prepping, she said, for a presentation to a client on Tuesday, and Dex, who had really only pretended to work since marrying Gav, had gone back to bed. As for me, I struggled to settle into anything productive or even relaxing. Lovely though it was, something about Fossil Cottage, with its thick walls and sombre quiet, reminded me of a tomb.

Consumed by a need to get away and clear my head, I shoulder my rucksack and head down the muddy path to Fortuneswell and The Mermaid in search of Will. The pub sits on the corner of the high street where it joins the main road heading up to the top of the cliffs. Like most of Fortuneswell, it's unreconstructed and old-fashioned, with sticky swirly patterned carpets and dark wood fittings, a world away from the carefully constructed retro ambience of so much of London these days. There's Will, pulling a pint for an old man with a seagoing face. He clocks me, nods and passes the pint to the old man.

'Bit short,' the old man says, piling a heap of coppers on the counter. Will tells him not to worry, then turning to me with a broad smile on his handsome face, says, 'Hi there. How was the view?'

I take a seat at the bar and at Will's recommendation order a bottle of The Mysterious Mer-Chicken.

'It's a saison, brewed in Blandford, not far from here,' he says.

'Saison?'

Will pours a finger of beer into the glass, invites me to try it.

'Tell me what you can taste.'

'Spicy and sort of tangy? Maybe a bit fruity?'

He raises his eyebrows and tips me a wink. I like Will.

A couple arrives and he moves across the bar to serve them. In snatched conversation between customers, Will suggests we meet up tomorrow afternoon and I say absolutely, yes, and we're swapping phone numbers when a group of anglers comes in and Will is suddenly preoccupied. I'm finishing up my beer and thinking about getting back to Fossil Cottage and forcing a conversation about the drowned woman, when in walks the policewoman from this morning, dressed in jeans and a Fair Isle sweater. Spotting me at the bar, she comes over, winks at Will.

'So he's got you on the Mer-Chicken already.' She takes

the bar stool beside me. Her eyes dart between me and Will. 'Come across any more fossils?'

'A couple, down at West Weare, not counting the couple in the pub here.'

She smiles politely at my bad joke, waits till the anglers have been served then catching Will's eye orders a pint of Golden Glory and another bottle of the Mer-Chicken for me.

'You two know one another?' asks Will.

'We do now.' Julie raises her glass. 'To new friends.' Once Will is out of earshot she adds in a soft voice, 'You could do a lot worse.'

'Speaking from experience?' Julie shrugs. 'It's a small island. Everyone dates everyone eventually. It was a long time ago.' She rolls a simple wedding band between the fingers of her right hand. 'Six years next July. Kev. Works at the station at Weymouth West. I'm with the Port Police. Coppers end up marrying coppers. Saves the moaning about shift patterns.'

'Anything juicy happen since I last saw you?'

'Like I said up at the café, it's mostly petty stuff. The Port Police generally handle boats going missing, insurance fraud, smuggling, that kind of thing. We get accidents on the cliffs and the quarries, the occasional tourist mishap. Domestics. Couple of those in the early hours. It's always worse at this end of the week.'

A tic starts up in my eye. 'There must be drownings.'

Julie shrugs, takes a swig, nods at my beer. 'You should

try the Golden. Proper beer.' A short, balding man walks by, lays a hand on her shoulder. A greeting is exchanged followed by a single peck on the cheek.

'Well, I'll leave you two girls to gossip,' the short man says.

Right.

'So, drownings then?' It has taken me some courage to work up to this and I'm keen not to leave it. 'So if you find someone in the water, like a body, how do you know if it's a suicide or an accident, or something worse?'

Julie thinks for a moment. 'Obviously, if there's stab wounds or something like that. Otherwise, there might be a history of mental illness, or previous suicide attempts. They might have left a note. But basically you don't, not always.'

'How far would the police investigate?'

She rubs a hand over her chin, feeling for the contours of the jaw. 'So far as we can, but sometimes there's not a lot to go on. It'll go to the coroner, but if there's no real evidence one way or another the coroner usually returns an open verdict.' She finishes her beer.

'Get you another?'

'Why not? If you're offering.'

Will has been joined by an older man behind the bar. The older man chin flicks to Julie and salutes. I order a pint of Golden for Julie, a half for me.

'She's trying to get you drunk, Julie,' the older man says, winking.

'She's bloody welcome to try, Trev.' She lifts her beer

and thanks me. 'Your good health.' Takes a long draught, puts the glass down and begins picking the cuticle of her left index finger with her right thumbnail. Trev is off at the other end of the bar now, serving a customer. 'Why do you want to know about drownings?'

'Oh, a neighbour, is all. I was just curious to know what happened to her.'

'Have you searched for press reports? Failing that, if the case went to the coroner, the inquest lists are all online these days. If you know where the inquest was held you can apply to look at the coroner's report. So long as you've got a name.' Her eyes narrow. 'But you said she was a neighbour, right?'

'Yes, a neighbour.'

'Sorry to hear that.' She meets my eye. There's an angle to her jaw that suggests puzzlement. The eyes deepen. Then she reaches for her beer and whatever notion is in her head is gone. 'We're being a bit bloody morbid for a Friday afternoon, aren't we?'

17

Cassie

God only knows why I did it. For all her faults, my mum never left me in the dark about the difference between right and wrong. Stealing's wrong, love. Don't ever be a tealeaf. An honest day's drinking for an honest day's benefit payments, that's the way. Mum's mantra, that was. Yeah, and maybe I should have listened.

But, of course, I didn't. At ten you don't know much but what you do know is that your parents, and people like your parents, aren't the people adults are referring to when they talk about good role models. In fact I used to steal from Mum all the time, skimming her benefits before she had a chance to drop most of it on cheap vodka. If you can call that stealing. Which, officially, I suppose, you can.

The point is, nothing is straightforward. People do stuff, terrible stuff sometimes, without the faintest idea why. Who can say they know why they do all the things they do? Maybe some of us know why we do some of the things. Maybe that's the best human beings can manage.

Sylvette are due to play the headliner set at midnight on the main stage, and the audience is gearing up, getting their drinks and snacks, using the loos. The usual insane queues. Still sober enough to use my head, I decide to venture to the periphery of the festival site, the part of the venue furthest from the river on the boundary with Tench Street, see what I can find away from the crowds. And there, under a row of London plane trees, sits the thing I'm after, a clean-looking toilet trailer with no apparent queue outside.

Of the six cubicles three are busy and two appear to be out of order. One cubicle is free. A woman is at the sink, hands hovering and swooping around the terrible bird's nest that is her hair. The face in the mirror is thin and anxious and part obscured by the hands, which rove around and above it like a troupe of spiders.

'Are you next in line?'

No response. I repeat the question and am shocked when the woman turns to see how rough she looks. Or not rough, necessarily, but haunted and very possibly ill.

'Are you OK?' She returns my expression of concern with a glazed slow blink which does not invite conversation.

I want you to know now that I have no clue as to what I'm about to do. Until an instant ago I was thinking only of relieving myself and getting back to the stage in time for the next set. Now, the idea floats in my head that I should try to get the thin woman to the first aid station or at least into the care of friends because she's in no fit state to be on her own. 'You really don't look well. There's a first aid place outside. I'll walk with you.'

A vacant stare. No one at home.

Still nothing, but when I make a move towards her, her body turns away. It takes her a second or two to reach the empty cubicle and shut the door behind her. The lock clicks.

What to do?

I tell myself that maybe it's not as bad as it looks. She just needs to throw up. I decide to wait, turning back to the bank of sinks to check I haven't got bag lady hair. There, lying abandoned on the shelf beside the basins, is a small tote, in green fake leather with a zip top. Beside the bag sits a comb.

Most likely this belongs to the skinny woman. She's too out of it to have remembered. I should go over to the cubicle and let her know. I should pick up the bag and knock on the door of her cubicle and pass it underneath. The gap's big enough. If I bend I can see her shoes. Cheap shoes with ill-fitting straps. She's sitting on the toilet seat, with her face to the door. Not being sick, evidently.

I reach out for the bag and swing it into my chest. The zipper is undone and one side sags a little under its weight, partially exposing the contents. In among the usual bag flotsam – a phone, a purse, some tampons, a lipstick – is something else. For an instant I feel myself pull back, shocked.

The person whose profile I see in the mirror as my hand dips into the soft interior of the bag is someone who looks like me but does not inhabit the same body. My heart is quickening but I'm not listening to my heart. In some other life, if it had contained something other than it does, perhaps I would have stood by guarding the bag until its owner reappeared. This would have been more like me. But none of this is what I do. Instead, my mind begins to stitch together an excuse in case I'm caught.

London, bomb threats, can't be too careful.

Some part of my crocodile brain, the deep reward centre, the one scientists trigger in rats until the rats forget to eat and starve themselves, that part is firing like mad. There is a woman who is both playing me and at the same time is me. Not an imposter exactly, but another version. But both women are telling the same tale. They're saying they need this, that money, *this* money, can change everything. A fragment of a moment later it is decided. After that, adrenaline takes over and in the blink of an eye it's done.

I have just become a criminal.

I know what you're thinking. You're thinking that would never happen to me. But believe me, it might. Because nothing is straightforward, least of all the human heart. At some point or other, we all become mysteries to ourselves.

I am at the door when one of the toilets flushes, the cubicle at the end opens and a young, lank-bodied woman emerges and heads for the sinks. The bag is where I first noticed it, jammed up against the mirror behind the sinks. It looks the same as it did before, though, of course, it's not.

I am half in and half out of the door now, my face and

body obscured by the dark, and from that half-hidden place I watch as the woman spots the bag, checks back at the other cubicles and glances up at the ceiling in search of CCTV and begins to empty it of what remains of the valuables. Before she notices there is a witness to the crime, I'm out, weaving around the crowd and only stopping once I'm clear of the food stalls to catch my breath. In the pocket of my jacket, taking up all the space, sits a roll of fifty-pound notes. And a voice in my head is saying, who brings so much money to a festival? As if chastising myself for my carelessness, some part of me already making that my problem, as if it is me who has been careless and I have only myself to blame for it being stolen, because, who *does* bring so much money to a festival unless they are up to something really immoral, like ticket touting or drug dealing? It's the work of an instant to make that money illegitimate, up for grabs, belonging, almost, to anyone.

Even me.

18

Cassie

Afternoon, Friday 30 September, Isle of Portland

Julie doesn't know anything about the farmer's market mentioned in the handbook at the cottage. The only market she is aware of is on Saturdays in Weymouth. The small supermarket in the high street keeps long hours but is almost entirely stocked with ready-meals and bags of crisps. She offers to show me the greengrocer, the only place, she says, I'm likely to get decent veg for our evening meal. Taking my leave of Will, I follow Julie out into the high street and down a cobbled alleyway to the side of the church, to a general store, which sometimes sells farm produce but often closes early on Friday afternoons. And randomly at other times too. The owner is a sculptor. He once showed Julie a vulva he'd carved, complete with inner labia and a deep vagina. He'd painted it in pink and purple hues and invited her to touch it.

'I told him, what you have in mind for that thing, the paint job will rub off in weeks, plus you might hurt yourself. Sad really. Harmless though,' she says, adding cheerily, 'There's lots like that on Portland.'

Once we get to the greengrocer's front door, Julie points to a man in a brown jerkin who is smiling and waving. 'Name's Joe. If he offers to show you his sculptures, remind him you've just popped in for a bit of rhubarb. Though, maybe not rhubarb. Maybe potatoes. Yeah, potatoes. He probably won't though, because you're not from round here and you look like you can handle yourself.' She holds out a hand. 'And good luck.'

'Oh, I can handle the Joes of this world,' I say, taking the hand. Her palm is dry and papery but the grip as firm as you'd expect from a copper. I want to believe that the pervs and creeps haven't a prayer with me, but it's not true, is it? I saw what I saw in the alley and I ran away.

'I meant, with Will,' Julie says, laughing, and for an instant I'm taken aback, afraid that I might have just said what I said out loud. My eyes flit to Julie who seems unperturbed.

'If we don't see each other again, thanks.'

'What for?'

'The beer, the advice, for telling me what fossils are.'

'Did I tell you that?'

'Yeah, you said they were fool's gold.'

She throws back her head and lets out a bark. 'Oh, I did, did I? Well, we're all fools for something, aren't we? By the way, that neighbour you mentioned. She got a name?'

'Marika Lapska, why?' The words tumble out without my properly thinking them through.

'I could do a bit of digging around if you like?'

'Oh no, no. I mean, that's really kind, but no.'

And with that Julie reaches out a hand, pats my shoulder and turns on her heel back up the cobbled path beside the church.

I watch her go, pause for a moment before entering the shop and think of texting Anna, who is the weekend's chief meal planner, then remember that there's no signal in Fossil Cottage. I've just walked across the threshold into the shop when my phone buzzes with a text. Gav: *At sister's. Soz abt this a.m. All a bit weird. Pls don't tell Dex.*

Glad, I tap out in reply, *Fine re Dex.*

Receiving a quick *x* back from Gav, I'm about to slide the phone back into my pocket when the screen lights up. This time it's Anna on a voice call. Anna has never been very good at solitude, which leaves her with no one to boss or fuss over or control. Anna doesn't mind what company she keeps so long as it's never her own.

'I thought you'd be at the cottage. Bo isn't back yet and Dex is still asleep. I've had to go halfway down the hill into town to get a signal.'

I explain I'm buying stuff for supper.

'Oh, Cassie, how sweet of you. I was going to make Bo drive us into Weymouth when he got back from his hook-up. You'd think supermarkets in these places would stock all kinds of lovely local produce but they never do. All they ever sell is cheap booze, massive bars of chocolate and fifty shades of Doritos. But if you can find some nice stuff locally . . . Listen, since I'm already halfway into town, why don't I come and help you carry the shopping up the hill?'

I've been hoping to have some time to sit on the bench at the church by myself and search the coroner's records, try to find out whether Marika's death was suicide or foul play. Do police turn out for suicides? I suppose they must. But perhaps if I whizz through the shopping there will be a few minutes before Anna arrives.

'Meet me in the churchyard?' I check the time on my phone, add a half hour and turn my attentions to the piles of vegetables in plastic trays.

'Hi,' a man's voice says. 'Holidaying here?'

'Hi. Actually, I just came in for potatoes.'

Fifteen minutes later I'm sitting on a bench in the church-yard plugging 'Tower Hamlets coroner's court' into my phone then tapping 'Marika Lapska' into the search box.

Nothing.

Is it too soon? Do all records go automatically online or only some? If it was a suicide would the coroner's report still be in the public domain? I realise I should have asked Julie a few more questions. There must be some record of Marika's body being pulled from the Thames. It's not possible that a young woman drowns in the Thames in the twenty-first century and there is nothing at all about it on the internet. It's simply a matter of finding out where to find it.

'There you are.'

Anna appears, from behind the war memorial, looking a little flustered. 'What did you get?'

'Potatoes.'

Reaching for the bag on the bench beside me, she peers inside. 'I thought you'd be in the pub making a play for Will.'

'I think the Spar has broccoli.'

'Seriously? The greengrocer had literally nothing green?'

'It's a long story.'

Anna gives me a good long stare. 'Don't tell me you were too distracted.' A smile breaks out. 'You were. How completely brilliant. Sooo, tell all.'

'We're meeting tomorrow afternoon. He's working till then.'

'God, how delicious! I miss my single days. Sometimes it feels like I'll never have sex again. When you're a mother . . .' She looks at me with a condescending air, then pats my arm. 'You'll understand one day.'

I shoulder my rucksack. Anna picks up the bag of shopping. The pavings around the war memorial are set at odd angles, making Anna look a good foot taller than me. We set off.

'I've been thinking,' I say. 'I'm not going to put this one in the Big Black Book.'

Anna stops and offers up a wintry smile. 'Cassie, darling, don't be such a spoilsport. Me and Dex are *dying* to see what he looks like in the buff.'

'It seems, I don't know, a bit shitty. It's not like we met on some hook-up app.'

'Well, maybe, but let's be real, that's all this is ever going to be, isn't it? He lives here and delivers milk for a living.'

'Which means what, exactly?' It's rare I get irritated with Anna, or, rather, it's rare I actually express it. Because I know what Anna's like and I still remember her when she was happy and those two things together break my heart.

Anna cocks her head and presses her lips into a disapproving line. 'Why are you being so weird, Cassie? This isn't still about that Wapping thing, is it?'

'No. You've all made it very clear what you think about that.'

As we're walking down the street Julie appears from the dry cleaners and almost runs into us. She smiles and waits to be introduced, and then is off down the road in the direction of the cliffs. Anna watches her go.

'Isn't that the policewoman from yesterday? You two seem to be great friends all of a sudden.'

'She's a mate of Will's. It's a small town.'

We turn off the high street and begin to make our way to the steps which give onto the path leading up the hill to Fossil Cottage. But in some as-yet-indefinable way, Anna is right. The Big Black Book and Marika Lapska are connected, at least in my mind. I've been uneasy about both these things for weeks now, even before I knew Marika's identity or that she had died. But my uneasiness on Marika's behalf never came to a head. It never led to action. How much easier it was to forget her when she had no name. I was a witness to her objectification in the hands of her rapist and all I did was objectify her further. Wasn't that what we were all doing, to one extent or another, by photographing people who did not know they were being photographed, scoring their sexual performance and putting images of them up on the Cloud which showed them at their most vulnerable? No one asked for that, they never gave their permission.

'I think we should close the Big Black Book down.'

Anna seems surprised for a moment, then irritated. 'Why would we do that?'

'It's too bloody dark.'

'Oh you are a funny one, Cassie. It's just a bit of fun! It's not as if anyone knows anything about it except us.' She pauses, her eyes narrowing. 'Oh, this is about that woman.' She pauses and, putting her shopping bag down in the brush of ferns and dogwood on the verge of the path, rests her fists on her hips. 'We both saw how out of it she was. My guess is that it was either a horrible accident or she killed herself. But who knows? People can be very unpredictable when they're off their faces. In any case, it's a bit late to grow a conscience, isn't it? Given what *you* did earlier that evening.

'Anyway, darling, you said the police aren't pursuing it, isn't that right?'

'That's what Gav told me.'

'Is that what you were talking to that policewoman about?'

'No, of course not!'

And so we carry on up the hill towards the sheltered bowl where Fossil Cottage sits, the atmosphere between us soupy and thick. Halfway up the hill Anna stops and catches her breath for a moment. Above us, the falcons are mustering for their twilight hunt.

'I think it's just best not to say anything to either of the boys, don't you? About what we said earlier? Bo doesn't have to know and I don't want Dex to think we've been gossiping behind his back.'

We go in the front door, past the creepy statue of the Mer-Chicken, through the Farrow and Ball hallway into the kitchen-living room in silence. Before now it has never occurred to me to be afraid of Anna, but now, I can see that perhaps I should be. Dex is lying, one leg slung across the sofa, right hand scrolling through his phone, left clasped around the neck of a bottle of Corona. His eyes lift briefly from the screen. Anna walks past him into the kitchen area, sets her bag on the counter and fills the kettle.

''S'up?' Dex says idly.

You have three friends, and they are more or less the only friends you have in the world. More than that, over the fifteen years you've known them they have become your family. One has been your lover and betrayed you in a way that remains raw. The other two have also been lovers. Only one of these two is unhappy. The other is careless of the other's feelings but he has never done you any wrong and he's brilliant and the most fun a person can be. So tell me this. Who is most deserving of your loyalty?

Anna spins about. She's looking at me, her brow lifting. Say nothing. 'Gav call?'

'Yeah, we spoke, he's fine. He's with his sister.'

'You've been out?'

'Only to get a phone signal.'

Forgetting the coffee she was about to make, Anna goes into the fridge, brings out a bottle of New Zealand sauvignon, fetches two glasses and places the ensemble on the breakfast bar. I pour for both of us then take mine over to the wing back chair opposite Dex, who picks up the beer bottle which is now sitting on the carpet beside him and shakes it in his ear. 'Oh, Dexter, I see you've drunk your beer. Can I get you another?'

Anna and I exchange looks. 'Remind me, which one of us is your server tonight. Is it your turn, Anna?'

'Don't even . . .' Anna says. 'Anyway, where's Bo? Still on his date?'

Dex shrugs. I guess.

Removing a pork joint from the fridge, Anna places it on the counter beside the oven to come to temperature, then leaving the kitchen walks through the living room, sits down on the sofa beside Dex and curls her feet under his knees. 'Cassie swiped right.'

Dex's eyebrows raise. 'The breakfast bloke?' Somewhere in my psyche I still long for Dex to be in the smallest way jealous, but there's never been any sign of that. Lifting himself up onto one elbow he passes me his phone, saying, 'What d'you think of that?' Anna immediately gets up and comes over. If there's one thing Anna cannot bear it's not being the first in the know. Bending her head at an advantageous angle, she takes a look at the specimen on the screen. This is the part that has always most delighted Anna: helping us choose our next Black Book entries.

'He's older than that photo,' I say, caught up in an obscure need to stick the knife in.

'And you know that how?' says Dex. I point to the green haze in the background.

'No one uses that effect any more.'

'He says he's thirty-two on his profile,' says Dex.

'People always lie on their profiles,' Anna says.

A pulse starts up under Dex's eye. 'He's just some guy who fancies a hook-up. I probably won't even bother. Anyway, as you might have noticed by now, older men are my thing. You know, especially the ones with terminal illnesses.'

He's looking away from us, then, just as suddenly, his head swivels back, and his face is sunny, as if nothing raw and agonising was ever said.

Is this why you approached Dex at the festival, Marika? The friendly, but inattentive, easy-going face? A face that says 'I won't be rude or aggressive or try to outsmart you'. A face which might just belong to the kind of guy who, for an easy life, will give in and buy whatever you want to sell him, if that's what you were doing. I wouldn't have blamed you at all for thinking this. He gives such good face, does Dex, it's frightening.

You couldn't have known that Dex's good face is a lie.

Take this one time. One of many I've witnessed over the years. We were on holiday. Camping on one of the Greek Islands. My head says Santorini, but it might have been another. We used to go to Greece as often as we could which was often in the early days. I'd get a bar job, scrape together my share in a few weeks, Dex would do a spot of gardening at his parents' house then hit them up for his half and we'd be off. We loved the dry, undulant landscape, elderly couples tending vegetables in their tiny patches of garden, white churches and terraces of olive trees populated by skinny cats. Another couple, about to move to a hostel a few miles further down the coast for a couple of days before heading home to – where? Rugby comes to mind – with a blow-up mattress to sell. At this point we're in the islands for another two weeks and sleeping on mats. So Dex hands over the money – it felt like a lot, though it almost certainly wasn't – we take the mattress and by two o'clock in the morning it becomes evident that the couple has offloaded a dud. Fully pumped when we paid for it, the thing is now half the size and shrinking. There's a leak somewhere but it's the kind of leak you'd never find. But Dex won't let the mattress lie. Puts on his trainers and hits the road. Outside it's a full moon which helps him find his way but also, perhaps, contributes to his craziness. It takes him several hours but he finally springs the couple in their hostel up the coast. They haven't even got up yet. By mid-morning he's back at our campsite with the money and a very bruised fist.

If there's one thing Dex can't tolerate it's being ripped off. Funny for someone in the art world, which is all about that, really. Is that what you tried to do, Marika? That roll of fifties I took from your handbag. Three grand's worth. Sixty notes. I know because I counted them. Did you take that money? Just as I in turn took it from you? Or did he give it to you? Did Dex buy something from you? What were you selling that evening, Marika? Was it more of those pills you had taken? Or something worse? Your silence, perhaps? Surely it's no coincidence that what ended up in your bag, and then in mine, was the same sum Gav says went missing from his house? But if Dex took it, what was it for? And here's another question for you, Marika, if you did steal that money: why was Dex carrying three grand to a festival? If I could ask you that question now, would you know the answer? Dex knows, of course, but I've a feeling he'll never tell me. And I'll never ask. He means too much to me to risk losing him over money. Or even over you.

'You're lucky Gav is so understanding about other men,' Anna says, steering the conversation to safer ground.

'Maybe it's a gay thing, or maybe an age difference thing. Or maybe it's just Gav,' concedes Dex. 'So long as I don't bring strangers to the house, he's always been super-cool.'

'How funny. We feel the same way about Fossil Cottage, don't we, Cassie?'

Turning back to me so that Dex can't see, Anna brings her finger to her lips. *Don't say a word.* Then, rising to her full height, she makes her way into the kitchen.

'Now, who's going to help make Bo-Bo's birthday cake?'

And so we pass the time before Bo arrives prepping the dinner, ignoring the elephant in the room, and, as so often, reminiscing about the good old days, all the time we spent together before our thirties got in the way: graduation week camping in the Brecon Beacons, the Black Eyed Peas gig where we all knew all the words, the weddings of people we never saw again.

We don't talk about the police or the money or Gav's illness or Bo's drinking. And we definitely don't talk about Marika Lapska.

A couple of hours drift by. The cake mix is beaten, whipped, stirred and baked.

'Who wants to help me decorate?'

'Let's get some music on,' Dex says.

'We'll probably be needing this too,' adds Anna, popping a bottle of prosecco.

A problem arises immediately. Anna wants to do a cream cheese frosting but a hunt in the fridge and in the pantry quickly reveals that there is none in the cottage.

'Let's just get drunk instead,' Dex suggests, but I know that look in Anna's face. Sort of crumpled, like a little girl. In Anna's world everything is either perfect or pure unfiltered shit.

'I'll run to the shop and get some. Won't take more than twenty minutes.'

It's snivelly outside, but not cold. I don't know what I was thinking saying twenty minutes. It's at least ten minutes downhill to Fortuneswell high street, then allow five minutes to buy the cheese, and another fifteen to get back up the hill. I'll have to hurry to make it in half an hour. I'm barely in town when my phone picks up a signal and pings with texts. Better check to make sure there's nothing urgent. I pull out the device, tap in the security pin and scroll down.

The usual blitz of marketing messages, something from one of my flatmates, subject line, *My granola?????!!!!!*.

And a single text from Will: *Msg from J re yr neighbour: police not investigating any further. Drowned while under influence of drugs. She said you'd know what she's talking abt. See you tomorrow.*

Thirty-five minutes have elapsed before I'm back at Fossil Cottage. The bottle of prosecco is almost empty.

'God, you took your time! We were about to call the police and report you missing,' jokes Anna. While I've been gone, she and Dex have tried smearing the chocolate cake in what looks like butter but it hasn't worked. Mostly, by the looks of things, they've been drinking.

'Well, I'm here now, bearing a world of cream cheese.'

158

We decant the cheese into a bowl and Anna goes at it at a very leisurely pace with a fork. Every so often, Dex, who is sitting at the breakfast bar, dips in a finger.

'I should have told you to get vanilla and icing sugar,' Anna says, looking a little crestfallen.

'It tastes bloody delicious. Just whack it on,' Dex says. There's a pause. If I'm going to say anything, it needs to be now, before everyone's too drunk to absorb it. There's no point in beating about the bush.

'I found out what killed Marika Lapska.'

Dex, his cheesy finger frozen mid-air, creases his brow in evident bewilderment and says, 'Who?'

'You mean, who killed her?' Why would he ask that? Unless he suspected something. I watch his shoulders fall and a sigh issue from his mouth.

'No,' he says, his voice sharp now. 'I meant, who's she? But now you've said that, of course, I know you're still going on about that woman at the festival.'

'She drowned.'

'Mate, of course she bloody drowned. She was found in the river.'

'All I'm asking is that we call Crimestoppers and leave an anonymous tip-off.'

'And say what exactly?' Dex is red-faced and about to blow. Which is not something Dex does, at least, not unless he's feeling ripped off.

'Christ, Dex, what do you think? We say we saw her.'

I watch his jaw tighten, the breath catching a little in

the throat, his fingertips forming little white moons where they are gripping the countertop. 'The woman I saw in the alleyway wasn't the same one as in the paper. Jesus, Cassie, how many times?'

Dex stares ahead, his body bristling. Then slowly rising from his bar stool, he turns and leaves the room. We listen to his footsteps climbing the stairs.

'Cassie, can you please not do this,' Anna says in a brittle tone. And with a flick of her hair she turns on her heel and bustles off up the stairs to deal with Dex.

A while later Anna reappears in the doorway, wearing a blank expression on her face.

'We need to have a little chat. There is something I should tell you. But it has to be between us.' She goes over to the sofa, pats the cushion and waits for me to join her. Looking directly ahead, she says, 'That woman. The one you thought you saw being, you know.'

'Raped?'

Anna's voice rises a notch or two. 'Cassie, we don't know that.'

'But anyway—'

'I had a little brush with her.'

This trip is turning out to be full of surprises.

'You said you had no idea who she was!'

Anna clicks her tongue against her palate. Generally if she's angry with someone she walks away. But here we are, sitting on the sofa in Fossil Cottage, and there's no escape.

'If you remember,' she says, emphatically, in a loaded

voice, 'what I said was I didn't know the woman. Which I don't. But whatever. She tried to get me to pay for her cab home. Some crap about not feeling good and how someone had stolen all her money. She was just a mess. Completely off her tits. To be honest, I found her a bit scary. I may have given her a little push. Not that any of that makes any difference at all to anything. It's just, you know, the police try to drag you into things.'

'You pushed her?'

Anna sits tall and crosses and uncrosses her legs. 'Just a tiny shove. She was being scary. Anyway, she lost her footing and had a bit of a tumble so I helped pick her up. She wasn't hurt or anything. But honestly, though, can you believe people? If *someone* hadn't stolen her money . . .' her eyes fixed on me '. . . she'd have called a cab and she'd be alive today, so I really think the thief is more to blame for this than anyone.'

'Including the guy who raped her?'

'The point is, if you carry on like this, it may just be better for you to go home. And if you insist on this police crap, you're really going to have to think about your place in the Group. We can't have disloyalty. We just can't.' She moves towards me and putting both hands on my arms, says, 'Plus you know it could backfire terribly and you could be the one getting hurt. So you must drop this, you know, or . . .' She drifts off, then pulls away and stands hands on hips, as if waiting.

By the time Bo returns a while later a semblance of calm

has been restored, and although anyone with a fraction of a talent for the nuances of mood would notice the tension in the cottage, Bo isn't anyone.

'Been up to anything interesting while I was gone?' His eyes buzz around the room. Anna smiles and blinks, very deliberately, first at Dex and then at me.

'Nada,' says Dex.

We wait for Bo to pour himself a glass of wine and fling his body onto the sofa. Then Anna says, 'So, tell us everything.'

How, what, when?

Her name is Rachel. She lives in a flat in a terrace of houses near the lighthouse. There's no need for any further details. We're not interested. What we are interested in is how dry her lips were when Bo went to kiss her, and how he'd had to pull away and moisten his own lips with his tongue before going back in again. How she'd laughed when he first touched her right nipple and given a little gasp when he touched her left. How she had asked him to start off with her back to him, as if spooning but without any of the intimacy, as if she regretted kissing him. How she leaned back into him. How she sighed when he entered her then fallen silent, as if she were being interrogated. Which, in a way, she was.

'You want to see her?' Bo asks. He's teasing. Seeing her is the whole point of the Big Black Book. He takes out his phone and scrolls. And there she is, all of a sudden, asleep and sweetly smiling.

In our earlier upset we've forgotten the actual cooking and at eight, just as we are about to eat, discover the pork loin, uncooked, under a plate on the counter.

'Takeaway?' offers Bo.

No phone signal. Internet ordering doesn't seem to have reached the Isle of Portland.

'Oh fuck it, let's just drink,' says Bo.

And so Anna lights the candles and brings in the cake from its hiding place in the pantry and there's a flourish of birthday hoorays and we all sing 'Happy Birthday' and we eat cake for supper and are happy. Or making a very good job of pretending.

'A toast to Rachel, and the Big Black Book,' says Bo.

Rachel, Rachel. If only you knew.

But Rachel doesn't. Rachel will never know. In our world, Rachel is just a number now, an entry, a trophy, a token. A small cog in the machine that is the Group. A little part of a big, dark secret.

We raise our glasses: 'To Rachel.'

'And especially to us,' adds Anna.

19

Anna

Anna has never been a fan of music festivals. The combination of mud and bad toilets, staged hedonism and awful boho outfits has never appealed, though she's naturally careful to hide that from the Group. After all, no one likes a spoilsport and everyone likes Anna, because she makes it her business to be liked. Being liked is all part of the game, the game she's been playing, one way or another, all her life, the only one she knows.

In the taxi on the way over to Ollie's, Anna recalls a dinner party held by her parents in the house with the red roof and the owl in the garden. Where was that? Farnham, which means that Anna must have been six. Yes, six is the red roof and the owl. By the time she'd hit seven they'd moved yet again. So Farnham, then. She remembers sliding down the stairs, unable to sleep, and her father taking her onto his lap. He adored her back then, though he was also never at home, so there wasn't enough of his regard to offset her mother's obvious distaste and almost none at all after the divorce. Small plates of profiteroles sat in front of everyone around the table. Profiteroles. So glamorous. Not unlike Helen herself. Anna remembers her mother's hair, as teased and puffed as a mushroom cloud, and the look of disapproval on her face. She remembers her father's meaty breath in her ear. 'Have mine, darling, but don't let your mother see.' She remembers him cutting at the little shells with a fork and spoon to make them easier for her to eat, the joy of the warm chocolate sauce and the cold cream in her mouth.

It didn't last. Nothing good in that house ever lasted. Anna recalls her mother rising from her seat and walking to the end of the table, those few seconds of dread before her mother leans down and, whispering softly so no one else, not even her father, can hear, says, 'People don't like greedy girls.'

Then something happening to her face, a kind of slickness, as if someone had popped her in the toaster for a spell, and taking Anna's hand, loudly now, so as to be heard by everyone at the table, saying, 'Go back to bed, darling. We don't want to get into bad habits, do we?'

She thinks now that's when it began. The food thing obviously, but also the idea that, when it came to love it was a bad habit to want more than was your due.

Over the months of their affair, Anna has wanted more but will never ask for it, not least because she is certain that Ollie has no more to give.

People don't like greedy girls.

Isaac wouldn't like her either, if he knew how insatiable her need for love was, if he ever saw beyond the façade. Anna makes it her business to ensure he never does. Luckily, Isaac is a very loyal person rather than an observant one. He's easily put off the scent. Her infrequent and largely dutiful bedroom encounters with him appear to be sufficient to do just that. So long as they are having sex, however tiresome and underwhelming, it won't occur to Isaac to look too closely, or in that particular territorial way men sometimes do with their kids, at baby Ralphie. If no one tells him, Isaac's very unlikely to find out. So long as she guards against anyone telling him, Isaac will never work out for himself that Ralphie isn't his kid. Bo certainly won't tell him because Bo doesn't know. Beside herself, only Cassie knows and only then because she guessed. This is one of the reasons why, along with good manners, Anna has never mentioned her husband's name to Ollie, though her lover knows she's married. What he doesn't know, he can't use against her.

Visits to Ollie usually have to be planned days ahead but tonight presents an opportunity to act spontaneously. A short text exchange in the lavatories does it. Ollie is out drinking with some mates but it's nothing he can't cut short. As for Anna, she's had her excuse formulated more or less since she arrived.

The Uber pulls into the familiar block of warehouse apartments. Anna can never quite remember what the building is called – is it Cinnamon or Cinnabar or maybe

Cardamom? But if she ever gets dementia the postcode will be one of the few things she'll always recall: SE1 4RY. Just across the river from Dex and Gav and a five-minute walk from Bo. She pictures Isaac sitting beside her aged bird-like frame, her liver-spotted hand in his, a puzzled look on his face. The absurdity of it makes her laugh out loud. The driver's eyes flick to the rear-view mirror and she feels the need, suddenly, to reassert herself before the laughter turns to tears.

'It's best to turn left into Tooley Street,' she tells the Uber driver now. 'It's the block on the corner with the big picture windows.' She likes Ollie to press her up against those windows, loves the feel of the cool glass on her skin, imagines the view from the outside. She gets out of the cab and crosses under the walkway to the entrance, keys in the flat number and is buzzed into the atrium. A former eighteenth-century grain store, the building has been expensively reinvented to look just industrial enough, a style borrowed, so far as Anna can tell, from waiting-room magazines in posh dentists' offices. The effect is impressive, architectural, studiedly uncosy, the opposite, in fact, of the warm spiciness suggested by the name. She passes into the immaculate foyer with its bank of mail boxes and in one corner, beside the double lift, a modern console table accessorised by a single orchid freighted with pure white flowers, something of a cliché these days. Over the months there has been quite a turnover in orchids. They're never watered, never tended, only ever replaced by some unseen hand.

Quite often the corridors smell newly cleaned and the large warehouse windows are fiercely shiny but the maintenance always seemed to happen by magic. There's none of the cheery, comforting mess of wheelie bins and shabby front gardens which dominate Anna's street in Queen's Park. In her texts to Ollie, she calls the place the CCO, or Centre for Covert Operations. There's a precision to it and a hardness she associates with espionage or chemical warfare research. Everywhere else but here she's the greyhound, or maybe the lurcher: beautiful, lean, a stupendous performer, but pliant, happy to pretend to be none too bright; but in this industrial-enough building, surrounded by the uninventive trappings of corporate money, she's able to leave her greyhound/lurcher self behind. This stripped brick cube is where Anna McEvoy gets to play the urban fox.

Ticking across the parquet floor in her heeled sandals, she reaches the lifts (which should really be called elevators in a building with such New York loft pretentions) and presses the call button. It occurs to her that, in the months she's been coming here, there has never once been a family either inside the lift or waiting for it. Not a single child, nor any sign of one. A respite from her ordinary life.

The doors open and she steps inside, pressing the button for the seventh floor. On the way up she searches for the tiny bottle of salt spray she keeps in her bag and wilds her hair a little. Ollie likes her to look as if she's just come off the beach, not the easiest thing to pull off in London. But she's good at the business of pleasing and manipulating men. Or boys, as she prefers to think of them. It's another reason the place makes her feel so comfortable. Something so reassuringly masculine about it. In feminine worlds she feels rather lost and panicky.

The lift heaves to a stop. She steps out into the corridor and waits a microsecond for the motion sensitive lights to click on. At the end of the corridor, the door to apartment A is already ajar. Ollie will be in the shower. He's finicky about his hygiene, which is one of the many things Anna likes about having sex with him. If she gets there in time, she might join him. She pads down the carpet, enters the apartment and closes the door behind her. The sound of running water from the shower room, as predicted. On the table in the living room is a bottle of champagne, two glasses and a couple of lines of coke along with a rolled twenty. The bottle is as yet unopened, which is unusual. She goes over and perches on the leather sofa, being careful not to stir the air enough to blow away the lines. Ollie likes to do coke before sex. Anna thinks he's probably got an 'issue'. Coke has never really been Anna's thing but tonight Isaac is on Ralphie duty and it feels different somehow. She picks up the rolled note and hoovers a line – there will be more where that came from – pinches her nose and blinks. Her heart begins to tick and everything gradually brightens into sharp focus. How perfect, she thinks, stripping off her clothes and leaving them draped over the modular sofa, that no one has ever suspected this. Not Isaac, who'd hardly notice if she had stranger sex on the sofa beside him if a big match was on, but no one in the Group, the people who, after all, know her better than anyone.

Naked now, she heads into the bathroom.

In fact it's a wet room, all marble and hard surfaces, one of those fashionable domestic installations designed to make the householder feel they might be in a boutique hotel somewhere exotic but unthreatening. Hong Kong or Buenos Aires, rather than, say, Kinshasa or San Salvador. In her own house she would have hated it, all those sharp edges for Ralphie to hurt himself on. But here its very anonymity, the air of bland luxury, excites her in a way that nothing at home ever did or does.

Ollie is in the shower and waves at her to join him. Through the steam she catches a glimpse of his erection, which is presumably what he intends, since he has positioned himself rather artfully against the glass. He's probably had a line or two already. She thinks about the full-length picture window and wonders if there's any way of enticing him out of the shower and into the living room. For a man with almost no sexual boundaries, he's oddly shy about having sex against the window, worried that someone with a river-view flat on the other side of the bridge and a telephoto lens might take a picture and post it on social media. Anna has thought about that too, which is why, whenever they do it against the window, she always hangs her head so that her face isn't visible, which makes the whole experience slightly uncomfortable, obviously, but worth it for the possibility that someone she's never met will spot her naked body and want it and not be able to have it.

Tonight, though, there are to be no negotiations. Ollie is too coked to wait. She opens the shower door and goes in. The trick with having sex in Ollie's shower is to avoid the flip-down seat because the slats dig into her flesh and also leave unsightly marks. She must also remember to stand clear of the water which otherwise washes away her natural lubrication and makes sex not only slightly painful but also – unforgivably – a bit squeaky. Naturally it isn't possible to say any of this to Ollie. God, it's all so complicated. Not for the first time a surge of envy shoots through her. Oh, to be average-looking like Cassie and not have to worry about inelegant noises or unflattering angles. Men have sex with women like Cassie for fun but they have sex with women like Anna so they can feel like kings.

Ollie takes her in his arms a little too roughly, then in a flash, spins her around and presses her up against the glass of the shower. It'll all be fine once the coke really kicks in. She'll begin to enjoy Ollie's heavy-handedness. If he's as blasted as she thinks he is, he'll be able to hold off his orgasm. Which will give her more time to settle in. At some point she'll think about Bo. There's always a point when Bo comes into it.

Later, when they are back in the living room, he in his expensive loungewear, she in her festival outfit, he cracks open the champagne. She throws back a glass overly quickly and feels slightly bilious.

'I'm so sorry I can't stay,' she says. This isn't true, but telling the truth would be both rude and unwise, as it so often is.

Ollie smiles and stays her with his hand. 'We need to talk.'

Please, she thinks, not a declaration of love. Not a state of the union address. Not a plea for her to leave Isaac. To her surprise, though, it isn't that. It's the opposite. In a calm voice Ollie explains that he's met someone. 'Someone real,' are his exact words. This will be his and Anna's last meeting.

Anna's stomach is a sour mash. Champagne and coke only add insult to the injury. How could Ollie have sex with her knowing he was going to dump her right afterwards?

'Don't be angry,' he says, 'we were going to have sex whatever and I just thought it would be more fun this way. I was actually trying to be considerate.'

The acrid mess in her stomach rises up into her throat and makes it hard to focus. She feels her insides dissolving. It's almost as if someone has thrown her across the room. The humiliation is a roar. She's more wounded lioness than urban fox now. A panic rises then, suddenly, as if by some as yet undiscovered neurochemical process, her brain has reached a point of absolute clarity. Or maybe the coke just makes it seem that that way. Her eyes pendulum from one expensive object to another, landing finally on a blue vase on the side table. Helpless in the face of her own rage she picks it up and spinning on her heels gallops forward. After that it all gets rather confusing and blurry, as if someone has wrapped baking paper around her head. She remembers coming at Ollie with the vase in her hand but the only thing after that she can be absolutely certain of is stepping out of the cab in Wapping some time later with a stranger's hand on her arm. The owner of the hand, a small dark-haired woman with an East European accent, looks rough, ill or maybe out of it. A scarf – some tacky blue and yellow thing with pom-poms – hangs limply around her neck.

Can't she see Anna's preoccupied, not in the mood. What? She's actually asking Anna to pay for an Uber for her? A complete stranger? Is she mad?

No, no, no, girl. I'm not taking you on. I've got problems of my own.

20

Cassie

Why are we drinking so much? Cassie asks herself. Anyone would think we are trying to obliterate some shared memory, a secret only we know. It won't go away, that memory, that secret. It will sink into the deeper layers of our friendship until, returning to the surface some day, it will begin to destroy us from the inside. It will eat us alive.

Twit twoo.

Fool's gold.

If I could speak out right now, what would I say? Would I start with the money I took from Marika's bag? A roll of fifty-pound notes bundled in rubber bands. Would I say I took it because I knew Marika was so wasted she would never remember the encounter? Would I confess that I did not stop to think why Marika might be carrying so much money at a festival or what might happen to her if it was stolen? Or would I start with what I witnessed in the churchyard? Would I say I was not alone? Would I say I saw what was happening and I chose to protect myself?

We catch up and stumble down the cliff path together onto the pebbles, wilding the night air with our whoops and shouts, made more frantic by booze and dope and the desire to get out of our heads, together, now, here, where nothing can touch us.

'Who's going in?' Bo says, peeling off his jacket. Soon enough he and Dex are naked and howling across the pebbles and bundling themselves into the waves, leaving me and Anna at the shoreline goose-bumped and trembling and wishing we too were men who could do these things and only regret them later.

Marika was under the influence of drugs. Death by drowning. Police saying it was an accident. That it probably wasn't even the same person.

What I saw could have been a casual hook-up.

The men are beyond the break now and all that remains visible of them is a crease in the silvery grey reflection of the moonlight upon the swell.

As I'm unbuttoning my blouse Anna is saying, 'You're not actually going in?'

'I've changed my mind.'

And oh, the sea is brisk, the moon grabbing at the water which rises only to shrink back like a whipped dog, baring pebbles with a growl. Once the water reaches my thighs, I throw myself into the curl of a crest and begin to swim until, finding myself a whorl of water where the temperature is, inexplicably, much warmer, for a while I allow myself to bob on the chop. While I am floating an odd feeling comes over me. It seems that I have drowned and am the revenant Bo mentioned. Drowned and dead and come back to the living with a message. Dex is on the other side of the swell now, waving me over.

'Come here, the water's bloody amazing.'

And so I raise an arm over my shoulder and begin a slow, inelegant front crawl in moonlight but soon I can no longer hear or see Dex and the water is darker now and thicker and unfriendly, worrying and jostling at my legs, and it's like when a man you don't know very well suddenly pins you to the bed a little too hard or for a little too long and even as you are trying to make sense of what is happening, or even as you are asking the man to back off and be gentler, there is a part of you that is at the same time thinking, *So this is it, this is how I will meet my end.*

My arms are whirling, and my legs kicking out, but the current only increases its grip. I can feel myself being drawn further from the beach, out into the dark expanse, and there is a banging inside my skull where my mind is trying to escape, a kind of hopeful denial in the face of what is now unmistakably danger. How did this happen, and so quickly? It was only a moment ago Dex was waving me over, only a moment more since I was thigh deep in moonlit water, turning to wave to Anna on the beach. And now the sea has turned on me. The waves on which I was bobbing are pushing me out to the point of no return. I can hear myself shouting, 'Dex! Dex!' but Dex does not appear. Bo is nowhere to be seen and Anna is a dim speck on the strand of beach beyond the shallows. The water is cold. How did I not notice when I went in how cold the water was? Or perhaps I did notice. It seems so long ago now. Am I losing touch with what is real? I am moving, but I'm going nowhere. I am stuck somewhere between the air and the water. The salt is in my eyes and in my nostrils. I am kicking, kicking and going nowhere. Am I beginning to drown? Is this what drowning feels like?

Is this how it felt for Marika?

From the corner of my vision I can see Anna standing by the shoreline, silhouetted in the moonlight, watching me throwing my arms to get her attention. A cloud passes over the moon and I am suddenly thinking about the supermoon at the festival, and about Marika, and I am wondering if that is what I deserve, to be where Marika is, able to tell her that I am sorry I stole her money and I am sorry I stood by while something awful happened and I did nothing because I was a coward and I was afraid.

A voice rises up from the waves and I am thinking, is that the voice of the undertow? Is that the voice of the water? The voice is saying, 'Cassie, over here!' My eyes are filmy with salt but I am looking and looking because the voice is not the voice of the water or the undertow. It is Dex's voice. And I'm calling back but I am swallowing water and the water is taking my voice back down into my body.

Something touches my arm and I think it must be something that has come up from the water but when I turn towards it I see it is a hand on my arm and the end of the hand is Dex. He's looking worried. He's saying, 'Are you OK?'

'Yes, OK thanks.'

He smiles and shows his teeth. 'You went a bit weird there for a moment.' He flicks his head towards the shore. 'Want to go back now?'

So I raise one arm over my shoulder and scissor my feet then raise the other arm and I keep on doing that, with Dex beside me, until I can feel myself rising up on the wave and dropping down onto the shore side of the breakers and I rise, dazed and exhausted, up onto the pebbles and hobble my way through the shallows and onto the beach with Dex following on behind.

Anna comes bustling over. It's cold suddenly. The wind, which felt balmy before we went in, is now sharp-edged and unwelcoming.

'Cassie, darling, I saw you waving, but I didn't know . . .'

Just then Bo emerges from the sea, whooping; shaking his arms free of water, he picks his way across the pebbles towards us, skin mauve in the moonlight.

'Fucking hell, it's bloody freezing. Whoever thought that was a good idea?'

Anna turns and reaching out a hand, touches my shoulder. 'Darling, you're shivering.' She takes off her jacket and wraps it around me. 'Here, have this.'

'No bloody sign of the Mer-Chicken, but I spy with my little eye a couple of fine Mer-Cocks,' Bo says.

'Put them back in their coops before they freeze to

death,' says Anna and the men, rubbing their legs back to life and scraping the sea from their bodies, pull their clothes over damp skin and still haw-hawing, race each other across the beach towards the path back to the cottage. I watch them go with an odd feeling of panic.

Suddenly my legs are going and I'm skipping across the pebbles, not wanting to be far from Dex or to be left alone with Anna.

Later, as I emerge from the shower, wrapped in a towelling robe, I can't help but wonder what it was that got me out there on the waves. When I go downstairs to join the others, Bo, dressed only in a towel, is pouring hot chocolate into mugs. A fire is flapping in the grate.

'Anna and Dex are in the garden, having a smoke.'

Through the French doors are two figures, bundled inside duvets, with their backs to me.

'You want some of my famous secret recipe boozy hot chocolate?'

'What's the secret?'

'I can't tell you obviously, or it won't be a secret.'

'Then how do I know there is a secret?'

Bo taps his nose. 'There's always a secret.'

Leaving my drink inside, I take two mugs of chocolate and head out into the garden. Anna and Dex have their backs to me but hearing the door slide open, Anna's head turns and in the light from the living room and the moonlight her skin looks almost synthetic and not quite human. She smiles and waves me over but when she thinks I'm not looking I see her right foot swing out and press Dex's.

'This is good,' Dex, says, taking a sip of chocolate. On one cheek sits a small sparkle though whether it is water from his wet hair or a tear I can't tell.

'Isn't it, darling?' says Anna, in an intimate tone. Then Dex's eyes join in with his smile and he is fine again and I have to suppose they had been talking about Gav because what else could they be talking about when there is absolutely nothing to say? Dex's smile fades and a silence falls and in the quiet some dark bud begins to blossom and I sense immediately that whatever Dex is about to say, Anna would prefer him not to. The hand not clutching the hot chocolate finds its way to mine and gives it a gentle squeeze.

'Listen, Cass, whatever Gav said to you about me and that woman please take it with a sack of salt. He's ill and he's fucking paranoid and it's really bloody wearing. For the record, that girl the police came about? I bought some weed off her and the bloke she was with thought I was trying to rip her off so it got a bit hairy. Obviously I wasn't about to tell the cops that so I made up something on the spot.'

'We should just stop talking about it. Let's just stop,' Anna says, holding up a hand. She turns her face to me and in the angle of her lips I detect a warning.

Just then Bo pokes his head around the French windows. 'Ladies and arseholes, the performance is about to recommence.'

And so we all troop in and one by one make our ways to

bed knowing that there is no performance, or, rather that, all of this is a performance. We're a side show, a circus act in a big top, straining to keep each other so occupied we can ignore the elephant in the room.

21

Dex

10.45 p.m., Saturday 13 August, Wapping

It's been ten minutes since Bo went to the bar and Dex has already forgotten all about beer.

The Radials are halfway through their set and his mind is back in the noughties. Wasn't he listening to 'Turn right then left then right again' when he first got news of 7/7? Yeah, that's right, he was. Oh, and hang on, wasn't Cassie there too? Now he remembers. Summer of the second year, they were doing their best to stay up in Oxford for as long as possible, doing shitty jobs. Well, no, Cassie was doing a shitty job working in a bar. Dex had that law office internship through his dad. Way back when they were on speaks. Before he discovered his real sexual identity. Even now the memory of his confusion back then burns. All that mutual masturbation in the dorms at school. That miserable git of a housemaster telling him it was just a phase, that all the boys went through it. The awful coming-out conversation with his parents, his mother's tears, his father standing with his back to him, saying he'd never have named him after one of his great jazz heroes if he'd realised what a disappointment his son would turn out to be. He's glad they're estranged, actually. He's better off without the reactionary old bastard. Now he thinks about it, weren't he and Cassie saving up to go to Greece? Santorini, was it, or one of the other islands? No, no, he remembers now. It was the Mani. They wanted to follow in the steps of Patrick Leigh Fermor, well, Cassie did. The romantic in her. What was that paragraph which so struck him? Taking out his phone, he taps in the search window and brings up a pages of quotes, locates what he's looking for and reads as if for the first time:

It might be argued that the decorous little services of the West, the hushed voices, the self-control, our brave smiles and calmness either stifle the emotion of sorrow completely, or drive it underground where it lodges and proliferates in a malign and dangerous growth that festers for a lifetime.

His breath catches, throat swells like a frog's and he feels himself almost slayed with grief. Everything he's let go, the horrible stiff-upper-lipness of his horrible upbringing. Cassie helped but it wasn't really until he met Gav that he was able finally to divest himself of it. If he hadn't read that paragraph all those years ago would he ever had had the courage to reject the future that had been mapped out for him?

Hadn't his parents done everything they could to try to

rip him off, to trick him into a life of pretence and quiet despair? And for what? Respectability? Convention? If it hadn't been for Cassie and, later, Gav, he might have slipped into the mould they had already prepared for him. When he thinks about Gav, though, his heart stumbles. Dex has always been given a long leash, Gav never even trying to impose his own monogamous impulses on his husband. There has only ever been one condition. Play by all means, but if you're going to play, play away. Gav has never asked anything else of him, except, perhaps, a willingness to feign interest in opera and modern dance, but still Dex hasn't been able to find it in himself to comply. Plus his earlier encounter wasn't the first time he'd ordered in. Why? Laziness? The path of least resistance? Maybe. Or could it be some twisted combo of revenge for his financial dependency coupled with a secret desire to get caught? Mate, best not go there.

He tunes back into the music, moves a little to the beat. The Radials! Irresistible. The dance area comes alive as everyone begins flinging their bodies around. For a moment Dex is transported. Someone pushes past and sends him off balance. He swings an arm out to stay himself and sees the culprit hurrying away. A small woman with dark hair, dressed in red. She turns for an instant, doesn't see him, but in that moment a sharp stab of recognition hits him. Oh, but, hang on, isn't that the pizza delivery girl from earlier? What's she doing here? His eyes scan the space beside her for signs of a companion, but she's scurrying off towards the edge of the dance area. Alone, he thinks. It's a bit sad, actually. Who goes to a festival without their mates? He feels for her, a foreigner in his town, his capital. He should buy her a drink. Yes, be magnanimous. He muscles his way through the crowd towards her waving and catches her eye. She's surprised to see him, which, yes – he suddenly wonders if he isn't being a bit creepy. Maybe that's why she seems ill at ease, a bit embarrassed.

'Hey,' he says, 'fancy seeing you here.'

'Yeah,' she says. She's trying to sound nice but Dex is pretty sure she's faking it. Her breathing has quickened and her eyes are darting from side to side as if she's looking for an escape exit. He's intrigued now. Why is she being so odd with him? Almost as if she's scared? Or maybe it's not him she's afraid of, maybe there is a man somewhere who doesn't like her talking to other men. He scopes about. Nope.

She gives him an odd, lopsided little smile. Her pupils are tiny, like two poppy seeds which have flown off a bagel and landed in her eyes. Oh, so that's it. She's taken something and it's making her paranoid. She's basically off her tits. Well, OK, whatever, maybe he won't offer to buy her a drink, then. He'll duck out as gracefully and as quickly as he can.

'Top band,' he says, thinking even as it comes out of his mouth, Christ, who says that? He's out of practice.

Her face immediately softens into an expression of relief. 'I am leaving,' she says.

'OK, well,' he says. 'Thanks for bringing round the pizzas.'

She catches his eye. Her pupils are minuscule, positively reptilian.

'Maybe I stay bit longer,' she says.

It's then he spots Bo, processing through the crowd, carrying two bottles of Corona high above everyone's heads like an icon at a religious festival.

'OK, well, bye then,' he says, assuming this will be the last he sees of her. He thinks of saying, 'Have a nice life,' but it sounds overly aggressive, so he decides instead as he's moving off to give her a little wave. She waits until he's a way away to return the gesture before disappearing into the crowd.

22

Cassie

Morning, Saturday 1 October, Isle of Portland

I wake, lean across the bed to the stool that serves as a bedside table to check the time on my phone and realise that it's not there. There is a little alarm clock on the shelf below though which reads ten thirty. No owl last night, or none I remember and no flashbacks of the awful moment in the sea, so the drink did at least do its job. I know the smell of drowning now. It's a briny, rancid scent, like old vase water. That's not something I'm going to forget. The wine has also left me slow and unable to think properly but that's a small price. It's not like me, all this sleeping. But I haven't been like me for a month now.

Coffee might help. I get up and pad downstairs. The living room is still a mess of empty bottles, overflowing ashtrays and what look like the wrappers from a year's supply of Lindor chocolate balls, none of which I can recall eating. My phone is lying on the kitchen table. Did I leave it there? How odd. I remember it being on the stool beside my bed. But it's here, so I must be wrong. I'm becoming careless and forgetful. Random message to self: stop drinking and change phone passcode. It's been 1108, my birthday, for as long as I can recall, but that feels a little less like a day to celebrate now that I know it was the last day of Marika Lapska's life.

Someone has begun clearing up in the kitchen. There is washing up on the counter top and a cafetière still half full of lukewarm coffee. Otherwise no signs or sounds of life, unless you count the cottage. We gave it a trashing last night and it took its revenge, fussing and creaking all through the early hours. It's quiet again now, but awake and brooding, licking its wounds.

The slow crunch of gravel under tyres comes in from outside. Through the glass pane in the front door I can see Bo's Audi heaving to a stop. The engine cuts and there is a moment of unidentifiable music from the stereo before the driver's door opens and Anna steps out, looking as fresh as a cheerleader, clutching a couple of bags.

I go over to the front door and wave. That dazzling smile. She approaches, gives a comedy swerve to avoid the Mer-Chicken and lands a kiss on my cheek.

'Cassie, darling, you're awake! Are you OK?' She hands the bags to me, swings off her coat and pulls at her ballet pumps. 'I thought we could probably use a fry-up after last night's dinner debacle. Bo back from his run yet?'

'I haven't seen him.'

'Oh, in that case he's probably gone to the beach. He

was keen to do some more fossiling. Apparently, last night's storm will have brought them up.'

'Was there a storm?' Perhaps it was this and not the house that woke me.

Anna's brow creases. 'Don't tell me you didn't hear it? God, the thunder was enough to wake the dead.'

In the kitchen Anna fills the kettle, digs around in the shopping for a packet of coffee and spoons the grounds into the big cafetière.

'Are you hungry?' She checks her watch.

I shake my head.

'Dex has gone off to meet someone, one for the Big Black Book, I think, so it's just us. I thought we might go horse riding later, though if we're going I should ring and book.'

'I don't ride.'

Anna looks as me as if I'm mad. 'Everyone rides. You get the coffee on and I'll nip up the road in the car and call the stables.'

An hour or so later, we're at the riding school in Easton, a couple of miles from Fortuneswell. Anna has found a hat to fit among the spares and is helping saddle up the horses with one of those teenaged girls who hang around stables. I'm in the tack room with another, even younger-looking, trying on hats and feeling oddly dissociated.

'Let's try a seven and three quarters?' The stable hand fetches a hat from a line hanging near the door then slips it over my hair. 'How does that feel? You've ridden before?'

'Ish, and not for a long time. I don't really think of myself as a rider.'

The girl fiddles with my chin strap and stands back to admire her work. 'Hayley's putting you on Jason? He's, like, literally bombproof? You'll be fine?'

Outside in the yard, Anna is absorbed adjusting the girth of a chestnut horse and only notices my arrival when alerted by the restless movement of the animal.

'This one's mine,' she says, patting the chestnut on the flank. 'Yours is the roan over there. They always put their less confident riders on him. I've told her you're rusty but sound.' The speckled pony is drooping its head in the sun, half asleep. 'Hayley's just saddling up her mount.'

Anna stands up with her back leaning against the chestnut's flank and gives me the once-over.

'You look brilliant, like you were born to it.' Anna has reached for the reins and is pulling them tight. A light foam bubbles from the horse's mouth onto the stable yard.

'I don't really know whether this is a good idea. I don't feel great.' There was a storm last night, but it did not wake me. The owl did not wake me. I thought I heard the house moving but perhaps I was dreaming.

You'll dream about your future.

I saw you waving but I didn't think . . .

'Last night, in the water . . .?'

'We were all disgracefully pissed, weren't we?' Anna laughs. She cocks her head. 'Are you OK, Cassie?'

That's a good question though it has no answer. I open my mouth to speak but nothing comes out. If I keep what I know about the drowned woman to myself, if I do nothing to make amends, part of me will die with her. If I speak out, I will lose the only friends I've ever had.

'Anna, about last night . . .'

Anna's eyes flare. In the tremble of her lips do I detect something like panic? Then there comes a clatter of hooves and a lean woman with a wind-leathered face appears on a dappled grey hunter and the relief that comes off Anna is like a quiet spring breeze.

The woman introduces herself as Hayley and directing herself to me says, 'Is that helmet a bit loose maybe?' In an instant, Anna comes over and adjusts the straps but even with the straps tightened, the helmet still wobbles when I move my head.

'I think I might need a smaller size.'

'That one looks perfect to me,' Anna says.

Hayley slides the stirrup buckles up into their keepers and turned her attentions back to me. 'So, all good? Had much experience in the saddle?'

Anna winks and laughs. 'You bloody bet she has.'

Hayley smiles and pretends not to get the joke. 'Jason will go easy with you. He's a grand old boy. Oh, have you tightened their girths?'

'I'll do it,' Anna says, going round to where Jason is standing, half asleep, one back leg bent, the hoof tip resting on the stone paving of the yard. Leading the animal to the mounting block she grabs the stirrup on the animal's far side to help me up then returns to the chestnut, springs up, swings over and gently kicks the animal into a turn.

'We'll set off then, shall we?' Hayley goes on ahead along a muddy path.

Quickly we leave the stable yard and the surrounding shorn paddocks behind. The horses seem relieved to be on the march along a path surrounded by still green bracken. A skylark rises, peeping to draw attention to itself and its now presumably empty nest. Before long the chestnut overtakes Jason and slots itself in behind Hayley's mount. They're used to this, Hayley's horse up ahead and Jason, with his soothing plod and sleepy face, making up the rear. The morning is bright with yellow sunlight. It is cold, though, and my fingers are growing numb. Jason, feeling it on his flank, dips his head and sneezes. There's a general sense of well being, of horses and humans companionably treading paths that have been trodden a thousand times before. We're making progress almost without being aware of it. I begin to wish I'd brought gloves like Anna who has, of course, come fully equipped. Behind us, out of sight, lies the stable yard and beyond it, to the north, Fossil Cottage and the quarry. To our left the sea is air force blue, ripped and foamy in the breeze. Up ahead now, a dip in the land gives out to a slope at the top of which lies the grey stone immensity of the Young Offenders Institute.

Hayley and Anna are way ahead, and deeply engaged in conversation. This too has happened without my noticing but Jason is content to lag behind and I'm not minded to kick him to catch up. In fact I'm beginning to regret this whole enterprise. Something is not right in my head. We plod on for a while until, with a sudden explosion of feathers, a hawk dives into a nearby bush and emerges seconds later with a pigeon in its talons. The movement seems to energise Jason who begins to trot after his stable mates. No tapping the reins seems to slow him and I can't bring myself to yank on his mouth. Eventually I resign myself to the trot, rising and falling in the saddle, my hat bumping against my skull, alarmingly loose. I can no longer see the other two now. For the first time being on Jason feels a little unsafe.

As it turns out Hayley and Anna are not far away, just over the brow of the hill, waiting for me. They have both dismounted and Hayley has her back to Anna and is rooting around in a saddlebag.

'Hello, darling! Hayley thought we could do with a warm-up. Are you OK?'

Why does everyone keep asking me that? In a fond voice, the kind women usually reserve for animals and kids, Anna goes on, 'Oh, just look at Jason-boy. What a good pony.'

Hayley turns and presents us with what looks like a flask. Her mount stands passively by, evidently used to this part in the proceedings, his breath noisy in the still air.

'My famous chai,' says Hayley, handing the grey's reins to Anna and pouring the tea into three small plastic beakers. She passes one to me.

'You have a problem back there? Anna said you'd be fine to catch up with us.'

I invent a story about readjusting my helmet, which in truth still feels loose and Hayley has just begun to move towards me to check it when Anna says, 'It's fine, honestly. You're just not used to wearing one.'

Hayley smiles, reassured.

The chai is delicious and surprisingly boozy. I go round the back of a small, windblown tree to take a pee. On my return Hayley is standing a little way off with her back to us, talking on the phone, while Anna has hold of the horses.

'Here.' She hands me Jason's reins. Just then Hayley finishes up her call and comes over, apologising profusely. We remount and set off once more. Emerging from a small copse, we find ourselves on a long, flat plateau ending in what looks like another quarry. Off to one side is a short row of quarrymen's cottages whose back windows overlook the sea. Soon, Anna and Hayley have pulled ahead again and appear to be deep in conversation but I am beginning to get the sense that something is off, either with the horse, or perhaps with me. Jason is skittish now, as if bored or uncomfortable. I shout out but the wind carries my voice away and my anxiety only serves to unsettle the horse even further.

Anna and Hayley are halfway across the plateau when Hayley turns and shouts, makes some forward motion with her arm. I'm assuming she's telling me which direction to go, so raising a hand to acknowledge her I twirl it to signal that I can't hear, but Hayley has already turned back and in an instant she and Anna are off on a gallop across the meadowland. So that's what Hayley was signalling. Picking up on all that equine adrenaline, Jason begins to tap dance, blowing air from his nostrils. Pretty soon he's not listening to anything I might be telling him with the reins or my body. He's used to this gallop, it's part of the routine, and he's not going to be denied it. We are both at the mercy of some primal wildness over which neither I nor the horse have any conscious control. I hear myself cry out, knowing that I am lost to the horse and he to me. Any attempt of mine to slow him down will fail. He's moved directly from a trot to a gallop, his neck stretched long and forward, nostrils flared and breath sawing the air. There's nothing for it but to hang on and hope for the best. We're thundering through the grassland, the horse wheezing with effort, flecks of foam loosening themselves from his mouth and flying by me like silvery arrows. Halfway across the ground grows uneven, and Jason's body seems to pitch and roll like a small boat on a stormy sea. The saddle is careening madly from one side of his back to the other and this only serves to further destabilise his gait. Immediately I draw the reins tight and press my calves against the animal's haunches in the hope of improving my purchase but regaining my balance only seems to encourage Jason to speed up. He's locked his jaw around the bit. He is all wild energy now. With every motion of the animal's legs, the girth slides wildly, threatening to tip me off. The helmet has fallen over my eyes and I can see almost nothing ahead. I fiddle one-handed with the strap but within seconds the thing has fallen across my forehead again. The only way to see where I'm going is to pull the release tab and watch it drop but the impact seems to alarm Jason further. Me yelling, screaming, *Anna, Anna!* only serves to panic him. My feet feel as if they are jammed into the stirrups. This is not sustainable. Sooner or later I am going to be unable to stay on and when I fall what will happen then? Will I be dragged or trampled? What if I am thrown? My head is unprotected now. Isn't this how people break their necks, snap their backs and crack open their skulls?

The quarry is upon us. There's a change in sensation as hooves come off the soft earth and begin to hit against chalk. A great scoop filled with the rubble and spoilings of hundreds of years of digging stone lies before us. A terrain of rabbit warrens and invisible sink holes. If Jason gallops into the midst of all that we are both doomed. He'll trip and I will sail right over his head.

If I believed in any kind of God I'd be praying now.

I close my eyes and cling on to the animal's neck. Moments later, with no warning, the horse grinds to a sudden and miraculous halt, the girth slips, my feet break shy of their stirrups and I feel myself being catapulted into the air. Complete weightlessness, a formidable lightness of being. I want it to last and last. But nothing lasts, not forever, and though time is slow and the microseconds long, I can see the ground coming up fast and I feel my arms come up to protect my head. There's a terrible thunk. Every part of my body feels jarred and compressed. For a few seconds I think I have blacked out and when I come to everything seems warped and blurry. My face is pressed against the grass and I can't move anything. A familiar sound digs its way into my consciousness, perhaps it's this that pulls me back. My chest feels weighted and I'm winded and coughing. But I am OK. I can feel my neck turn and though one eye is gummed shut through the other I can see a blur of pale beige topped with blue which gradually comes into sharper focus. Can that be Dex? It is, I think, it is. What's he doing here? Dex racing towards me, yelling my name and behind him, in a robe, is a dark-haired young man.

'Mate, are you OK?' Dex is panting and shock is registering on his face.

I can stand. With Dex's help, I can hobble. He is pointing to one of the quarrymen's cottages. 'Can you make it that far?'

Yes, I think I can.

We reach the door about the same time as the young man, who is clutching the horse's reins. Nothing readable in his expression though this may be because of the filmy curtain behind my eyes.

'Is she hurt?' the man asks Dex.

'Not badly, no. I think she's just in shock. The horse?'

'Not a scratch.' The young man's name is Trent. I know

this because Dex asks him to take me to the local hospital while he sorts out the horse.

There is a pain in my chest and through the mist of adrenaline my limbs feel heavy but I already know there is nothing broken. Maybe I've cracked a rib. That might account for the pressure in my chest, but there's nothing medics can do for cracked ribs. All the same, there's no way I'll be able to walk back to Fossil Cottage.

'Not hospital.'

'Okay, but you have to wait here with Trent.' Dex says.

I'm in no position to argue. We agree that I'll rest at Trent's house until Dex has found Hayley and taken Jason back to the stables. Then he'll return in a cab and bring me back to Fossil Cottage. That way I won't be alone. Just in case.

OK then.

Trent, who has been making a quiet study of his feet all this time, pulls Dex to one side. 'Maybe you should get dressed properly first?'

I can't tell you anything now about Trent's house except how it smells. Rank and spicy and unmistakably adult. Once he's settled me on the sofa, Trent, aware of the reek, takes to opening the windows. How slow on the uptake I've been. I put that down to the shock of the fall. But I've caught up. I am most definitely fully in the picture. Trent was on his way to becoming another entry in the Big Black Book. Not that Trent would have known or even suspected it. Because it's creepy. The whole idea is off.

The smell of sex now fading, Trent makes tea and fetches me a couple of ibuprofen before making his excuses and going off to get dressed. When he returns, in jeans and a tight T, he's all nervous chatter, muttering about how it is on Portland and how nice it is that the island is attracting more weekenders and not just climbers because the climbers are too focused on climbing to be interested in having any fun. And on and on. I'm barely listening. My chest is leaden and my limbs are like poured concrete but nothing in my body is as heavy as the feeling of foreboding, of there being something ungraspable, some malign energy, which has singled me out.

I thought you were waving.

If you put the ammonite under your pillow you'll dream about your future.

'Dex told me you two were an item way back,' Trent is saying.

'Yes,' I say, taking a sip of tea. 'Did he tell you he's married?'

I watch Trent's face go blank, the eyes dart then drift inwards. He's irritated and disappointed, but none too bothered. It's only a hook-up after all.

'That's really his business,' he says, limply.

'I suppose it is.'

From inside my jacket pocket my phone rings. It's Anna.

'Darling, are you OK?' Realising they'd lost me, she and Hayley turned back and ran into Dex, who had told them that he'd been on his way back from his date when he'd happened to witness the accident. 'I'd come but we've still got the horses. Dex says someone's looking after you. I'm so sorry, sweetheart. We probably shouldn't have got so far ahead . . .'

The phone pings with a text message. It's from Will. *You OK? Still on for later?*

No longer listening to Anna and irritated by the presumption I tap out, *News travels fast. Bit bruised, but yeah, should be fine.*

A text pings back immediately. *News???? Bruised??? You OK?*

So now. The news of my tumble has yet to reach him. Will is checking in. Though why the first 'You OK?' isn't clear. Why wouldn't I be? My thumb scrolls through the thread, stops at three texts back.

Morning. Hope stuff from J useful? See you later?

Oh, so now the first 'You OK?' makes sense. Will is wondering why I didn't reply to this initial text, which he sent at ten this morning and the answer is, I hadn't seen it till now. Though that's odd because, even before I opened it, the message was marked as read at 10.05. I have no memory of seeing it then. Besides which, wasn't I asleep? Also, wasn't the phone lying on the kitchen table? Mind is playing tricks today. Too much booze. Stop drinking, Cassie, it's turning you into a zombie.

'Darling? Please say something. You've gone awfully quiet. You're worrying me.'

'Did one of you go into my phone this morning?'

A pause. 'Why on earth would any of us do that? Anyway, it's passcode protected presumably. Are you sure you're OK, Cassie? Dex told me you'd fallen on your head.'

23

Cassie

The masseuses are waiting for us to undress and still Anna is insisting on an inspection.

'Just let me touch it!' She's sitting on a fold-up chair in the corner of the massage area, elaborately releasing the heels from her feet.

'You are not touching my ink. It's sore.' I peel off my T-shirt and hang it on the makeshift peg.

Beside Anna, an expensive scented candle gutters. We are in a cordoned off area of the VIP pamper zone, paid for, like everything else tonight, by Bo. This is Anna's kind of terrain, though. She's become one of those over-groomed yummy mummies you see in certain London postcodes, all glossy hair, glowy skin and expensive acrylics, decked out in lululemon or Eileen Page, wielding pushchairs like shields.

Her lips soften into a pout and her hands move into prayer. 'Please, please, please, please, please.'

Anna's shoes are off now and she's pulling at the buttons

on her jumpsuit. Her voice softens to a whisper, repeats its plea. 'Please, please, please.'

'Stop it!' I'm laughing now.

She wraps herself in a towel and contorts underneath it, removing her bra. In the fifteen years I've known her, I've never seen Anna naked.

'I'm only really interested in why you chose an ammonite.' She pauses long enough for me to read the sly slant of her mouth. 'Is it because of Bo?'

'You're a monster!' I pull off my trousers and hang them on the back of the chair. 'Anyway, I already told you why I got an ammonite. That tattooist gave me a choice between that and a dolphin.'

'A dolphin? Just no.'

'Exactly.'

Anna lies down on the massage table, rearranges her hair and sinks her face into the doughnut. I wait just long enough to see how it's done before clambering onto the adjacent table.

A moment later the curtain moves and the two masseuses we saw earlier waiting at the pamper area entrance reappear, exchange brief greetings and busy themselves mixing oil. The taller one of them, a lean woman with cornbraids, comes over and waits for me to put my head in the doughnut before arranging my arms flat on the table. The feeling of her hands, sweeping across the broad width of my back, are those of the best lover you never had and the oil smells clean and comforting. Tomorrow I'll be just another millennial struggling to make ends meet in a city that, with its gig economy, insane work hours and outrageous rents, is doing its very best to drive me away. Plus I'll be sporting a cracking hangover. But let's not think of that right now. Let's live for the moment just a little. Let's live for tonight. Because tonight is the night I am a birthday queen sitting in a VIP tent at a cool festival with my besties while someone who is probably paid even less than me massages my shoulders and pedies my feet.

The massaging stops and for an instant it feels like some small part of me just withered away with it.

'Is that tattoo new? I shouldn't really . . .'

Anna says, lifting her head from the doughnut and directing herself to the masseuse, says, 'Pretty please, it's her birthday,'

'I don't know . . .'

'We'll tip like you won't believe.'

The masseuse smiles and shrugs. 'Well, OK. Happy birthday. I guess I can work around it.' Pouring a little more oil on her palms, she begins to push at my flesh anew.

Silence falls for a while as the masseuse turns to my lower back, pressing her fists into the muscle either side of the spine and sending warm waves up into my shoulders. Beside me, Anna has begun making appreciative little grunting sounds. I'm conscious of thoughts slipping from my mind and falling onto the floor like cut hair.

'God, isn't this glorious! I hardly ever do this sort of thing these days. Never have children, darling, they eat you alive. So expensive too. We're practically penniless.'

The thoughts instantly pick themselves up and fly back into my head. It's not a good feeling. I don't know how I'm going to make the rent this month and I'm already late with last month's payment.

'Oh God, let's not talk about money.' The masseuse stops momentarily. When she restarts there's a different energy to the movement.

'But, darling, you just paid to have a tattoo so . . .'

'Were you listening when I was telling the story in the pub? The guy did it for free. He had a kink.'

'Oh yes.'

Silence falls again followed by the resumption of small grunting sounds from the other table, then silence once more.

'Just a thought, why don't you ask Bo to lend you a couple of grand? Or Dex. Ask Dex.'

'No! Anyway, you know how Gav is about money.'

The masseuse tries valiantly to stop me fidgeting. In the space of five minutes I have become the nightmare client; tense and broke.

'Well, ask Bo then. You know how brilliant he was with me.'

'True, but I'm just useless with money. You were run over by a lorry. You nearly died. You had to take a year off.'

It happened when Anna was cycling to work. A lorry turning left, the usual thing. The attending emergency doctor said that, though she was horribly bruised and with a fractured pelvis, a broken arm and several broken ribs,

Anna was lucky to have escaped with her life. Bo, Dex and I took eight-hour shifts at her hospital cubicle. When Chris and Tricia, Anna's parents, finally flew in from Nice, where they'd taken early retirement, they spent most of their time shopping saying that Anna, who was by then in a medically induced coma, wouldn't notice, made a huge fuss about the ropey coffee in the hospital cafeteria and left two days later. Bo was a champion. This was a couple of years before he hit pay dirt with his dating app. The money Bo gave Anna for her recuperation was the stash he'd saved in order to quit the tech job he hated and sign up to study for a PhD in palaontology, which, naturally, then never happened.

'Poor you, though, you had to deal with Chris and Tricia. I have that sweetheart Dr Bukhari to thank for putting me in a coma so I didn't have to.' She pauses to fire instructions at the masseuse (*Ooh, yes, just there where the knot is. Lovely*) before going on, 'Anyway, having money doesn't make you any happier.'

Outside, a group of festival goers passes by laughing loudly.

'I'd be happy to give it my best shot.'

She turns over and waits for the masseuse to rearrange her towels.

'Sometimes all you really want is the one thing you can't have. Or the one person.'

The lean woman with the cornrows stops massaging and asks me to turn over.

'But you've got Ralphie.'

'Yes, darling Ralphie. I adore him, you know I do. And I love his dad, in my own way.'

'Isaac?'

'Of course Isaac.'

There's a pause. I wonder if this might be the time to speak about Ralphie, and what I know. It's just us, for once, and the mood is light.

'Anna? Are you ever going to—' Her eyes sideswipe. Waving off the masseuse she sits up and clutches at the towel. Then in a voice laced with warning, she says, 'Don't, Cassie, just don't. And don't you dare ever say anything to you know who. Not ever. I wish you hadn't guessed but you did so we can't do anything about that now. If you did tell I wouldn't be friends with you any more, you know that, don't you? And nor would you know who.' Swinging her legs over the table she reaches for her clothes and using the towel as a screen, slips them on.

'I'm sorry, I didn't mean to snap, especially not on your birthday. Of all four of us, only Bo really got a decent set of parents. Ironic, really, you'd think that would make him keener to be a parent himself.'

A phone pings. Peering at the console table she reaches out and peers at her device. Her face, sunny for an instant, suddenly darkens.

'Oh bum. Ralphie's woken up and Isaac doesn't seem able to comfort him. I'm so sorry, darling, I'll have to go,' says Anna, regretfully. 'But listen, I can jump in an Uber, settle Ralphie, and whiz back. I could be by your side again come midnight. You'll hardly notice I've gone.' She bends over and lands a kiss on my head. 'You look absolutely gorgeous, by the way. Why don't you find some nice bloke to swipe right? There must be loads here. You won't even miss me.' She squeezes my hand. Her eyes are dark mirrors and in the dim light of the VIP tent she looks invincible. 'Don't ever be a mother, darling.'

24

Cassie

Afternoon, Saturday 1 October, Isle of Portland

Dex and I have been at the cottage for over an hour now. In the cab on the way over there had been a discussion, begun by Dex and more painful than cracked ribs, because it seems increasingly unfixable.

'You know, Cass, we'd all understand if you just wanted to go home,' Dex says. It hadn't occurred to me to go home. Now, it seems, the idea has been discussed behind my back.

'Why would I go home? In any case, my home is here with you three.'

Dex takes my hand and squeezes it. 'You just seem a bit out of step with the rest of us right now.'

'Is that what you and Anna were talking about last night when I brought out the hot chocolate?' *When Anna pressed a warning foot onto yours.*

'No, I mean, I don't remember. But no.' Dex knits his brow and goes on, 'All I'm saying is, first there was that thing in the sea, and now the horse thing. You seem to be having a really shit time. I just wonder if you wouldn't be better off in London?'

The cab pulls into the little drive and crunches onto the gravel.

'Just think about it, OK?' Dex says, helping me out of the cab.

Anna is waiting for us at the front door. 'Well, that was all very alarming, wasn't it?' She has laid a duvet on the sofa in the living room in preparation for my return and fetching a cup of tea and a fistful of ibuprofen wonders if I shouldn't go to the hospital for a check-up.

'I'm OK, just a bit bruised.'

I watch Dex disappear upstairs with his cup of tea.

Sitting down beside me and gently moving my hair from my face, Anna says, 'They were terribly cut up about it at the stables, as well they might be, given that they promised your horse was bullet-proof. You could sue them, you know.'

'Hello, it's me, remember? When was the last time I got myself together to do anything? In any case, it sounds odd but I'm really having trouble remembering what happened.'

Already the events seem like a thick stew through which only small parts of the whole are visible.

'You shouldn't be so hard on yourself.' Anna is running her hand through my hair now. 'I do love you, Cassie, darling, and it's because I love you that I'm wondering, maybe, since you had that horrible accident, it might be better for you to be at home in London right now? I'm worried that you might feel worse here, away from everything familiar.'

'You're familiar. So is Dex and Bo.'

'Well, OK then.' She picks up the cup of tea and takes a delicate sip. A penetrating silence descends on Fossil Cottage. 'That's why we're still friends, really, isn't it? Because we always agree on the big things.'

It has been nearly two hours since Jason and I parted company and Anna has yet to ask me a single question about how it happened. And, to make matters odder still, the more I try to remember the day's events, the hazier they seem.

25

Dex

The pizza arrives a little earlier than Dex had been expecting and the ring on the doorbell catches him newly showered but still naked.

He throws on his bathrobe and trips down the stairs, remembers on his way that he double-locked (paranoid that Gav would return and catch him) the front door and as he goes by the console table in the hallway yanks on the drawer where the key habitually lives.

A small, dark woman is at the door with the order. Dex thinks he recognises her. On Bo's recommendation he and Gav have started ordering from the Great Big Pizza Company so she's probably delivered here before. He's usually focused on the pizza, he thinks, with a twinge. London is so anonymous. How many people do you pass every day without taking much notice? He takes the pizzas and asks her to wait on the doorstep so he can find her a tip. She looks like she could use one. He figures undernourished or maybe a bit druggy. Turning his back he moves into the living room, deposits the pizzas on the table and goes over to the cabinet where Gav keeps a bowl of coins, turning the tiny key and scooping up a handful. These he dumps in the pocket of his bathrobe, then reties the bathrobe where the belt has come loose.

When he goes back into the hallway, the woman is still waiting on the stoop. Fabien, as his Grindr date has styled himself, is now standing at the top of the stairs, though still wet from the shower and covered only in a small towel.

'Do you have, like, a fresh towel?'

They've had their fun and in the post-coital phase, Fabien is failing to grow on him. Particularly now he's dripping all over Gav's silk Nain rug.

'I told you, in the big grey armoire,' he says, holding a staying hand up to the pizza deliverer.

'Arm? What does that even mean?'

Mate, thinks Dex, your name is Fabien, you're French. Armoire is French.

'The cupboard, in the bathroom, where towels are usually kept.'

'I think I might have tried there already,' Fabien says.

Christ on a bike. Have I literally fucked this man's brains out? Dex thinks.

'Sorry about this,' Dex says to the pizza woman.

Yomping up the stairs two at a time, Dex clatters towards the main bathroom and points to the large cupboard, which seems to satisfy Fabien, then turns and makes his more measured way back down the stairs and is surprised to see the woman still standing there, patiently waiting. She must be desperate, he thinks, handing her two twos and a one, a very overgenerous tip, but to include having to wait while he dealt with the cockwomble upstairs. She smiles and he smiles and harmony is restored. He swings the heavy front door shut and relocks, then is about to remove the key and put it back in the console when it strikes him not to bother. Fabien, or whatever his actual name is, will be leaving in the near future.

Truth be told, Dex would really rather his date leave now. The frisson is having company in his and Gav's bedroom when Gav has expressly forbidden it. Bloody good word, frisson. Anyway, now that's done, leaving Dex with a sense of business completed and, beneath that, a vague sense of unease, guilt probably. Still, it would be astonishingly rude to kick the man out without so much as a drink and a bite.

He calls, 'Pizza!', takes himself back into the living room, switches on the TV loudly enough for Fabien to be able to hear upstairs, lies back on the modular sofa and opens the box marked American Hot. A few minutes later Fabien appears, dressed, primped, smelling of Gav's aftershave and no doubt ready for his next Grindr appointment.

'I think I'll just go. Do you mind?'

Does Dex mind? His mind is dancing an Irish jig.

'Mate, do whatever you need to do,' he says to his soon to be ex-friend in as measured a voice he can muster. He looks at the boxes sitting on the table in front of him, picks up Fabien's. 'Want this to go?'

Fabien looks at the box and is embarrassed.

'No, please, I insist,' Dex says, standing and thrusting the box in Fabien's hands and thereby saving himself the trouble of finding a place to dispose of the box before Gav sees it.

Having shown Fabien and his pizza out, Dex shuts the front door, and stands with his back to it for a moment, feeling a mixture of relief and pleasure and guilt, but mostly relief. He moves into the living room and folds a slice of American Hot into his mouth. What a shame, he thinks, that there's no Grindr only for interesting people, or, at least, guaranteed not-bores. You'd think Bo would be able to come up with an algorithm for that. Give Bo some ones and zeroes and he can come up with anything.

He's looking forward to meeting up with the Group now. Why is it, he wonders, that he's never been able to make any other really long-lasting friendships? What does that say about him and about the Group? Maybe it's because they've all been through so much together: growing pains, minor university triumphs, finals and that awful low period when they basically graduated into the midst of the world financial collapse, then his break-up with Cassie, wedding to Gav, Anna's accident then the birth of Ralphie. Looking back on it now, the months and years they spent together seem so full of incident and feeling. They were living at a kind of emotional intensity he'd never experienced before and hasn't with anyone else since. Even with Gav. Particularly with Gav and most definitely recently. Dex's other half has been grumpy and out of sorts lately. And all that weight loss. Dex wonders whether his hubbie is trying to reclaim his youth. Whatever, it isn't working. No, for all the pain and tensions, the break-ups and the betrayals, he never feels so alive as when he is in the company of those three. They are the colour in what can often seem a world painted in fashionable but no more desirable drabs. Their voices are his favourite music. God, he thinks, interrupting his own reverie, I'm beginning to sound like some nutter in a cult. Don't want that, do we, Dexter mate.

He finishes his pizza, gets dressed and at the appointed time takes off down to the river and makes his way along the Thames Path. A sentiment flies into his head fully formed. I bloody love London on a summer's evening when the air is balmy with the fug of garden flowers and petrol fumes and there are people lying out in the parks and strolling along the river path. There is no way I could love it more. Being able to be here, in the magic of a dimming twilight, with the lights of the city blinking on, walking towards the people who I love and who love me, and with the prospect of hours of music and laughter and dancing stretching ahead, this is what joy is. That's even a little bit poetic, he thinks.

He reaches the Prospect of Whitby in high spirits and makes his way through the pub to the Group's usual table at the back in the bay window with a direct view of the river. Cassie and Anna are already seated and chatting animatedly. A warm scent of briny mud and detritus floats up from the murky water. His eyes float over the familiar plaque explaining that from this pub drunk men were rowed out to the middle of the river, robbed, tossed overboard and left to drown. Every time they come here, which is often, Dex says that's what he'll do to Bo, one of these days, and Bo always says, do it, man, because you look across the water, that's my river-view flat right there and I'm a strong swimmer. But no one's really going to throw anyone in the water. Obviously.

Cassie spots him making his way through the crowd and waves. Dex comes over and slides onto the bench. Two pint glasses of beer and a large wine glass still half full of white wine sit on the table alongside a bag of crisps and a small tray of salted nuts.

'Where's Bo?'

Cassie gestures towards the gents'.

'Can I get anyone a drink?'

He's waiting at the bar when Bo approaches, alerted by the women, and helps him carry the round back to the table.

'Happy birthday, Cass,' he says, putting another beer in front of Cassie and beside it, the present he's bought her.

She opens the box and takes out the ammonite pin, backs away as if unnerved then, letting out a hollow, uncertain laugh, presents her right arm to him, where there is what looks like a new ink etched into the delicate skin of the wrist. A blue ammonite.

'Wow, how weird is that? I didn't even know you were into ammonites. I must have just picked it up somehow.'

'You two always were on the same page,' Anna says.

Cassie reaches out the newly inked arm and gives Dex's hand a squeeze. Smiling, she looks at each of us in turn and says, 'At this table is all the love I need.'

'Oh God, please, no emoting, or not yet anyway, we've a long night ahead of us. Hey – you got that today?' Dex asks of the ink on her wrist. It looks new and sore.

'Wait till you hear how,' Bo says.

'I can hardly,' Dex replies. His curiosity about the tattoo surprises him, given how long it's been since he had any claim on Cassie's body or on her sexual self. Plus, the oddness of the coincidence. Group mind, Dex believes in that, some invisible pool of energy they tap into from time to time. It's as if they have become a single complex living organism. A coral maybe. Something like a coral, with each part separate but only capable of survival inside the colony.

'I'm afraid I came empty-handed,' Bo says, the crisp packet sitting suspended in his hand in mid-air.

'Dude, this entire evening is on you,' Cassie says, raising her glass in a toast.

Dex waits for a cue from Anna then joins in the toast but it kills him a bit to do it. Anyone can buy festival tickets. Anyone as rich as Bo, anyway, whereas he, Dex, put real thought into his present. And as became quickly obvious just now, he couldn't have chosen better. Literally couldn't. Why does Bo insist on stealing the limelight? Every bloody time. All his adult life Dex has been the side show, the other guy, the straight man to his friend's giant fucking ego. Why isn't it enough for Bo that he got the best body, the best degree and the best career?

Now Bo has even spoiled Dex's interest in Cassie's tattoo. He half listens to the story, about some blond guy with a Tolkien obsession who's had a whole body tattoo of Middle Earth, but he can no longer really focus. The story is actually quite funny but of course Bo has hijacked it by laughing hysterically and spraying his beer all over the table.

'Ha ha,' says Bo. 'So if the guy was Gandalf, that makes you Shadowfax, Casspot.'

'Because?'

'Ridden by Gandalf,' Bo says, explosively.

Anna and Cassie are both giggling like schoolgirls now. It's unseemly, and stupid, almost as dumb as Fabien and his ridiculous pretensions. Dex feels the spleen rising in his gullet and knows it for what it is, raw envy repackaged as contempt, yet cannot stop the dark energy growing and billowing inside until it bursts out of him and he hears himself saying, 'What are we, fourteen again?'

'Or maybe you are Galadriel, Casspot?'

'Who's that?' says Anna, still laughing. This is awful. They are all ignoring him.

'The Lady of the Golden Wood,' Bo goes on.

More raucous laughter. Ha ha ha. Followed by a descending chorus of snorts and giggles and expressions of merriment.

'You're a funster, mate,' Cassie says. There's a moment

of stillness falling while the others collect themselves. Dex watches Bo taking a long draught of his beer and reaching for the bag of crisps. You weren't that funny, he thinks. If Cassie hadn't been so ready to laugh.

Dex raises a hand to his throat and feels for the Adam's apple. A joke is hiding in there somewhere if only he can find it. But the moment leaves and it's now too late. Bo is talking about the old days on the Isle of Portland collecting ammonites. Another clear encroachment on Dex's territory. It was he who bought Cassie the ammonite brooch. If anyone should be talking about ammonites it should be Dex.

'There was this myth that if you put an ammonite under your pillow it would make you dream of your future,' Bo is saying.

'Does it work?' asks Cassie.

'I have no idea,' Bo says, evenly.

What? Dex can hardly believe what he's hearing. How can Bo talk such crap. He's a scientist, for God's sake. 'What a crock,' Dex says, more forcefully than perhaps he intended.

'Maybe I'll try it with Dex's pin tonight,' Cassie says, ignoring him.

Oh, so now it's a pin? Since when did his gift become a pin?

'Brooch,' he says, het up now, his brow sweaty and tense, stretched over a mess of white noise.

'I think you probably have to use a real one,' Bo says, picking up his crisps and offering them around.

When they reach him, Dex says, 'I don't think so thanks, mate, I had a pizza with my date before I came out.'

'Trieste with double mozzarella?'

'What?' The moment the word enters the air Dex is aware of sounding defensive.

'Pizza,' Bo says. 'That's what you always have.'

Dex blinks, trying to recompose his face, kicking himself for being so reactive.

'Whoa,' Bo says, holding his hands up in surrender. Dex catches Bo's eye and pretends to laugh it off. Why didn't he just say a friend came over? Why was he dumb enough to be so evasive? Now it looks as if he has something to hide.

The only way out of this is to change the subject. Saying, 'So, do you want to hear about my date or not?' and not waiting for the answer, he launches into the story of what turned out to be his semi-disastrous date. Transferring the encounter from his and Gav's house to a fictional pad in Elephant and Castle – even the Group can't know he breaks Gav's golden rule – and embroiders the story, embellishing all Fabien's ridiculous pretensions and bolting on a growing atmosphere of farce. As he observes Cassie and Anna getting more drawn into the story the cloud of murk inside his mind begins to clear and lets the sun back in. Then, all of a sudden, this:

'Did you get that skinny, dark delivery girl?' Bo shovels a large crisp into his mouth and bites down on it.

In a flash Dex feels his sides crumble, like an unstable

cliff. Left with the uneasy feeling that he's messed up and momentarily lost control of the situation, he says, 'What?'

'Pizza delivery.' Dex looks about, trying to appeal first to Anna then to Cassie, but is met with blank looks.

'Mate, what's with the pizza? No one cares.'

But of course Dex does care. He cares because he thinks Bo is sniffing him out, trying to catch him in a lie and that line of thought has set him off in many others, no less disturbing. He's wondering now whether he really did leave the console table drawer closed, perhaps he left it open. He thinks about the money in there, how stupid it was to keep the spare key somewhere like that, his own foolishness in insisting on locking the door from the inside.

'No reason.'

Well then, Dex thinks, relieved. Let this be an end to it.

But Bo, who is running his fingers down his pint glass, isn't finished.

'I'm just surprised they deliver all the way down there,' Bo is saying. 'Because the flyer says a one-mile radius and I reckon Elephant's got to be at least one and a half.'

For a moment Dex doesn't respond to this, hoping that Anna or Cassie will come to his aid and end what has become a conversation over which Dex no longer has any control and does not know how to stop. The atmosphere reminds him of a visit to the municipal tip he once made at the height of summer. The same still, rancid fug. He doesn't know what to say but he knows he can't just say nothing. Beside them Cassie and Anna are inspecting their drinks glasses and shooting each other long, low looks. The only way he can think of to respond is to meet the challenge with a counter-challenge.

'Mate, are you out of your mind?' he says.

Bo swings his head around like an owl's as if to say, 'who, me?' There's an amused bonhomie in his expression, the eyes wide, the lips curled up at the edges which Dex senses is fake and because of this, rouses in him feelings of such hostility he could cheerfully punch his friend. 'I don't think so, do I sound it?'

'Frankly, yes,' Dex says, already feeling that he's got Bo on the back foot and is taking back the power. 'Because, why the fuck else would it even occur to you that I'd lie about a pizza delivery?'

26

Cassie

Afternoon, Saturday 1 October, Isle of Portland

A while after tea and the conversation with Anna, Dex comes bounding into the living room, clocks me and Anna sitting at either end of the sofa, slumps into the wing-back chair beside the sofa and switches on the TV with the sound muted.

'Have you decided to stay?'

'I'm thinking about it.'

Dex spins around and crosses his arms over the back of the wing chair. 'I think you should go. We can get you a cab or wait for Bo to come home and drive you to the station.'

'It's beginning to sound like you want to see the back of me.'

'Of course we don't want to get rid of you, Cassie, darling, do we, Dex?'

In the chair Dex is biting his lip. His whole face has become brittle and he's shaking his head as if he's disapproving of the question. What's that all about? Is Dex going to cry? Anna too has seen it. Getting up she goes over and plants a kiss on the top of his head.

'Darling Dex, we're all really so sorry about Gav. Poor love, you always were such a sensitive boy.' Yawning and making exaggerated Pop-Eye arms to suggest tiredness, she goes on. 'While you make up your mind, Cassie, I'm going upstairs for a nap.'

Dex waits for her to leave, then rises from his spot in the wing chair and turning to me but without catching my eyes, says, 'Fancy a tea or something stronger?'

'There's some co-codamol in my sponge bag.'

'Done.' He returns, bringing with him the foil of pills and a whisky chaser and sits beside me.

'I'm not trying to get rid of you, but I think maybe for your safety . . .?'

'What does that mean?'

'Only that you had a bump to the head and if you were home you'd be nearer to an A&E. Just in case. I'd go with you on the train, but Gav's coming for me on his way back to Exeter and I can't face the scene if I'm not here. He's being unbelievably demanding and unreasonable at the moment.'

'Please, Dex, stop fussing over me. I'm OK. Let's change the subject. How's about a card game? I'll beat you at two-player poker if you like, then you'll be sure I'm OK.' When we were dating, Dex always beat me at poker, but I've practised a lot since then, and now I'm good.

A smile appears on his face. 'OK, then, why not?'

He goes over to the bureau, fetches a deck of cards, returns and curling his legs under himself, begins to shuffle.

We're a couple of hands in, it's Dex's play and the cards are in a fan in front of him when the question presents itself.

'You didn't go into my phone this morning, did you?' It wouldn't be hard for Dex to guess the password.

He looks up from his cards, looks at me and frowns. 'No, of course not. Why would I do that?'

'You wouldn't and you didn't.'

He mutters a disapproving grunt before his face lifts and a smile appears. 'Oh, I get it, you're trying to psyche me out.' He wags an admonishing finger and lays down a flush. 'Clever clogs, but I'm afraid you failed.'

We play a few hands. I don't try to win but I try not to lose either. Dex pours himself a whisky. I wet my lips on mine, biding my time. On the sixth or seventh hand, in a tone as close to a summer breeze as I can muster, I say, 'That money Gav was going on about, you don't think the pizza delivery person could have taken it, do you?'

'No, like I said, Gav already spent it and he's just forgotten.'

I fan the cards in my hand. Why would Dex lie unless he met the fake Frenchman at his and Gav's house in Lovat Lane and had pizzas delivered there? Didn't Bo say his pizza place only delivered within a mile? Marika Lapska was dark and thin and, as I know from the report of death in the paper, worked for a food delivery company.

What happened to Marika that night before the terrible

event in the churchyard? I'd allowed myself to believe we were just doing the sensible thing, that any rational person would avoid trouble at the end of a festival – but a terrible thought has occurred to me. What if I wasn't the only one with a motive for remaining out of sight? What if we all had reasons for not coming forward?

I know now that Anna refused Marika's cry for help at the taxi rank. I know Dex had a run-in with her too. Were we all a malign influence on her life that night?

Did all of us actively contribute in our different ways to Marika's death?

Are we all to blame?

'Your move,' Dex says, interrupting my thoughts. He draws an oval in the air. 'That poker face right there? There is literally zero expression on that face. It's like you're not even alive. You are alive, though, right?'

There comes a knock on the back door. Dex gets up to answer. It's Will.

'I heard about the thing at the stables. Is Cassie OK?' I can see him moving his head, trying to edge around Dex to see if there's anyone in the living room. Instead of letting him in, Dex stands blocking the view into the living room. I cannot see his face, but the angle of his shoulders gives off an air if not quite of hostility then of unwelcomeness.

Dex waits until the other man has finished, and in a chilly tone, he says, 'Luckily, she's fine, so . . .'

'Hey, Will.' I've risen from the sofa and hobbled over.

Since tumbling from Jason, my body has stiffened. I'm young, but evidently no longer that young.

'I'm so sorry about what happened.' He takes a step around Dex and leans in to give me a hug. From his spot in the utility room by the back door, Dex watches him beadily.

'Can I have a word? In private? The car's in the drive, if you don't mind.'

From his post, Dex feigns a kind of cool detachment but his eyes follow me and as I'm closing the back door his face says, *We'll need to talk about this later.*

Outside, the ravens shift and murmur in the trees.

'What the hell was all that about?' Will begins, once we are safely installed in the Land Rover and he's put the heating on.

'I don't know. He seems to have come over all protective.' Will looks at me sideways, as if he's deciding whether to carry on.

'Obviously, you're entitled spend time with anyone you like . . . but your friends . . . You know they're kind of weird, right?'

'Are they?'

'Look, I know I've only just met you all, and I don't really know how to explain it, but you just don't seem comfortable with them. It's like none of you trust each other.'

'Well, we do. More than anything.'

Will pushes his fingers into mine until our hands are

clasped. Our eyes meet for a moment before Will looks away.

They say that however you bring up a child it will feel normal to them. Kids adapt to all kinds of strange situations and quickly lose any sense that the situations are strange. I've read the articles. Who or what is to say what is normal?

But is this normal? Me and Anna and Bo and Dex.

'I don't know you very well, Cassie, but I know those people at the stables, they're really hot about safety. They wouldn't have let you out of the yard without doing all the safety checks. They would have checked that girth.' He pauses, pressing his fingers together, searching for the right words. 'Look, I'm not going to lie, Hayley said something to my friend that I think you ought to know.'

Will looks at me and swallows. There's genuine concern on his face.

'No, it's fine, I'm not hurt or anything.'

I don't want Will's concern. It doesn't interest me. All I want is Anna and Bo and Dex.

The heart beat rising. *What did you do?*

They say if you put an ammonite under your pillow, you'll dream about your future.

Go away, Marika Lapska. I never knew you. Why don't you go and haunt someone else? I took your money but I don't owe you anything. I don't know why you died but you were out of it. I know I didn't kill you.

My arm is on the door release.

'Please don't go. If you don't want to see me later, that's fine. Just hear me out. I think your friend Anna might have done something unintentional.'

Unintentional. That means it was an accident.

'It doesn't matter.'

'Yes, it does. Hayley saw Anna fiddling with Jason's tack when you went off to go for a pee. Maybe she thought she was tightening his girth and accidentally loosened it?'

Our breath is hazing the windscreen. Will reaches out and turns up the blower and in that action I get the sense that he's about to back away from me, from the group, from all of us. And it's a relief. Honestly, it really is.

'It's OK, I'm not going to be suing your friend Hayley or posting some bullshit on Twitter or whatever, if that's what you've come to check up about, so you don't have to worry.'

Will smiles but I can see he's hurt. 'It wasn't just that, obviously. I wanted to make sure you were OK.'

'. . . to have sex?' He turns to look at me.

'Are you always this cynical?' Am I? Who can I ask but the only people who really know me? And Will isn't one of them.

'I'm sorry. I get it, I really do. You're anxious to protect your mates at the stables.' Will nods and smiles. There's a pause in which each of us takes the other in. That's when Dex appears in the front porch, standing, hand on hip.

'Is everything OK, Cass?'

The hand on the door release, popping it open, me

shifting my weight, making to leave and as I'm about to, Will reaching for my hand again and squeezing it, Will saying, 'Please come over later, not for sex, not for anything. But just because I'd like to . . .' He leans over and plants a kiss on my forehead. 'And think about what I said.'

I reach for the car door, let myself out, feet scrunching across the gravel. Without waiting for me, Dex turns and goes back inside. The Land Rover's lights arc across the bushes. I wait in the porch, beside the statue of the Mer-Chicken, until the red tail-lights have disappeared down the driveway.

Family. I've been saying the word so long I've forgotten it's supposed to mean something. Will is right. My friends are weird and hostile to outsiders. And it is odd about Anna.

And all this is absolutely, perfectly normal.

27

Bo

Bo isn't big on having women round to his place. The exceptions to the rule being Anna and Casspot, obviously, but otherwise, no thanks.

The female smell lingers over everything. He prefers to see them in hotels, or, if pushed, on their own turf. Which, generally, means having to interact with them in parts of London much less salubrious than London Bridge. It's mad how far people live from the centre of London these days. All the travelling and the hotel bills. Seventy, eighty quid. Another thirty or so for the Uber. It's an expensive habit, but he sees it partly as field research. He'd charge it to his business account but that would make it all rather too public.

He's home now, though, in the apartment (OK so it's a flat but no one calls multi-million-pound homes with direct views over the water 'flats' these days), getting himself ready for the much anticipated night out. Sooner or later his phone will ping with a text to say that Anna is outside. The only woman who knows his secret. She'll nag him about it as usual and he'll issue all the necessary reassurances and then she'll stop and they will both look forward to a good night out.

It's irritating that tonight didn't go to plan, but he's had things go wrong before. Interruptions. Women suddenly changing their minds. (God, why are women so flighty and unreliable?) It's hardly a big deal, but it's vexing and not ideal given that she's already had a drink. A small one, but still. In an hour from now she'll be feeling distinctly off-key.

He doesn't wish her ill, but really, to back out like that when they'd already started. And for what? A shitty work call from a shitty employer about a shitty job delivering pizzas.

It's really Anna's fault, this habit of his. No guilt. God, how beautiful and vulnerable she looked after the accident. Her face, her delicately boned shoulders, the bird-like clavicle, the parts of her body left untouched by the lorry's wheels seemed jewel-like and evanescent. What was it about seeing her prone and unconscious which had so aroused him? Even now, he still finds it difficult to think about. Her vulnerability, perhaps, her complete lack of power. As she hovered somewhere between life and death, everything about her seemed miraculous. How powerful that had been! Even now he only has to think about her lying alone and unconscious in that great, faceless London mausoleum of the ill, to become almost painfully aroused. Sitting beside her then, he knew that something inside him, some wholeness, some kernel of normality, had shattered into a thousand pieces. For the weeks she remained unconscious, Anna was his Sleeping Beauty and he her Beast. Not that he would ever have said anything so corny to her. Or to anyone. Life was now a before and after. Before he had always thought of himself as a perfectly normal bloke. Afterwards he sensed something breaking away. The fuel that powered his decency. Now there were only fragments of that old Bo left. He had become a dark distortion of himself, a black hole, drifting in Anna's orbit without ever being able to land.

Even now he's never really spoken about that time, afraid that if he did, it would puncture the intensity of this memory. If anything, his response to the mental image of Anna's helplessness has only grown stronger and more powerfully arousing over the years. The memory is no respecter of banality or the mundane. He can be brushing his teeth or microwaving a ready-meal and a tiny fragment of the whole – the way the sweat collected in her jugular notch for example – only has to flash for an instant across his mind for him to grow wretched with desire.

And yet, the real Anna is no longer of any erotic interest to him whatsoever. Hasn't been since Ralphie's birth, obviously, but also for quite a long time before that. The last time they had sex (and yes, he's done the maths but prefers not to think about it) it was more or less a mercy shag. They are so much better off as friends.

Speaking of . . .

The expected text from Anna pings. He checks himself briefly in the mirror, puts on his light cashmere hoodie and heads out of the apartment. The cab (it's a Prius, it's always a Prius) is parked up on the opposite kerb side, with its indicator lights flashing. As he crosses the road Anna spots him and gives a little wave. If it were Cassie in the vehicle she would lean across and push open the door for him, then budge up obligingly to make room but Anna isn't Cassie. Anna just sits and waits. A model of composure. He gets in and says hi, but knows better than to bounce all over her like some overgrown puppy. She waits until he's settled himself then leans in and kisses him once very lightly on the lips.

'How was your date?' she enquires.

'She didn't show so I just got a pizza instead.' He makes sure she's not looking at him when he responds. She's not as good at detecting his lies as she thinks she is, but why take the risk.

'Ah, poor Bo-Bo.' She pats his knee. He rewards her condescension with a stern look, which she meets with one of her enigmatic smiles. He's not sure she believes him, but so long as she stays off his case, it doesn't really matter.

'Good that I came early, then. Nice to have a chance to catch up before the others arrive. I hardly ever get you on your own these days, darling.' He checks the rear-view mirror. They are crossing London Bridge now, and to his relief the driver is occupied with the flow of traffic. Nothing incriminating has been said, or will be, but you can never be too careful. The pizza delivery girl will almost certainly have had to cry off her shift but she'll have no idea why she isn't feeling great. The likelihood is she's already back in her shitty flat way out somewhere in zone zillion, sleeping it off. In a few hours she'll wake and hardly remember a thing. No harm done. Not the way he does it. Not with the amount of research he's done. In any case, so long as she doesn't tell anyone she's feeling odd or do anything drastic like go to A&E, she won't connect this encounter to anything. Tomorrow she'll wake up and remember nothing. It's a 99 per cent probability he's in the clear.

'You look great by the way,' he says.

'None too shabby yourself, Mr Bojangles.' He smiles to himself, pleased that she still thinks him worth flirting with. If it hadn't been for the accident, could he have settled down with her? He's asked himself this question a thousand times and always comes up with the same answer. No, because it would have been too much. All that feeling. He would have ended up hating her. Aside from desire, hatred is the only feeling he can really pin down. Every other emotion is ungraspable, like a little dog running up and down inside a tunnel. He desires and, less often, he hates. Sometimes he wonders if desire is just the flip side of hatred. When he's not feeling one or the other he's almost a robot. It has occurred to him more than once that there might be something about him that isn't quite normal.

'You'll be nice to Cassie tonight, won't you?' Anna says. They are driving along Lower Thames Street now, the

Tower of London tremendous and yellow in the floodlights. Ahead is the supermoon, massive and awesome.

'Of course. I'm always nice to Cassie. And Dex.' Another reason he could never have been with Anna. Her patrolling. She's always doing it, whether over their friends or over his dates. Sometimes he wishes she'd just leave him the fuck alone. But he can never tell her that. Not since the terrible time she arrived unannounced and let herself into the apartment with the keys he'd forgotten he'd given her after a wobble with Isaac and discovered his habit. Bundling a semi-conscious woman into a cab with Anna going mental. It's why he uses hotels almost exclusively these days. It's a safety issue.

It's why he's already regretting the pizza delivery girl.

28

Cassie

Evening, Saturday 1 October, Isle of Portland

'Happy birthday, my darling Bo,' Anna says, scooping the flute from the table. We raise our glasses to our lips. The wine is a cold wave, more like sea water than champagne. A mountain of seafood awaits and there is more wine. And I am feeling a great deal better.

'To fifteen bloody great years of friendship,' Bo says.

'To the four of us,' Anna says, smiling at me as she says it.

Nothing is said about the police or the festival or the missing money or the assault in the graveyard or the drowned woman. Here, tonight, for the next few hours while the wine is flowing we are at one with our memories and our stories, and in the fun palace of our friendship there is only room for laughing, drinking and making promises to each other that we may or may not keep, while in the middle of the table a pyramid of empty shells and broken claws grows up around us until it blocks our view of everything but here and now. Tomorrow the shells and broken claws will be picked clean of their flesh by gulls working through the rubbish and left for the tides to crush into grains of sand. But that's tomorrow. Tonight, right here, right now, is all the love I know.

Though perhaps, just maybe, not forever.

By eleven I am at Will's front door in Fortuneswell. I am not drunk, only, perhaps, a little worse for wear. He greets me in a lopsided manner, one hand white from the effort of holding back an enthusiastic yellow dog.

'This is Baxter,' he says with a smile. 'Do you mind dogs? He's not mine, I'm just looking after him.'

'I love dogs.' Dex and I would talk about getting a dog, though, of course, we never did. He waits for me to move into the hallway then closes the front door and lets go of the dog, which shimmies and sniffs at my feet.

'My old boy died a couple of months ago. I really miss him. Having a pet says something about a person, don't you think?'

We move into the living room where Will has set a fire. He shows me to a worn sofa, and offers me a glass of whisky then disappears for a moment and reappears with a tray in the shape of an ammonite onto which he's stuck two glasses, a bottle of Bell's, and a tumbler of ice.

The cottage is like the best fossil beach you never quite found. There are fossil cushions on the sofa and fossil wallpaper and a fossil rug on the floor. The real things are lined up on shelves, where most people keep books, ranged along the window ledges and hanging in box frames on the wall.

'Apologies for all the fossil-themed knick-knacks,' he says, taking a seat on the sofa beside me. 'Presents from Mum when she didn't know what else to get me.'

Will picks ice from the tumbler and adds it to our glasses. 'I'm glad you came. I thought maybe you wouldn't show up.'

'Because of the fall?'

He pauses, his whisky glass like a talisman in his hand. 'Not really that so much. Though how are you feeling?'

'Much better, actually. Almost human.'

Will smiles and raises his glass. 'Here's to being almost human.'

The whisky unfurls in my gut. It's good. Full of substance in a way that prosecco can never be. I put my glass back down on the coffee table.

'I really meant, because of what I said about your friends,' Will goes on. The dog comes up and pushes his snout against my hand.

'We must seem a bit odd to you.'

'Not really. Just a bit close, maybe.'

'And that's a bad thing how?'

'It's not, necessarily. But is there any real space for anyone else, I wonder?'

'I'm here now, aren't I?'

'Yes, and I'm glad.'

I lean towards him and take a kiss. His lips are wet and his breath saturated with the whisky. He smells, as he did the first time I saw him, of sandalwood. Reaching out he very gently pulls me to him. The palm of his hand is warm and surprisingly hard around my cheek.

'You know what first made me want to kiss you? The way you took my hand. You didn't shake it, you just squeezed.'

'Did I?'

'I thought, once you'd met Anna . . .'

'Anna's the sort of woman men think they should like but we rarely do, not really. I think she knows that but she doesn't seem able to do anything about it. Do you remember after I'd dropped you at the top of the hill? I felt your eyes on me as I drove off.'

'I'm good at staring.'

He pulls away and taking my hands in his, says, 'I didn't mean that, obviously. I meant more that there's something steady about you. Something absolutely rock solid.'

'Ha! That's funny. I am the least steady person I know. I'm thirty-two years old and I'm still in a shared flat working at a job I don't particularly like and living from hand to mouth.'

'It's what makes you different from your friends.'

I can feel myself pull away, keen, all of a sudden, to be back at Fossil Cottage playing some silly drinking game and sharing a spliff with the Group.

'Oh, so we're back to them. It's obvious you don't like them, but I have no idea why you're being so negative. It's rude and I really don't appreciate it.' A tide of feeling has risen up in me. My throat is suddenly tight and there's a hollowing in my belly. What the feeling is though, exactly, I'm not sure, but I'm struck by a sudden impulse to cry. Tonight was a chance to redeem the night of the festival, to forget about Marika and the money and the police. To do one simple but almost impossible thing: to turn back time and make it right. We so nearly made it. How close we were.

He's risen from the sofa now and put another log on the fire. Turning back to me but not sitting down, he says, 'I'm sorry, but it's not a question of liking or disliking them. There's something about them I just don't trust. And I don't think you should either.'

I feel my limbs tightening before a spring. Two hours ago, my mind had already leaped forward into a future with Will, with all five of us together, a future in which I was no longer the junior partner in the Group, the hanger on, the urchin. A future in which I'd proved myself by bringing another member into the Group. A future in which I was finally worthy. But now all that's gone. Will has robbed me of that. 'Thank you for your extremely frank opinion, which, by the way, I didn't ask for, but they are my friends and of course I trust them. Why wouldn't I?'

'I don't know but I think you do.'

There is a moment to go back then, an opportunity to rewind, to walk out of the door and return to Fossil Cottage and to pretend that none of this is real. That what I saw in the churchyard and what I did in the toilet trailer at

Wapping Festival, that none of that ever happened. That everything is perfectly normal.

The choice is quite clear now. I tell him everything and betray the Group or I leave.

Rising to my feet, I hear myself say, 'I'm sorry but this is really not going to work out.' Even as I say the words, I realise that they sound far too final, but it's too late to go back. You can never go back. I should know that by now.

I watch his shoulders sink, a knot appear on his forehead. The mouth which only moments ago I was kissing tightens into a thin line. Sensing a change in the energy of the room, the yellow dog comes over and digs its nose into his hand. Will takes his eyes from mine and turns himself to the dog. I am to understand that he will not try to stop me or beg me to return.

Outside, the moon has risen and shrunk, like something left in the oven just long enough to become unappetising. There are lights on in the cottages around and the scent of wood smoke. I set off down the road towards the high street, interrupted, briefly, by the entreaties of a cat.

Were we always like this, the four of us, too tight for comfort, the bonds between us secured with unsayable secrets? Did we always seem such a mess, so unlikeable, so sinister? Was there never a more innocent time, a time when were really were young and sweet and full of promise and not simply pretending to be all of those things?

There was, there was. It is so bright in my mind that my eyes are dazzled by it.

At this table is all the love I have.

But is that enough? I have reached the Spar now, its gaudy window strung with early Christmas chocolates and a local druggie slumped in its doorway. God, this place. Perhaps I should have gone home. Why didn't I? Anna and Dex wanted me to. Were they afraid of what I might do here? Were they afraid of what I might say? It is wild here, much wilder than Tottenham, which is itself pretty wild. But here it is sad and wild and beautiful. The peregrines are roosting in the cliffs now. Above them, on the island's high ground, the prisons give off a sickly light. Within the walls of the prisons, life is regimented but it's all pretend, a thin barrier pitifully unequipped to push back the chaos. There are moths in the light of the street lamp and bats in the air. There are feral goats resting on West Weare. The crows are in their rookeries. On Chesil Beach the sea pounds the shingles. Halfway up the hill Fossil Cottage listens.

The druggie says, 'Spare any change?'

From my pocket I pull out a tenner and two pound coins. 'That's all I've got so there's no point in following me.'

He takes the money, gets up and toddles off up the hill to find his fix.

A single lamp illuminates the yew tree in the churchyard and from somewhere nearby an owl hoots.

What did you do?

You know the answer to this question. I have explained it to you over and over, Marika.

We did nothing because there was nothing to be done.

Because you are not my call, Marika.

Because caring is too dangerous.

I did nothing because – please understand this – at that table is all the love I have.

But it's too late for any of that. Something is buried inside me. It lies under layers, unseen but implacably there. I will never be rid of it now. Whatever I do it will never go away. But sooner or later it will make itself known. It will come out of the rock, it will rise to the surface, it will tumble onto the beach, it will be washed in by the tide. And then we'll see. Then we'll hold it in our hands. We will turn it over and see that it is not made from fool's gold after all. We will see that it is real.

At the churchyard I turn and make my way back to Will's house.

'I'm sorry.'

'Don't be. Come in.'

It has been a long time since I have slept with anyone I cared about. Not since Dex. Far, far too long. So long I've forgotten how intimate it can be. It's lonely out there in algorithm land. Love mapped out in a language of ones and zeros. People reduced to profiles and matches and clicks. Human hearts written up as score sheets in a Big Black Book.

Afterwards, while Will is sleeping, I sit on the side of the bed and reach for my phone. It's so automatic but until now it hasn't occurred to me that it is really a kind of betrayal, a kind of theft. I won't do it. Not any more.

To be honest, I don't think I'm well in the head. Beside me lies my sleeping lover but I have no memory of sex at all. It's the strangest feeling. Is this what concussion feels like? A wooziness, a kind of mental nausea, a swirling of the neurons and a blank where there should be thoughts and images and the memory of sounds and smells. Maybe I should have gone to A&E. Maybe I should have gone home. I will. I will go to A&E. I will go home. But not tonight.

Will stirs, reaches out an arm and finds my waist, realises I am sitting up and, rubbing at his face, props himself on his elbows, his eyes wide with disbelief.

'You're not going, are you?'

'I feel a bit weird.'

From somewhere outside a siren starts up, so loud and sudden, it has me jumping out of my skin. Will reaches out and strokes my face.

'It's OK. Someone's just escaped the YOI. Happens once in a blue moon. There's only a skeleton staff at the weekend. He'll probably be off the island by now. Please stay here.' He sits up, takes my hand and curls his fingers around mine.

'I'll only keep you awake.' I'm pulling on my clothes now. If I don't leave now I will have no choice but to betray them. And then I will have nothing.

'I like being awake. If you're here, I'd rather be awake anyway.'

Pulling off the duvet, he rises, naked, from the bed and in a calm voice tinted with regret says, 'If you really must go, at least let me take you in the car or if you're not feeling well, maybe we should go to the A&E at Weymouth.'

'Thanks, but all I need is a bit of air.'

Outside, a single streetlight shines milky light onto a wet pavement. The street is deathly quiet. A bird calls, not an owl, some other kind. In the distance the water sighs over the pebbles on Chesil Beach. Anyone trying to get off the island tonight will have a time of it.

At the corner of Will's street I retrace my steps towards the Spar and the churchyard and there, sitting in the bus shelter with a man, illuminated by the light in the churchyard, is Bo's date, Rachel. I cross the street and walk along under the street lights to the path leading up to the cottage. Everything is quiet. The shrunken moon has spread its silveriness across the black mass of the sea. To the right are the lights of Weymouth. To the left, the darkness. I am tired now. My head is aching and my chest feels wrung out. I want to fall asleep and not dream about the drowned woman or about anything at all.

By the time I reach Fossil Cottage I am so heavy in limb and heart that I can barely make it inside the door. I do not want to go up to my room. I do not want to pass by Anna and Dex and Bo asleep in their rooms. I do not want to walk under the urchin or see the waves thump and suck at Chesil Beach through the little window or feel the ammonite of fool's gold which sits under the pillow like an accusation. Tonight I want to stay here, downstairs, where there is nothing to challenge me. And so, pulling off my shoes, I stumble onto the sofa, tug the sofa throw over myself and in the soft breeze coming though the open crack in the French windows try to sleep. But Marika rises up in my mind. Marika who seemed so out of it in the churchyard that she looked more rag doll than human. Tonight, just tonight, I want to forget. Tomorrow I will walk away.

It's still dark when I am next conscious but already my pulse is thrumming, the instinctual part of me alert before my mind has had time to catch up. I sit up and rub my eyes and in the clearing blur of red veins against a black background in the shadows on the far side of the room, a shape forms.

'Dex?' My mind, still half in sleep, begins to stir and rise.

No response comes. The shape resolves into the form of a man.

'Dex? Bo?' My voice is taut and full of fury. Every sense scrambles. I'd like to scream but nothing comes. If this is not a dream then what is happening to my body? My nerves are busy sending panicked messages but everything is frozen. I want to get off the sofa, I have the urge to run, but my body is shapeless and my limbs are soft and floppy. I want to speak but my voice has gone to ground.

The figure has emerged from the shadows. Outside, the owl is hooting. A chill breeze comes in from an open French window. Are you directing this, Marika? Is this your show? Your revenge? If it is, I deserve it, I do. Only not now, Marika. Now I need your help. But I know what's coming and it's not you, Marika, is it? What's coming is only more horror.

For a moment before the hand clamps around my mouth I can feel his body pushing through the stillness, then it's over. Nothing more to be done. My head jerks back. Monstrous insects buzz just below the surface of my brain. I cannot rid myself of them. The heart is ticking somewhere beyond the fringes of my body. I've separated and come apart. A voice, spring-loaded and unfamiliar, hisses, 'I need the fucking car keys.'

Something chill and unyielding is pressing into my skin. There is a knife at my neck. The shadow jerks my head back once more. Its palm is sweaty on my lips but the hand is trembling. For an instant I feel myself dematerialising then a brief, abominable pain flares. Whoever is on me is as scared as I am and that makes him unpredictable and dangerous.

Without moving my arm I point to the outline of Bo's daypack on the floor.

The shadow growls, 'Get up.'

And so I rise but unsteadily. Something strange is happening to my body. It began yesterday after the fall from the horse. A gradual disarticulation, the parts working loose from one another. I'm in pieces. I'm falling apart. I want to say this but the sound of my voice has slowed to a long moan only I can hear. An arm is around my neck now, the palm still clamped against my mouth, the glint of the blade just visible in my peripheral vision. We stumble a few paces. Pushing me to my knees the shadow reaches for the pack and jams it in my face. I do what I'm asked, open the zip and pour the contents onto the floor.

A light comes on in the hallway and, there, at the bottom of the stairs, stands Dex. For an instant the three of us, the empty daypack and the mess on the floor, are all part of the same tableau while our minds try to catch up with our eyes. But it cannot last. We are the cartoon characters chased off the cliff, suspended in mid-air and about to plummet.

'He has a knife!'

A mute, destructive energy surges through the room. How will this end? Time grinds to a halt. For a moment no one breathes. Then, all of a sudden I see Dex rush forward. Something clatters to the floor, there is a dark blur beside me, the smell of piss and sweat. A pair of legs flashes past and something warm and tasting of metal pools across my lips and I am alone, all of a sudden, on my knees amidst a scatter of objects with cold air coming in and a roar in my head and in the background a tinny voice shouting, 'Call 999,' and I know instantly that no such thing can be done because there is no phone signal.

A moment later there are hands on my arms, lifting me up, and I am back on the sofa but now it is safe because Anna's arms are around me and her right hand is wiping something cold and wet across my face.

'It's OK,' Anna says. 'She's OK. It's just a nosebleed.'

So you see, Marika, I have people, and my people will intervene.

'Christ on a bike. What happened?'

'I woke up and he was already in the room.'

'Did you get a good look at him?'

Did I? No.

'It was really dark and I'd only just woken up and I think I must have drunk too much or eaten something because I'm feeling really out of it.'

Running her hands through my hair, Anna says, 'I expect it's just the shock, darling.'

'He ran off,' Dex says. He's come back into the room now and he's panting and wired. 'I didn't really get a look at him. Too dark.'

'You hear that siren earlier? Someone escaped from the YOI.'

'Was he after Bo's wallet?'

'I don't think so. He asked for the car keys.'

'Did he get them?' Dex says, bringing over the tea and setting it down on the coffee table beside the sofa. 'Where is Bo? And why the fuck isn't he here?'

I point to the keys which are lying on the carpet beside all the other detritus of Bo's daypack – a battery pack, a foil of pills, his monogrammed leather sunglasses case.

'He had a skinful last night,' Anna says.

'Well, wake him up! I'm going to drive up to wherever there's a phone signal and call the police. Bo needs to be down here with you guys in case that clown comes back.'

Beside me, Anna stops stroking my hair and holds up a hand. She's looking at Dex. Something unfamiliar passes between them.

'Do we really want to get the police involved? We're going home soon. Not to mention the fact that your name will come up as someone the Met questioned last week, Dex.'

There is a pause. Dex, who has moved a couple of paces towards the hallway and the front door, stops, and in the tilt of his head I can see the cogs turning as he considers what Anna has said.

Then, with a long deep breath, he turns, and walks back to where we're sitting, closing the living room door behind him.

29

Cassie

It's been three or four hours since the intruder broke in and, having caught a couple of hours' sleep together in her bed, Anna and I are already up and downstairs, me with an ice pack pressed to my nose and Anna with the bag of filter coffee in her hand. Dex is in the shower. Bo is still asleep, incredibly. He slept through the whole shebang. The doorbell rings. I check my phone. Nine a.m.

Anna says, 'Are you expecting Will?'

'Nope.'

She goes to the kitchen window, peers out, 'God, no, it's that policewoman friend of yours. You didn't call her, did you?'

'Of course not.'

We both scan the room and Anna is already going for the door when I spot something lying beside the sofa and reaching down, find the foil of pills. I turn it over and check the name of the drug printed there. Nothing I recognise. I drop it in the pocket of my robe then, thinking better of it, fish it back out and stuff it underneath the sofa cushion. Plausible deniability. That's what they say, isn't it? The door is open now. From the hallway, sounds of female voices drift in. Seconds later the door into the kitchen-living room opens and Julie steps inside and coming over, hand outstretched and in a cheery, declamatory voice says, 'Hello again, Cassie.' She's in her uniform now, her hair tied into a tight bun, all business.

'That nose looks sore. You get that falling from the horse?'

'Oh, you heard about that.'

'It's a small island.'

'PC Blythe has come about someone who escaped from the YOI last night, but we didn't even know anyone had, did we?' Anna interjects, pointedly, sidestepping Julie and making her way towards the kitchen.

'We were just making breakfast. Would you like a cup of tea or coffee?'

'Coffee would be great. It's been a long night.'

'Take a seat,' I say, gesturing to the chair furthest from the sofa. Anna returns to the living room.

'The others are still upstairs,' she says. 'Bit of a late one.'

Julie smiles and says nothing. The kettle sings and Anna goes back into the kitchen.

'Did you find him?'

The non-committal smile once more.

In a bright voice, Julie says, 'Has Will been round today?'

'We didn't need any milk, so . . .'

The policewoman nods and smiles as if this answers her question.

A moment later Anna returns carrying a tray on which sits a large cafetière, a jug of milk and three mugs.

'Well, then,' says Anna, taking a seat beside me. 'How can we help?'

A couple of tracker dogs has traced the escapee as far as the hedge at the back of the cottage. From here the trail then led back down towards Chesil Beach. Julie wonders if we heard a disturbance, saw anything or noticed anything missing.

Anna shakes her head slowly, as if she's only just thinking this through. 'Nope, I can't think of anything,' she says, finally looking at me. 'We didn't see anyone, did we?'

'We heard the siren . . .'

'. . . but we thought it was a ship,' Anna says, 'we're Londoners so . . .' She tails off then leaning over the table, presses the plunger and in a casual voice, she says, 'Have you caught him yet?'

'Yes. He was apprehended on the other side of Weymouth a couple of hours ago. Shoplifting, poor kid. Hungry, got no money. They always get caught.'

Anna fills a mug and pushes it over towards Julie, taps at the milk bottle.

'I thought we had some sugar but it turns out we used it all on a cake.'

Julie smiles. 'This is fine.' Then, pulling out a notebook,

she continues, 'So, you were where when the siren went off?'

'Oh, we were here in bed, weren't we, darling?'

I turn to look at her but there's nothing written on her face but a faint flicker of a smile.

'All four of you?'

'Not in the same bed, obviously.' Anna's smile grows wider. 'That's right, isn't it, Cassie?'

Julie scribbles something in her notebook, stops and reaches for her coffee. 'And before then?'

A tiny tic starts up in Anna's eye. She hasn't anticipated this.

'Oh, well, we all had dinner at the Crab Shack, then we went to the pub down by the quay.'

'The Mermaid?'

'No, the other one. The Quarryman, is it?'

'What time would that have been?'

'Maybe half ten.'

'And you were all there?'

Anna casts a sideways glance at me. She's giving me permission to tell at least part of the truth.

'I was at Will's house. By the time I got back everyone else was asleep. I didn't turn on the light because I didn't want to disturb anyone,' I say.

'But you checked all the rooms?'

'Excuse me?'

'You said everyone else was asleep.'

'The three of us came back from the pub then went to bed,' Anna interjects, quickly.

'And when you got back, everything was normal?'

'Well, obviously, this a holiday rental, so we wouldn't necessarily notice. But nothing of ours was missing, if that's what you mean.'

Anna reaches for the cafetière and tops up everyone's coffee. Nothing to see here.

'I'd like a quick word with the others. If you could ask them to come down?'

'Oh,' says Anna, looking puzzled. She's unused to her having her charm go unnoticed. 'I don't think . . .'

'All the same,' says Julie.

'Of course.' She rises and disappears up the stairs.

Julie clears her throat. 'So, did you get anywhere with your neighbour?'

My heart jumps.

'The Coroner's reports.'

'Oh that. I forgot about it, to be honest.' I'm doing my best to sound neutral.

Draining her coffee, Julie says, 'Will likes you. He's a good guy, Cassie. Don't, you know . . .'

'Mess with his head?'

She glances at me then looks away. I have irritated her. The atmosphere is broken by the reappearance of Anna trailing Bo who comes and sits on the sofa beside me. While I make the introduction, Anna brings another couple of mugs from the kitchen and pours out the last of the coffee. Moments later Dex appears, wet-haired and green-hued.

Julie waits for the men to settle, then asks each in turn

259

to describe the evening. She lets them get as far as the Quarryman, then says, 'So how did you get back here?'

'We walked,' said Dex. 'Didn't we?' He does his best puppy dog look. 'Tbh it's all a bit of a blur.'

From the other side of the sofa Anna flares her eyes. 'We asked the barman to order us a cab but he said there was only one serving the whole island and it being Saturday night . . . so yes, all three of us walked back together.'

'Staggered more like,' Bo says.

Julie smiles but it does not reach her eyes.

'So, you got to the pub around ten thirty. When did you leave?'

Bo looks at Dex for affirmation. 'Just after midnight? Before that siren thing went off anyway.'

'And you didn't see anything untoward when you got back to the cottage? No lights on that weren't on before, no door open, nothing taken?'

Bo shakes his head. 'Nope, nada, though we were wasted, or at least I was, so . . .'

Anna rises to her feet. 'What we're all saying, PC Blythe, is that none of us saw anything.'

30

Dex

Dex really isn't into lighter-skinned guys, though that makes him sound super-superficial, so the one buzzing the video entry right now leaves him feeling deflated. Fabien is almost blond. On his profile pic he looked darker. But then it was a dick pic. Anyway, now his date is at the door and, evident blondness aside, he's none too shabby.

He pops the lock and goes to the door. Naturally Gav will assume he'll have gone on Grindr. The moment he gets home he'll be wanting the minute-by-minute. Dex obliges, though, in all honesty, he finds it slightly creepy in a way he doesn't when sharing with the Group.

'Hi, Fabien?' he says, inviting his date to step inside and take off his light summer jacket, using the few seconds while Fabien is occupied as an opportunity to check him out. Naturally, he'll have to invent a location other than the house for the date when talking to Gav or the Group. He thinks about it for a moment and settles on Elephant and Castle. Yes, Fabien looks the Elephant and Castle type.

He goes to the console table, pulls out the drawer and fetches the spare set of house keys. It won't hurt to lock the door from the inside. What if Gav came back early? Not that he will. But what if?

Jacket off, his date does a twirl in the hallway, craning to get a better look through the half-closed doors in to the drawing room and the study.

'What a beautiful house. All that art.'

Dex smiles blandly – all Gav's – and leads Fabien into the drawing room. He's never been very good at the pre-liminaries, would actually prefer just to get down to it but it's trickier, somehow, in your own home. The need to be hospitable, a generous host.

'Ooh, this colour!' exclaims Fabien pumping his arms up and down as if playing air drums. Interiors are also Gav's domain. Interiors, art, the stuff they go and see. Most of their friends, even. All Gav's.

'Like a beer?'

Fabien runs his finger along the wall. 'Let me guess? Incarnadine? Or Nancy's Blushes.' He chuckles, amused with himself. On the wall now, where he touched it, is a long greasy smear.

'Please,' Dex says, 'don't do that again.'

Fabien raises a single eyebrow. 'I'll have a glass of champagne if you've got it.'

There is some, Dex knows. Gav always keeps a bottle in the fridge, though not generally for the use of his husband's lovers. Christ on a bike, though, really? Champagne?

When he returns from the kitchen with a bottle and a couple of flutes Fabien is already perched, naked, on the sofa. Well, good, if that's how he wants to play it. He moves forward, doing his best to seem confident, though in fact, he's beset by worries, wondering whether he should move in for a kiss or maybe something else or, given he asked for it, pour Fabien a glass of champagne. Plus the indignation from before still lingers.

Dex puts the bottle down on the coffee table and sets the flutes beside.

'Now, or later?'

Fabien is staring at him as if he's gone mad, and maybe he has. There's a fit, young, naked bloke on his sofa and he's standing there, fully clothed, rearranging the glassware.

'Ooh, you look dangerous, unpredictable,' Fabien says. 'Are you dangerous, Dexter?'

Is he? Once he was, perhaps, in the old days. In all the good ways. All the ways Bo still is. A thought flies by. Has living with Gav made him old before his time? The idea so upsets him that he starts tearing at his clothes to get them off and prove to himself that this is not the case. He doesn't even want Fabien now. He only wants to feel more alive. He stands over Fabien, erect and ready, but even as Fabien takes him in his mouth, the thought keeps replaying in his mind that there is a part of him that is sad and afraid and although his dick is definitely into what is happening, a part of his heart remains in the hallway, wishing he hadn't opened the front door.

Afterwards, in the master bedroom, Dex hands Fabien his own bathrobe and wraps himself in Gav's which, of course, is far too big, then paces downstairs to fetch the remains of the champagne, even though the events of the last hour or so have done nothing to support the idea that there is anything to celebrate here, but the expedition is also an excuse to fetch Fabien's clothes, a gesture which, he hopes, Fabien will take in the spirit in which it is meant. The red drawing room still smells of early promise and it is with a melancholy air that Dex sweeps up Fabien's clothes and trousers and underwear, and his own, and brings them all upstairs and into the bedroom. There, Fabien, is still sitting on the side of the bed, with a vacant look in his eye. Did he just take something, speed or bath salts maybe? Dex wonders.

'Oh, I can't put those on without having a shower,' Fabien says with his nose in the air, waving at the pile of clothes.

'Of course,' Dex says, none-too-discreetly checking the time on his phone.

'And while I'm in the shower – Dex isn't it? – how's about calling for a pizza? I am starving.'

'No problem,' Dex says, kicking himself. What am I now? The valet? He doesn't want to be rude, but there's a cost-benefit aspect to every Grindr encounter and this one just swung into the red. 'I'm kind of meeting friends, though.' He smiles at Fabien and from his pained expression sees he has offended him. 'Although I don't mean, because, obviously . . .'

What will it take? Not much. He even has the Great Big Pizza Company number on his speed dial. Twenty minutes to shower, by which time the pizzas will probably have arrived, five or ten minutes of eating and small talk and he never has to see Fabien again. Besides, he's quite hungry himself and tonight is likely to be a big one, so he'll need to line his stomach.

'Fine,' he says. 'I'll get the food. You go ahead, take a shower in the bathroom down the hall. It's a bit nicer. Second door on the right. The towel on the rail is fresh and there are some others in the cupboard.'

This isn't true. The shower down the hall is no more or less nice than the one attached to the bedroom, but it's further away from any association with the master bedroom and Dex is now feeling shabby about having used the marital bed for his extra-curricular activities, knowing as he does how much it would upset Gav. 'I'll use the en suite.'

'I saw the ticket to the Wapping Festival,' Fabien says, out of nowhere. 'In the living room, on the mantelpiece.'

'Oh yeah,' Dex says. 'Going along with some friends later.' It suddenly occurs to him to wonder why Fabien's mentioning it. Oh God, he's not wanting to tag along, is he? No, no, absolutely not. Not in a thousand years. 'I don't think there are any, like, must-see acts.'

'The ticket said the Sylvettes. I love the Sylvettes. But so expensive.'

Dex tries to laugh this off. 'Yeah, but, I'm not sure it'll

be worth it. The acoustics are always really bad there. I wouldn't even be going if my friend hadn't already bought me a ticket.'

'Oh, well,' says Fabien, uncrossing his legs and rising from the bed. At the door he stops and turns. 'Aren't some of us the lucky ones?' And with that he turns and pads down the hall. At the door to the bathroom the footsteps stop.

'Hello?' Silence. 'Hello?' The second hello has an air of irritation about it. Christ on a bike, really? Champagne, sex and takeaway pizza and the guy still can't remember his name?

'Yes?' He pokes his head out of the bedroom door to see Fabien standing in the hallway with one hand on the bathroom door handle.

'I'm vegetarian. And I must have lots of mozzarella. Double mozz.'

Dex waits until he can hear the shower then speed dials Great Big Pizza, orders a Trieste for him and a veggie for Fabien, requesting extra mozzarella on the veggie.

'Thank you,' he says, winding up. 'I must have lots of mozzarella.' God, Fabien is a pain.

He's still in the shower room towelling himself dry when the doorbell rings. Throwing on Gav's robe, he pads down the stairs to the hallway and peers into the drawing room. The first thing that hits him is the greasy smear. Something about it suddenly makes him feel despondent and, when that clears, almost murderous.

Are you dangerous, Dexter?

Try me.

A knock on the glass of the front door brings him zooming back into the present and the hallway. Through the frosting he can see a person of small stature standing holding a couple of pizza boxes. He goes towards the door then remembers it's locked from the inside.

'One moment,' he says.

A thin, reedy woman's voice speaks back to him in an East European accent. He turns and walks back to the console table, opens the drawer, takes out the keys, and, without closing the drawer, approaches the front door.

31

Cassie

11.45 a.m., Sunday 2 October, Isle of Portland

If I can pinpoint the moment when it first seriously occurs to me that the Group is floating into dangerous waters, it is Sunday morning, at The Mermaid.

It's a warm day and the sun has turned the sea into a rippling space blanket. The path from Fossil Cottage gives out onto a huddle of honey-coloured stone hunched over the great belt of Chesil Beach. It's quaint and lovely. It's too late in the morning for the falcons and even the crows are quiet now. Earlier, as Julie was leaving, the sound of bells reached us from the church, but the congregation has dispersed leaving only a junkie slumped against a tombstone and the vicar has shut and locked the church. No owls but then owls stay out of the light. The only hunter out here in the sun is me. I am hunting for the truth, but the truth is evading me.

I should have left when Dex and Anna wanted me to. It's too late now. I am already tangled in the seaweed at the shoreline. When the tide comes in I may drown.

'Something's going on and your friend PC Blythe isn't telling us what it is. You need to find out,' Anna said, as we walked down the hill. It wasn't a suggestion. I knew that the moment she said it. It was in her voice and in her eyes and in the way she wound her hand in mine.

This is a test. Of my love and of the love that comes back to me.

At this table is all the love I have.

The door into the public bar at The Mermaid opens into a hoppy, welcoming funk. Will is serving and doesn't notice me straight away. When he does, his face brightens and he waves me over and I feel that there is something bad in what I am about to do but I am going to do it anyway.

'Hey, Cassie. How are you?'

As I near his jaw tightens and a crease appears in his brow. He says, carefully, 'What happened to your nose?'

Already from his face I can tell he's not quite sure whether to believe my answer. Secrets and lies make easy bedfellows. Easier than people. Easier than the truth.

When I was young my mother read to me sometimes. Not often, but sometimes. One of the stories she liked to read (because my mother always picked the stories) was *Pinocchio*. In the story Pinocchio's nose grows longer every time he lies. But in this version now, the nose doesn't grow longer. It simply thickens and goes purple. *Liar liar*. Lies have become so easy and so necessary.

'The horse. Bruising's only just come up.'

'You look like you need a stiff drink. Can I get you something on the house?' If Will is hurt about my leaving last night, he's doing a good job of not letting it show. Maybe he's not the type to hold a grudge. Maybe he just doesn't care.

You see what's happened to me? My nose hasn't grown longer. Instead I have grown. I'm becoming jaded and weary.

When I ask for a coffee he turns his back to me, fills a cafetière, and sets it alongside a cup and saucer on the bar. Perched on the saucer is one of those little caramel biscuits you more often get in continental Europe.

'Does it hurt?'

'Not really. I mean, yes, a bit, but I took some pills.'

'I felt bad about letting you go off on your own like that. I should have insisted.' His eyes reach mine and there's a steady look, an appeal to me to come clean.

'That's sweet,' is all I am able to say.

He lets out a yelp, somewhere between hurt and bleak amusement.

'What's so funny?'

A pause. His head is cocked and he's eyeing me through narrowed lids now. We're a moment from truthfulness. In another instant, it will all be said. The attack at Wapping Festival, the drowned woman, Gav and Dex, the escapee at the cottage and the sense that the Group is splitting open and when it does, terrible things will emerge. Awful, unforgivable things.

In that moment the door opens and in with it comes a burst of sunlight and out of it goes the moment for the truth.

'That's Ian from the brewery. I better just . . .' He smiles and waves to the figure behind me, then, 'Why don't you take a proper seat at one of the tables? I'll only be five minutes.'

The pub is pretty empty, the lull before the Sunday lunchtime rush. A couple of women are sitting at a table by the unlit fire, angled with their backs to me. I settle into a nearby table and begin idly keying words into the Google search box. Thames. Drowning. Wapping Festival. Isle of Portland. Prison escape. Nothing of interest. And then, something. Not on the phone but a few words overheard which set off an alert in my mind. Whatever it was has passed before I'm able to catch it, but I'm listening now. The two women have my full attention.

They are talking about a recent date. The one with mid-brown hair to her shoulders, from the back view I'd say in her early twenties, is saying, 'Obviously, I remember him coming round, we had a few drinks, then nothing.'

'You don't remember anything about the date?'

'No.'

'How weird.'

'I spent most of Saturday in bed. I just felt really out of it. I mean, we had a few drinks, but I really don't think I drank that much. Maybe I did, though.'

'You don't know the guy's name?'

'I'm pretty sure I did at the time but I've just forgotten it. I literally cannot remember.'

'If you two matched, he'll obviously be in your profiles, won't he?'

'I checked but he's deleted his profile from the app.'

By now I'm all ears, my pulse quickening, thinking of any excuse to walk by so I can see their faces.

'Wow.' There's a pause, then the other woman says, 'Do you think you should report it?'

Will comes over, nods to the two women and sits.

'So, Cassie, don't you think you should get someone to look at that?'

'Those two women, are they friends of yours?' I ask, ignoring the question.

I watch him crane his neck and turning back to me, in a low voice, he says, 'The older one is Alison Freeman. I was at school with her. Can't quite see the other one. I didn't serve them. Why?'

With impeccable timing, the woman with the shoulder length mid-brown hair gets up and makes her way towards the toilets. After a moment's wait, I get up and follow her. There's only one toilet and she's in it when I get there so I hang back and wait by the basin. The toilet flushes. The click of the bolt as it slides back. The door opens. My gaze lingers just a little too long. She meets it with a curious smile, as if trying to place me. There's an odd, uneasy moment when our eyes lock as she holds the door open for me.

It's Rachel, the woman I saw with a man down by the bus shelter next to the church last night. The woman Bo hooked up with on Friday. Big Black Book entry number 346.

32

Cassie

Someone should write a book about the hellacious freaks, dicks and weirdoes who cross your path when you're active on dating apps. The guys with twisted heads and rubbed-out minds, guys whose hearts are locked in underground vaults, guys with no discernible souls.

Not that I'm claiming any moral high ground here. Because me.

Someone should write about those guys. But someone should write about the good guys too.

Ink Man's real name is Jake but for the purposes of sex he likes to be called Gandalf. Really. Being Gandalf is what turns him on. That and the ink of Middle Earth on his back. Why we matched I don't know, except the Swipe app isn't very discriminating. I should probably tell Bo that. It's his app, after all. He developed it and it's the reason he's made all that money.

They've been predicting the end of romance. They've been saying the old black magic is over and the only spells my generation will ever get to write are carved out in ones and zeroes. 'You lot will have will never have any good stories about how you met,' Gav told me once. 'All you'll be able to say is that you met on some app. How sad is that?' At the time I was offended but also, Fuck you, oldie. If I was your age, all I'd have are memories of hanging around in parties and at clubs waiting for a guy to notice me and being ever so grateful whenever one did. My generation don't have to hang around waiting. We don't need to crush on some guy or trick ourselves into an imagined love just because we want to sleep with someone. We no longer have to stand at the party and smile and hope while some guy with a girlfriend at home gets his flirting kicks. We don't have to hang out with the duds or the creeps because they've waved their magic wands and turned us into doormats. We don't have to spend hours waiting by the phone. So maybe there are no stories, but, believe me, Gav, it's better this way. It's way, way better.

Me and Ink Man are just a hook-up but that's OK. I like Ink Man's profile, I like the look of him, his sweet smile, the way he's turned his body into a story, someone else's story, granted, but you can't have everything. He profiles well. We've messaged, we've Facetimed. He's sent me pics of his tats and his cats. Besides which, he's funny, cool, doesn't immediately scream narcissist or serial killer. Which, you know. Sometimes it's enough. Often, actually.

Tonight, Ink Man and I want the same thing. A brief

connection, a handshake in the dark. It's OK to want that. It's fine not to have to pretend.

And now we are meeting. His ink shop is just off the Highway, between a chippie and a bookies. The shop is closed and the blinds are drawn like he said they would be. Closed for business, open for pleasure. I ring the bell. Ink Man comes to the door with a warm smile on his face and a silver point cat in his arms and bolts the door behind me.

'Meet Miog,' he says, holding out the cat.

I chuck the cat under the chin. It slow blinks in return.

'Sweet,' I say.

'Not really,' Ink Man says. 'He's actually an evil genius.'

We're in the ink shop now, a glorified dive with a reception area to one side, a heap of ink and metal magazines on an old table surrounded by vintage barber chairs. The walls are mood boards of ink illustrations and photos of tattoos. The ink book lies on the floor beside the table.

'Amazing. You did all these?'

'Most of them.'

He brings me a beer, twists off the top. For someone whose work requires delicate movements, he has huge hands. As we knock back the ice breaker he takes me on a guided tour of the skin art he's most proud of. A wonderful full-back dragon, a wolf's head with a bottomless maw, a gorgeous, multi-coloured ammonite.

'That's my favourite,' he says. 'The Golden Spiral.'

'Which is . . .?'

'Phi, a perfect mathematical ratio.' He smiles. 'Except, it's not.'

'I'm confused.'

'It's why people want those tattoos. Because they think ammonites describe the Golden Spiral. You know, something mysterious and eternal.' He runs a finger along the image, leaving a smear of grease from his finger. 'In fact they're not Golden Spirals but I don't tell customers that. If they want to think they're getting the Golden Spiral that's fine by me.' He smiles. 'I can ink you one if you like.'

The conversation moves on inconsequentially. We finish our beers. Ink Man fetches two more. But something in the atmosphere has changed between us now and instead of chit-chat, or an opener to sex, an awkward silence falls. Until Ink Man gives a little cough.

'I may have brought you here under false pretences, but I thought you were cool enough not to mind too much,' Ink Man says, giving me the eye. 'What I really like, I mean what gets me off, is inking women.'

What Ink Man wants is for us to go upstairs to his flat, where it's warm, and there, instead of sex, for Ink Man to leave his mark on me in a more permanent fashion. Ink Man wants to ink me.

'Just a tiny, tiny one,' he says, pinching tininess with his fingers. 'Maybe on your wrist?' There will be no funny stuff. He won't be asking to film me. He can only promise me that the ink will be small and inoffensive and, above all, artistic.

'Will it hurt?'

'I'm not going to lie. I can give you a joint to smoke if you like, though. I won't join you but only because I need to keep a clear head when I'm inking.'

'I get to choose the tat?'

By way of an answer, he passes me a folder full of images of sea creatures. Dolphins. Mermaids.

Ammonites.

'Also,' he says, 'I'd like both of us to be naked.'

It would be so much easier to say no, to thank him for his time, to wish him well and to leave. To tell the others when they ask for today's entry into the Big Black Book that my date was a no-show.

Maybe that's why I say I'll do it.

And so we go upstairs to the studio, which Ink Man called Bree-land, after the territory in Middle Earth. From the small fridge in the tiny flat he fetches a couple more beers, cracks off the tops and chinks bottlenecks with me. His kisses when they come are warm and full of connectivity. From time to time Miog slides by and goes unacknowledged. Ink Man's mind hasn't wandered. He is absolutely in the zone. How rare that is! Ink Man is going to take his time and be in the moment. This is turning out to be everything a casual birthday hook-up should be. I'm having a lovely time.

That's the thing about online dating. The haters say it's superficial, you don't get to know someone, everyone is just pretending. But if I'd met Ink Man at a party, I'd have run a mile. He has a Middle Earth tattoo. As it turns out, that would have been my loss.

By the time Ink Man is ready to ink me, I'm ready for just about anything.

'What position do you sleep in?' he asks.

'Why do you want to know?'

'Trust me.'

'I sleep with my right arm under my pillow, mostly. That's how I wake up.'

The hand that is stroking my right leg moves to my right arm. He takes the forearm gently in his fingers and turns it over to expose the veins on the wrist. With his index finger he makes a tiny circle on the thin skin just above the wrist.

'I'm ready. Are you?' A verbal response is unnecessary. He picks me up and carries me to a chair.

'I prefer the Spektra Edge,' he says, taking a tattoo gun from a box beside the chair. 'I only use this one for special occasions. Trust me,' he says, and laying my right arm along the broad arm of the chair, the thin blue skin of the underside facing upwards, tells me to hold still. And I do, because part of the peculiar thrill of all this is its potential danger.

Time passes. Every so often Ink Man looks up and cranes his neck to rid it of crooks and aches and I take the opportunity to check out a few new lines, some new colour on the flesh of my arm. Then he bends his head and returns to his work and whatever he is working on is obscured once more. When it's done, he gently pins my arm and inspects his work under a magnifying glass. He wipes over the surface with some kind of fluid and he's done.

On my skin, now, only three or four centimetres across, in burnished hues of terracotta and blue, sits an exquisite ammonite. Ink Man inspects my face, keeping close watch on my reaction. I inspect the spot, still raw and a little bloody, where now an ammonite sits. It's a beautiful thing, a protective shell to keep secrets in.

'Why did you ask me how I slept?'

'If you put an ammonite under your pillow, you'll dream about your future. That's what they say.' He motions for me to wait, then returns in his boxers and a couple of beers and a blanket to keep me warm. 'If you're not going home straight away, sit for a while and have another beer, let the ink settle.'

He takes a seat beside me on the sofa and pulls on a few clothes. His arms are across his chest, the hands wedged firmly in his armpits, Middle Earth reaching beyond his boxers.

'So how is it a good thing to dream about your future if your future is about to take some terrible turn?'

'Forewarned is forearmed. In your case, literally.'

I stretch out my arm, ink up, and admire it for a moment. When I next turn to him, his head is leaning up against the back of the sofa, eyes closed, mouth a little open, fast asleep, so I creep over to my jacket, take out my phone and thumb up the camera. Behold Ink Man, Big Black Book entry 342.

33

Cassie

The early birds are arriving for their Sunday roasts and Will is back behind the bar in The Mermaid. Rachel and her friend are gone and soon I will be too.

Bo saw Rachel on Friday night. They drank too much. He stank of booze. But I saw a foil of pills in Bo's daypack. Rachel sensed the wrongness of what happened between them. One of these days she might realise why.

Have I stopped being a bystander and become a witness?

Nobody likes a tattle-tale. No one likes a snitch.

At this table is all the love I have.

Sometimes I get the feeling I'm standing alone in the dark behind a thick wall. There is a crack in the wall and it would be possible to put my mouth to the crack and shout, 'Is anybody there?' But what stops me is the fear that nobody on the other side will listen.

Marika Lapska knew this too. She found out the hard way.

Will comes over and slides onto the bench behind the

table. 'Sorry about that. Stacey's taken over for a bit, but I'll have to go back in a few minutes.' He takes my right hand, turns over my arm and taps the tattoo. He's got a similar ink on his bicep, only Will's is larger. I like Will. I liked Ink Man. In another time and another place. But the moment for personal intimacies has been overtaken by more practical, more pressing concerns.

I have come here to hunt for information.

I have not come here to tell.

'Did you see Julie this morning?'

'Yup.' Will is making some invisible drawing with his finger on the table.

'Did she mention that she came to the cottage?'

'I knew that, yes.' An indirect answer. Duly noted.

'She wanted to know if we'd seen that kid who escaped from the youth offender place. The dogs tracked him up close the cottage. But then she said they'd picked him up so we weren't sure why she really came.'

Silence. No eye contact. Does Will not know anything or does he just not want to get drawn in?

Regardless, I press on, 'I just thought you might know what's going on.'

He's nervy and uncomfortable now, eyes keep blading to the bar. His knee is jigging. He won't meet my gaze. Eventually, he says, 'Is this why you came down here? To pump me for info?'

'No.' Yes.

He takes a deep breath. His eyes are stormy now and his

jaw is set tight. Then, just as suddenly as it had arrived, the storm passes. He says, 'There was an attack on a woman last night. It's not officially out there yet and I'm really not supposed to talk about it. Honestly, it's fine, by this afternoon everyone will be talking about it anyway. Nothing stays secret here for long. Just don't say I told you, OK? I only know because, well, you know, Julie.'

'Was your friend able to ID him?'

'No. They think it was probably the kid from the YOI but he's a house burglar apparently, no record of violent crime. Plus, why would he take the risk of drawing attention to himself? So they're still pursuing other lines of enquiry. Anyway, that's all I've been told.' His eyes are filmy. Biting his lip, he says, 'Sorry. I know the victim, so, obviously . . .'

Here are the questions I want answered but dare not ask. Who attacked Marika Lapska? Did she jump or was she pushed? Why did she have three grand in her purse? And what was she really doing with Dex the night she died? Why did the police want to speak with Dex?

And now there are a few more questions to add to the list. Do police forces talk to one another? And when Rachel realises what happened to her on Friday night will she walk up to the crack in the wall and shout 'Is anybody there?'

'Was the woman seriously hurt?'

'I don't think so. Her friend said they'd been drinking in The Quarryman and left together some time after one thirty to walk home. The friend lives in that terrace by the allotments, so my friend left her at the gate and walked on to the quarrymen's cottages up on the plateau overlooking the sea. The attacker either followed her home or he was waiting for her. She can't remember much about the actual attack, apparently.'

'So if she can't remember . . .?'

'She says all she remembers is he ran off.'

My hands come up automatically and clamp to my mouth. There's a little rush of breath.

All three of us walked back together, Anna said.

But as we all know by now, Anna is protective to a fault.

As we all know by now: Anna lies.

I return to Fossil Cottage to find a message in Dex's handwriting sitting on the kitchen table.

Back later.

I am alone. The sun is out and ticking through the windowpanes. Somewhere a pipe is gurgling, otherwise the silence is both eloquent and a little eerie. Fossil Cottage wants us to know it is watching.

I could go now. I could. I could wave goodbye to the Group and to the last fifteen years. I could disappear without ever getting to the bottom of anything. But then how would I forgive myself?

The front door swings open and Bo bursts in looking sweaty and hung-over but also flustered.

'Oh, Cassie, hi. Can't stop.' In a flash he's bounding up the stairs. I can hear him rooting around in his bedroom, turning over clothes. I leave it for a few moments, then go on up.

'Looking for something?'

He wheels about. He wants me to go away and begins searching again then, realising I'm not going anywhere, stops what he's doing and with one hand on his hip, says, irritably, 'What?'

'Did you and Rachel do drugs together?'

Rubbing his hand over his hair, trying his best to excavate some memory from his addled brain. 'Probably. Who's Rachel?' Screws up his eyes, casually scratches his balls.

'Your date. Friday night?'

'Oh yeah, her. She had some home-grown, so we smoked a bit. Why?' He backs me out of his bedroom and very deliberately closes the door behind him. 'Listen, Casspot, I'm in a hurry, OK? They're showing the game down the pub.' I wait for him to go ahead then follow him back down the stairs and into the living room. He lifts the rug, moves a few cushions, swears under his breath.

'That bloke, when he emptied out my rucksack, did he take anything?'

'Not that I saw. What's missing?'

'Battery pack for my phone. Can't find the fucker.' He quits searching and from his position by the sofa, twists round to look at me.

'Why the sudden interest in Rachel?' He's on his phone now, frowning. 'I overheard her talking to a friend in the

Mermaid.' His shoulders fall. 'How would you even know what she looks like?'

'The Big Black Book?'

He slides his phone into his pocket. He's suddenly a great deal more focused. Intrigued or maybe wary.

'A woman was attacked last night.' For a second or two he's completely still, without breath, his Adam's apple suspended halfway through a swallow. It's like watching a TV screen on pause. Then he blinks and, going over to the sink, picks up a glass from the drainer and fills it with tap water.

'I think we should stop.'

Bo freezes. With his back to me he says, 'You're probably right.'

'I mean, we should stop all of this.'

I can see him gripping the glass in one hand. For a moment I think he might break it. Then the moment passes. He makes his way back into the living room, bounces over and lands a kiss on my cheek.

'Come here and hold out your hand and close your eyes.'

He takes me by the wrist and opening my fingers as if they were petals drops something cold and hard into my hand. 'I'm off to the pub. See you later.'

The front door slams. I can hear his footsteps across the gravel. When I open my eyes there's an ammonite sitting in my palm between the heart and the fate lines. I watch Bo strolling down the driveway between the trees, his hands jammed in his pockets, so sure of himself, so certain in the lie. We are coming undone.

You've been rumbled, Bo.

If Bo and Rachel had smoked weed, he would have brought the smell back with him, and I remember exactly how he smelled that night: like booze, and fresh air.

34

Cassie

Afternoon, Sunday 2 October, Isle of Portland

A human bark sends me to the window. The raggedy autumn trees give way to a partial view of Anna, standing on the path leading from the cottage to the village, flapping her right hand as if to relieve it of some itch or pain. Standing a couple of feet from her, with his body angled away, clutching his cheek, his head bowed, is Bo.

In all the years we've known each other I've never witnessed anything like this. Since we stopped being two couples and became the Group, our collective disagreements have always been over small matters of style or effort. Why will Bo never wear his seatbelt when he's driving but always whenever one of us is at the wheel? Should the washing up be done after the meal or left till the morning? Do we go camping in France or get tickets to Glastonbury? These questions were resolved without bitterness by allowing the person who cared the most (usually Anna) to have their way. I see now that this was a kind of moral cowardice, an unwillingness or inability perhaps to confront deeper discontents. We gave way to each other because the Group had become more important to us than the individual members in it. Maybe that's how all groups of people operate. Maybe that's OK. Evidently, it's not OK now. So what's happening now, Anna hitting Bo and Bo taking it, is fascinating and a little scary, a sign that we are at our end or the path to some new beginning?

Anna storms up the path into the driveway and heads for the front door. In the time it takes for her to reach it, I have already scurried upstairs to my room. The front door opens and slams shut. There are footsteps on the staircase. Not long after that, the front door opens again and Dex comes tumbling in, half-singing, half-rapping a tune whose provenance I'm in no state to remember. There are footsteps, heavier this time, and continuing up to the second floor. A quick knock, the bedroom door opening and Dex peering round the door.

'Oh, you're here. Are you feeling OK? Where is everyone?' He comes over to where I'm sitting on the bed and plonks himself beside me.

'Bo came back briefly then left again to watch the game at the pub. I thought you'd all gone somewhere together.'

'We did. We went for a walk but Anna stomped off on her own. Look . . .' He comes over to the bed carrying a small brown object on his palm, waving it under my nose and inviting me to take it from him, then takes a seat on the bed beside me.

'What is it?'

'Ichthyosaurus vertebra, apparently. Dino bone.'

Holding Dex's eye I turn the thing over in my hand. 'What was Anna so upset with Bo about? I saw them having a row outside.'

'You know what those two are like. So bloody touchy.' Dex removes the fossil from my hand.

'Heavy, isn't it?'

'That's because it's not a bone any more. It looks like a bone, it started life as a bone, but it's now become something else.' I hand it back to Dex, who checks it out, bewildered.

'A fossil, you mean?'

I've flustered him. He rises to his feet and the fossil, which only a minute ago seemed so precious, drops to the floor. 'Is this about that woman who got attacked last night?' He'd heard then. Or perhaps he already knew.

'I don't know, is it?' He takes a step back and twists his neck round to check the door, then goes over and gently closes it.

'Gav shouldn't have said anything, Cass. That was our thing. But it doesn't make any difference that you know, really. So the cops came round, so what? It was nothing. I got talking to her and some have-a-go hero decided to play the big man and it got caught on CCTV. I didn't even know her name.'

'Why are you lying to me, Dex?'

His palm goes to his chest in a gesture of surprise. 'What?'

'You knew Marika Lapska, didn't you? She stole your

money so she must have been at your house. Did you tell that to Gav? Did you tell it to the police?'

He takes a deep breath and blinks. A look of defeat comes over him. 'OK, right, so she came to the house to deliver a pizza and I got distracted and left her at the door for a moment. I didn't even know anything was missing until Gav got back later and texted me. I just happened to see her at the festival. Obviously she didn't know I'd be there or she wouldn't have showed up. When I confronted her she just got all weepy on me and denied it. I was probably a bit heavy with her, trying to check her bag, but there wasn't any cash in it. I don't know if she had some drug thing going on. Maybe that's why she took the money. She seemed pretty out of it, to be honest.'

'But you didn't say any of that to the police, or to Gav, did you?'

'Mate, look. I had a guy over to the house that evening. He could easily have taken the money. It was in the same drawer as the house keys and I had to open the drawer to open the door for the pizza. Gav would go ballistic if he knew – you know he's got a thing about me not bringing dates back to the house – and with this bloody cancer thing hanging over both of us, I don't want to put him through that.

'You know Gav had a CCTV installed at the front door. We've laughed about it, remember? It was a condition of the insurance apparently. High value art, blah, blah. There are Bridget Rileys in there, Anish Kapoors, a Grayson Perry pot.

He's got a Damien Hirst, for crap's sake. Why he's paranoid about strangers in the house. If I'd told the police everything they'd have wanted to see the CCTV and I didn't want to take the risk of Gav finding out. Honestly, when they came around I didn't even know that woman had died.'

'Is that why you didn't intervene when you saw Marika in the churchyard? She deserved what was coming to her?'

'No, of course not. I just thought she was probably wrapped up in some drug gang thing and I didn't want to have anything to do with it. And so, yes, I didn't do anything about it. But I wasn't exactly alone in that, was I?' He rolls his eyes, irritation in his tone. 'Seriously, this weekend is turning out to be a shit show.' And with that he's out the door, slamming it behind him, and racing down the stairs at a clip.

Some minutes later Anna appears carrying a mug of tea. 'What was that all about?' She comes over, lays the mug on the limed oak stool serving as a bedside table and sits down beside me.

'Just Dex being Dex.'

There's a pause while Anna takes this in and evidently decides not to pursue it.

'Anyway, how are you feeling? Did you manage to get some more sleep?'

'A bit groggy from painkillers, but fine.'

When she runs a hand through my hair it's as if some dark spider has made its nest there and is preparing to lay its eggs.

'Did you speak to Will?'

'Uh huh. Some woman got attacked last night. The police seem to think it was that guy who broke in here.'

'Oh, I see,' she says, her energy softening, moving her fingers once more across my scalp. 'God, Cassie darling, you were so lucky that Dex came down when he did. It could have been you. I was wondering, maybe the best thing would be for you to go home after all? Bo's gone off to watch the game, but his car's still here. I could give you a lift to Weymouth station. I think there's a fast train at forty-seven past the hour,' she adds, casually, as though the timetable was some factoid she had stumbled upon in the course of a mental rummage. 'I'm sure the boys would understand.'

A brief silence falls before I ask, 'What were you and Bo arguing about?'

'Oh, you heard that? It was nothing really. I just thought we all should have a late lunch together but Bo was being an arse about going to the pub to watch the game.' She smiles and pats my hand, a co-conspirator.

'You must have seen the woman when you were in there last night.'

'What woman?' Her expression is a perfect blank.

'The one who was attacked. Apparently she was drinking there and probably got followed home.'

'God, how awful.'

A space opens up in the conversation and into it falls the thick, grey, cosmic web of lies we have all been spinning, together and alone, long before the weekend, before the festival even. What is wrong with us? Have we forgotten how to tell the truth? Do we even know what it is any more?

'Are you OK, darling?' Anna says. 'Are you sure you don't want to go home? I really think that would be best.'

'I probably just need a walk.'

'In that case, why don't I come with you? We could go up to the quarry and look at the view?'

'I think I'd prefer to go on my own.'

'Oh, I see. Well, in that case, I'll be here when you get back. But don't be gone long, will you? You're obviously still a little bit in shock.' She's stopped stroking my head now and in an odd, hectoring tone in which it is possible to sense the faintest hint of a warning, adds, 'I don't want to have to worry about you.'

A little later, after Anna has gone downstairs, I pull on my walking boots and leave the cottage but I do not go to the quarry. I'm afraid Anna might follow me there. Instead, I make my way down the path into Fortuneswell. The peregrines are sailing over the cliff tops, calling and hacking. In the right-hand pocket of my jacket lies the ammonite Bo gave me. In the other, the one I found for myself. For fifteen years I have spun in the Group's orbit but lately I have been a bad comet, unruly and unpredictable. I'm spinning out, I'm going it alone. With a steady heart I make my way towards the bus stop by the church where Rachel and her boyfriend were sitting. I could go back and collect my things but there is nothing in Fossil Cottage I can't afford to lose now and everything in me is screaming it's too late. Now is the time for action. If I do not return soon, Anna will come looking for me.

Up on the road by the quarry a cream and green bus appears from around the headland. I finger the ammonite Bo gave me and think of Marika. There is too much to untangle. Too many lies. I think about the Mer-Chicken, the hideous, mythical beast invented to fill a gap in human understanding. The harbinger of death. This is what the Group has become. A monster of the imagination. A conjured creature which can now only bring misery and torment. Up on the headland the bus grinds to a halt. A solitary woman gets out and a thought flies by about Anna and how lonely she must be, trapped in her web of lies. How lonely all four of us are, stuck in our pretence at friendship. In the light of Dex's phone in the alleyway, I saw that clearly for the first time. We have not been best buddies for a long time. Perhaps we never were. What we are now is frenemies. The bus pulls out and picks up speed. The bus stop is still fifty metres away. Shall I? This is the time. It is now or never, now or I am lost.

As the bus roars around the final corner on the approach into Fortuneswell, I can feel myself rising from the pavement, sprinting, my arm flapping a signal. The sound of compressed air and a squeal. The whoosh of the doors opening.

'Nearly missed it,' says the driver as I step in. 'Where to, love?'

35

Cassie

The text comes through as the train is drawing into Southampton. I hit call back. There are no preliminaries. The voice is a knife to the jugular. 'I am so angry with you right now I don't know if I'm going to be able to be your friend. You promised not to tell Dex I told you about the police. And now I can't trust you ever again.'

No more avoidance. No more hesitation or creeping around or pretending not to know what has become common knowledge. The train is slowing. *You are now approaching Southampton Airport Parkway.*

'Don't tell me you're on a bloody train? You've just abandoned everyone?' No answer required. 'That chap you had a fling with just went to see him. Will, is it? He seems to know all about the police visiting Dex after the festival too. Now Dex is too scared to leave the island. He thinks the police are going to come after him about this woman who got attacked. For God's sake, Cassie, what did you do, walk round the island with a loud hailer? Who didn't you tell?'

'I'm sorry, Gav. It all got too complicated. The Group, everything.'

'You know what, Cassie? Fuck you. I don't use that language often, but fuck you.'

The world outside is dragging its heels. A series of drab warehouse buildings and box stores trudges across the windowpane. It's too late for an apology. Outside in the corridor between the carriages a few passengers have already gathered by the doors. A fishy smell of brakes is rising up from the tracks.

'Dex is really scared. Go back and give him some support. Do the right thing. Talk to this Will chap and get him to shut his mouth. Please. Before I have to.'

The next stop is Southampton Airport Parkway. Southampton Airport Parkway will be the next stop.

And so I find myself on the platform, waiting for the next train back to Weymouth and killing time surfing around a few of the local Portland news sites. A single line on a local Twitter feed noting the escape and re-apprehension of the young offender. No mention of an attack on a woman or Dex or Rachel. I consider calling Gav back, then think better of it. Right now, what is there to say? Gav is right. Dex is the man who rescued me from my loneliness. If I owe a debt to anyone in the Group, it's Dex.

The train to Weymouth trundles through countryside I had hoped to leave behind. A couple of stations further on from Southampton, a woman boards the train, stops at my aisle and makes as if to settle in the seat beside me, but the train is nearly empty and with one dark look, I hustle her away to another seat a few rows further up the carriage. As she turns to put her belongings up on the overhead rack she narrows her eyes and gives me the death stare. Too bad. I have something to do and I need to do it in private.

There's Wi-Fi on the train but it's not until we reach the outskirts of Bournemouth that a stable 4G connection appears. I bring the secure folder in the Cloud and click. Up come the Big Black Book entries, some of them pictures of men I've had sex with, captured mostly when they were unawares, their faces sometimes doughy in sleep, occasionally a flash of torso or a shoulder, an arm loose, skin still slick with sex sweat. Back and back I go, through thumbnail after thumbnail, trying to ignore the creeping shame because I need to be clear-eyed right now and to see this through this to its conclusion, to unpick the whole tangled mess of it.

If I don't who will?

In any case, it's really Bo's entries I'm interested in, pictures of sexual encounters which, most likely, not even Bo remembers. Each thumbnail needs to be opened and viewed with new eyes. What I'm looking for, I'm not sure. Something in the eyes, perhaps, a certain slackness of the jaw. There is a kind of drowsiness that steals over a person after sex, a kind of melting, but it's not that. I'm looking for people who seem incompletely shut down, as if, behind the drooping eyelids and the corpse mouth, something inside themselves remains silently screaming. People who look like Marika did in the alley that night. Back and back I go, inspecting each image, but nothing surfaces until I reach Lucy, Black Book entry 289 and there it is, the encounter I've been looking for, the one that had even at the time lodged itself in my mind. A young woman, early twenties with dyed pink hair. She appears to be asleep, but there's something which, even when I first saw it, troubled me. Back then I didn't understand its significance or maybe I chose to ignore it. But I clearly remember looking at that face and feeling unsettled. It's in the eyes which, though unseeing, are partially open, the pupils wildly dilated, and in the slack-lipped set of the mouth.

Most tellingly it's in the thin stream of foam pooling from the edge of her lips down the right side of her chin. Lucy isn't sleeping at all. She's overdosing.

Bo's dirty little secret.

Not so secret any more.

I did nothing for you, Marika, and I'm truly sorry. But this is what you have given me, the moral courage to act. I will not let this pass. The time has come for me to act.

The ticket collector appears, stops beside my seat, says a cheery 'Hello!' and waits to be handed a ticket. He checks it, scribbles over the date and hands it back. A young man trundles by with the coffee and tea trolley. By the time I return my attention to the Big Black Book something odd has started to happen. Entries are disappearing, one by one, a slow progression of deletions. A quick check confirms that this is not a signal problem nor the result of my fingers on the virtual keyboard. The Big Black Book is steadily growing smaller before my eyes.

But this is not Wonderland and I am definitely not Alice.

I tap into preferences and a notification appears on my screen.

Administrator access required.

In goes the password. Up comes the same message. The entries in the Big Black Book continue to disappear. I log out. In the few seconds it takes me to log back in more entries have vanished – too late, I fumble to take a screenshot but now, when I try to go into the settings, I'm automatically logged out. And that's when it hits me. Someone has logged in and changed the administrator protocols. That person is deleting the Book, entry by entry, slowly but surely erasing what has taken years to create. Destroying the evidence. By the time I get back to the Isle of Portland all that will remain of the Group's dark little secret will be a series of deletions. The Big Black Book is transforming in front of my eyes into the Big Black Blank.

36

Cassie

As the cab from Weymouth turns off the high street onto the road leading up to Fossil Cottage the signal bars on my phone slip away. I called Will at Weymouth station and left a message but he hasn't responded. It's too late now. Whatever is waiting for me is mine to deal with alone. It's raining and the trees in the little wood below the cottage, which once seemed so romantic, are strung with ravens, their sodden wings hunched against the weather. The driver approaches the driveway too fast and the gravel sinks against the undercarriage. No sign of Bo's Audi. The wind stirs the trees. Otherwise nothing moves. Then from the kitchen window Anna's face appears and vanishes just as quickly. I pay the driver and watch the cab slide back down the hill before heading heart-sick towards the front door. There are only two ways to escape the Group. I see that now. Either I'll be the death of it or it will be the death of me.

The door will not open so I ring the bell and wait. A long

301

time passes before the chain rattles, the lock slides open and Anna appears. Something about her has changed. Or maybe it's just the way I see her now; beautiful still but in the way that, at a distance, a snake is beautiful; the way a drop of mercury is beautiful when it is behind glass.

'I've come back to try to make things right.'

'It's too late, Cassie. We don't need you any more.'

'Dex needs me.'

Anna considers this for a moment, hand on hip, her shoulders hunched forward slightly as if she's about to spring. A coldness in her eyes. Then, turning her body away, she waves me inside. I follow her into the living room in silence. Only a day or two ago the cottage seemed cosy. Now it's dank and cold.

'Dex isn't here. He's at the police station helping with their enquiries.'

Anna's chest heaves, moving the skin around the collar bones. Her eyes on mine feel predatory. The set of her mouth could stop a stampede. 'What were you thinking, telling the milkman about that nonsense at the festival? You must have known he'd go straight to that awful snoop of a policewoman? How else would she know about it? Now they've put Dex's name into their computer or whatever and they've obviously put two and two together and made twenty.'

'They'll find out Dex is gay and it'll be fine.'

Anna, who has been pacing and clutching her fingers through this, suddenly stops and faces me.

'Oh, for God's sake, Cassie. Your little-girl-lost act won't wash any more. You told the milkman you and Dex were an item. This is all because of you, your spinelessness, your endless pathetic need for approval. Do you have any idea what you could be bringing down on us? Not just Dex. All of us.' She's in my face now. 'You do not keep secrets from me, do you understand? There are things you don't know. I have to manage all of this now. The boys, the Group, everything. And you are going to do whatever I need you to do.' She's right over me now, pressing her finger into my chest where the pain is. 'You. Do. Not. Keep. Secrets. Not from me. Not ever.'

'We've all been keeping secrets; from the rest of the world, from each other, even from ourselves.'

'What the hell is that supposed to mean?'

'Have you deleted the Big Black Book?'

The room falls silent save for the beat of the rain on the windowpanes, the sigh of wind down the chimney. Anna has slumped in the armchair. She is shaking and crying now but there are no tears. It's not sadness. It's more like fear.

'I have no idea what you're talking about but I think you should just shut up.'

'Don't do this. Don't lie.'

Her head shoots up and there's a wild quality to her. 'Explain to me how I would have done that, Cassie. I've been here, waiting for Dex to get back. There's no phone signal and no Wi-Fi.'

'Then it can only have been Bo. Anna, we need to find him. I think he's done something bad – really bad.'

Anna's eyes have turned inward now. In her mind, she's scrolling over everything she knows, trying to make sense of it.

I say, 'Where is Bo?'

'Out. At the pub. I don't know. Maybe he's run away, like you.' As she says this her arm floats out and into the air. Gone. 'The point is, Cassie, that Dex is being questioned right now, and you know he didn't attack that woman at the festival because you saw him with Bo on the other side of the alleyway. And you know he was here last night because he came down the stairs and saw off that bloke. We were here, Cassie, we were all *right here*.' She pushes a finger through the air for emphasis. Here, in this place, with the listening walls.

'But Julie . . .'

'You have to go down to the police station and tell them you know for certain Dex was here last night.'

'Why don't you tell them?'

She shakes her head. 'This is *your* problem. *You* took that money from the woman at the festival and that was why she couldn't get a cab. If you hadn't taken her money she would have gone home and she'd probably still be alive.'

'*You* refused to help her out!' I sound like a petulant kid and I hate myself for it.

'You know, I really do think you have a screw loose sometimes. I've always thought it. Who goes to a festival with that kind of money in their purse? You think it was

304

some giant coincidence that Gav loses three grand and it turns up in her purse and then in yours? Where do you think she got the money from? She took it from their house. Gav got home early. He went to the drawer and saw it was missing. He texted Dex to ask if he knew where the money was. Marika had delivered a pizza to the house. Dex saw her at the festival earlier in the evening and she was odd with him. So he went looking for her. He confronted her, but she denied it and Dex didn't find any money on her because you took it.'

'He told the police he didn't know Marika.'

'Oh for God's sake, Cassie. What happened to your brain? Why do you think Dex tried to pass it off on Gav's poor memory? That's what they were fighting about when you arrived. Dex had tried to persuade Gav that he'd spent the money and just forgotten about it but Gav was insisting the cleaner must have taken it and was threatening to sack her. Dex felt bad.'

'Why didn't he just say it must have been the pizza delivery woman?'

'He didn't want Gav or the cops to check the home CCTV because that bloke he hooked up with, the French one or whatever, came round to the house.' She flops onto the sofa, defeated, and putting her head in her hands, begins to sob. 'Oh God, this is all such a mess.'

'I'll give him the money back.' She shakes her head, sadly, and in her eyes is all the sorrow of years spent in the desperate striving for unachievable order. 'The money is so beside the point for Dex now.' She stops and, cocking her head, as if the thought had only just occurred to her, says, 'Your friend the policewoman would be very interested to hear about that, though. You know, if someone told her.'

37

Cassie

Afternoon, Sunday 2 October, Isle of Portland

The police constable guarding the Port gate can't or won't tell me when PC Julie Blythe is back on shift and once it is established that the information I wish to give isn't port business, loses interest, suggesting I head over the spit into Weymouth and report whatever it is I have to say to the police station there. The news that I'd rather wait for PC Blythe is met with a thin-lipped acknowledgement. The constable waves me inside and points me in the direction of the front office where I repeat my request over again and am instructed to wait until someone can see me. Which takes an hour during which time there's no sign of Julie. Eventually a woman in a wraparound dress bustles by, stops, walks back a couple of paces and says, 'Cassandra Levitt?'

We shake hands and the woman introduces herself as DC Kathy Taylor from the Weymouth station. Forties. Rotund in a welcoming way and with a calm reassuring manner. Routine. She swipes me through a set of swinging doors then swipes me again into a side office and offers me a seat in a grey plastic chair beside a Formica table, waits for me to take it before commanding the seat opposite, sweeping her dress flat underneath her as she goes. Opens a reporter's notebook. Plays see-saw with a pen between the fingers of her right hand.

'So? What's brought you here today?' Done this a thousand times. Ready for anything.

'You've got my friend, Dexter Walbrook, in for questioning.'

Her face remains inexpressive. She says nothing and waits for me to go on.

'We're renting the cottage just off the path up above Fortuneswell. Fossil Cottage?'

'Yes. It's pretty up there, isn't it? Lovely view over Chesil,' she says, in an effort to put me at my ease. 'You asked to speak to my colleague, PC Blythe.'

'She came to see us at the cottage.' I tell DC Taylor how Julie and I met, leaving out the connection to Will. She listens politely but I can tell from her glazed expression that it's something she already knows. 'I wanted to come in because I know Dex wasn't involved.'

'I see.'

I tell her about the lead-up to the evening, how I wasn't with the others when they had a drink in The Quarryman, how they left just after midnight and walked back up the path together and how, when I came in a bit later, everyone was in bed asleep. How I'd had a bit to drink and crashed out on the sofa in the living room.

'So you checked on your friends in their bedrooms before you went to sleep on the sofa?'

'Well, not exactly, but you can sense it if there's people asleep in a house, can't you?'

'But you didn't check.'

'Well, no.'

'So you don't actually know if they were all in their rooms?'

So far this conversation isn't getting either of us any further on than our discussion with Julie. It's time for the new information, a modified version of the truth.

'Actually, I do.'

She looks up from her pad, interested now. In the modified version of the truth I wake to the sound of someone trying to get in through the French windows. I scream and then Dex comes down and the rest follows on from what really happened. More or less. I do not mention that the intruder came into the house because it will make the initial lie seem larger and I want DC Taylor to think I am capable of telling the truth. When I'm done talking DC Taylor repeats the story back to me.

'Is that it?' she says, finally. She folds her hands over the desk and interlinks the fingers. Dresses her face in a bland, non-committal smile. 'Can you tell me why you didn't say anything about this man to PC Blythe?'

'We're only here for the weekend. We didn't want to get sucked into anything.'

'I see.'

'So, can you tell me when you'll be letting Dex leave? Now that I can vouch for him?'

'I'm afraid not, but you've been very helpful, thank you,' she says, rising to leave. The same gesture with the arm, this time in the direction of the door.

'There's something else . . .'

DC Taylor looks at me for a moment, unblinking, and as if frozen. Then the corners of her mouth lift and she sets her shoulders back and she approaches the table once more.

A line must be drawn and the burden of drawing it has fallen to me. I should have done it before, but I didn't. Start at the beginning and leave nothing out. Let's get this over as quickly and clearly as possible. If I'm the one who has to kill the beast, if it falls to me to twist the knife, then at least be sure the blade is razor sharp.

So I begin with the money and what Dex was doing talking to Marika, then what happened at the churchyard and how all of us witnessed the attack. And how we did nothing. It takes longer than I had imagined it would. I leave out a few details. No need to mention the drugs in Bo's daypack or the Big Black Book or Lucy with the pink hair or the fact that the only one of the Group I did not see that night after we left the Crab Shack was Bo. Anna is right. I do owe Dex. And I owe Marika. And in an indirect way I owe Rachel, though I'm not ready to tell that part now. There is a story to tell and it is lively in me but not all of it is yet clear. I could have prevented some of this. I could have made the difference, but I put love, or what I thought was love, on a higher plane than truth. That was my big mistake, and it wasn't just a bad call. It was a moral error. And so I will tell. I'll tell the whole thing, because it is time for all of this to stop.

38

Cassie

Two hours after I left Fossil Cottage to go down to the Port police, I'm back, standing in the porch, beside the Mer-Chicken, waiting for Anna to let me in. All around, the falcons are rising and the ravens are attacking them but the Mer-Chicken is as still as a stone. A harbinger of death, Bo says. What if that death is my own? I have kept an ammonite under my pillow and dreamed of my future and now I am afraid but I am also ready. There was a time, before Wapping, when I would have given my life for the Group. There may come a time when I might still have to. Anna, Bo and Dex are not my future. I know that now. Already Anna has said she wants nothing to do with me. The others will fall into line, just as they always have. I've become a snitch, a tattle-tale, a gossip. I've kicked love and loyalty in the teeth and set myself on another path. I have irrevocably broken the bonds of friendship. I have turned my back on the only family I have.

'So? Did you tell them?' Anna is standing on the

threshold, knuckles straining, gripping the jamb and blocking the entrance. Her eyes are wilder than I've ever seen them and she's rolling her bottom lip over her front teeth. A tiny bead of blood rises to the surface. There's something panicky in her voice.

'Yes.'

'Everything?'

'Everything they needed to know.'

'So what did they say?' A test question. If I pass, I will be allowed back into the cottage. If I fail, the door will slam in my face and that will be the last I will ever see of Anna.

'They said thank you and they'd consider it.'

She closes her eyes for an instant, pressing her fingertips against the lids in an attempt to relieve some inner turmoil. My response is not what she hoped for but as much as she knew she could expect. Gradually, the little pulse ticking in her clavicle slows. Collecting herself, she flashes a brief, unlovely smile, and in a brusque manner says, 'Yes, fine, come in.'

And I'm back, readmitted to the inner sanctum of the Group. Look how well I've done. What I've achieved.

If only Anna knew.

We walk down the passageway and into the living room. How could we ever have found Fossil Cottage anything but bleak?

Anna sits in the armchair by the unlit wood stove, limbs restless, hands working. Before her on the table is a half empty cafetière and a mug. It's time to tell the truth, to come clean, to say everything I know and take the consequences.

'We need to find Bo, Anna.'

Anna whips round, her legs now pointed straight at me, like javelins.

'You're sounding hysterical.'

'Let's stop pretending. Bo deleted the Big Black Book because he's drugging those women. He drugged Rachel, I think he probably drugged Marika and he may even have drugged me. We need to find him, or he'll do it again.'

'Do what? Where is all this coming from?'

'I don't know. But I think you do.'

I slide my fingers around the back of the sofa cushion where I'd pushed the pills, but nothing comes up. I'm standing now, with my back to Anna, peeling away the cushions, scrambling for the evidence. Suddenly, Anna's hands are on me. She is trembling but her grip is firm enough to spin me around and force me back into the seat. She's crouching beside me, her eyes lit with some terrible, gorgon energy, her hands clutching my shoulders, shaking me so violently I am afraid of her.

'Cassie, look at me!'

Despite myself, I do. Because she's Anna and because I still love her. 'Even if you're right, those women willingly hooked up with Bo. They knew what they were getting into.'

'Did they?'

'Everyone has their dark place, Cassie, including you. You think those women were so innocent? They swiped right for a casual hook-up with a cute guy they'd never

314

met. Those women wanted to feel lost. They wanted to be annihilated, wiped out by the act of sex. It was part of the fantasy.' Her fingers are drumming on her forehead like a blackbird summoning worms to the surface. 'There's no accounting for how dark sex can be. Anyway, if what Bo did was that bad, why did no one go to the police and complain?'

'Christ, Anna, this isn't sex. I don't know what this is. What Bo did was so bad precisely because he made sure no one was able to complain.'

We meet each other's eye and in that small instant a world of truth passes between us.

Suddenly, it's clear. All of it. Anna holding me back that night in the alleyway. Anna convincing Dex not to go to the police after the break-in. Anna always there, making sure that none of us knew too much or let anything of what we did know slip. Her debt to Bo, her love for him the shield she held around him.

'How long have you known?'

'I don't know. It depends what you mean by "known".'

For someone like Anna there is always a swerve, some charming euphemism or get-out clause. It's how women like Anna are raised. Honesty would crack the glossy veneer. Then God knows what might come seeping out.

'I saw you both down by the path. I saw you hit him.'

'Oh.' For a moment she seems flustered. Then she reaches out a hand and strokes my face. 'Darling Cassie, you always were so much nicer than me. You were so free of all that snobbery and bullshit the rest of us grew up with. You were the fresh beginning we were looking for. But over the last fifteen years we've grown up and you haven't.' I push the hand away. Anna steps back. Her voice is frosty now. 'All those principles you drag around behind you, all that virtue signalling. It's so childish. It's unattractive.'

'I'm going up to the car park to get a phone signal. Then I'm going to call Bo and tell him to come back. We can go to the police together, but we're going to the police.'

'He won't answer. He won't come. You'll never convince Bo he's done anything wrong. God knows I've tried.'

'They'll find out.'

'What will they find out exactly, Cassie? Whatever you told them, it's not proof of anything. None of those women would be able to identify Bo. It would all just be vague guesses and incoherent impressions. He's good, Cassie, he's careful. He knows exactly what he's doing.'

'There's bound to be CCTV somewhere.'

'So what if there is? That's evidence of nothing. Besides which, I am absolutely sure he didn't have anything to do with the attack last night.' There's a pause while a memory surfaces. 'That walk we took through the pebbles on Chesil Beach? You remember how the pebbles moved to cover our tracks? Bo is the expert at leaving no trace. Bo's profile on the apps he's used, the Big Black Book, it'll all be gone, erased. I'll bet he's already home cleaning up his hard drive or whatever it is you have to do. It's best this way. The police will soon realise Dex didn't have anything to do with what happened last night and we can go back to being us.'

'I don't think that's possible.'

She blinks, surprised by my tone and in a delicate sweep of her hands, pulls away and moves to the other side of the room. With her back to me, in a chilly voice, she says, 'Stop trying to fix what you did, Cassie. What you didn't do.'

As she's speaking I can feel her words drifting away. They say that regret dries up the soul. What they don't say is that the soul can drown in it.

'I can't just leave this, Anna. I'm calling Bo. We're going to confront him.'

'The truth matters, of course it does, but you people, the Group, Bo, are the only truth I know. You should know by now, Cassie, that I will protect all of you. I will say and do whatever's necessary.'

I've heard enough. 'Stop, Anna, just stop.' And for a moment she does. Then her head snaps up and her hair tumbles around her shoulders. She's laughing now in tiny, bitter peals. This is even more confusing.

'Oh Cassie, you really don't understand, do you? You're putting yourself in a great deal of danger.'

39

Cassie

Early evening, Sunday 2 October, Isle of Portland.

I'm on the road leading from Fossil Cottage up the hill to the quarry and the cliffs, one eye on the way ahead, the other on my phone's reception bars. Bringing up the rear a few paces behind me is Anna. She's calling my name but I'm not listening. I'm driven by some internal energy, possessed by terrible thoughts. I want Bo to tell me that none of them are true. I want him to say that when it comes to sex, women lie. We make things up. We're confused. We wilfully misinterpret, we say 'yes' when we mean 'I don't know'. I want him to say that we are strangers to our sexual selves and so we let things happen to us that only afterwards feel wrong, that the woman with the pink hair did not wake up because she was a drug addict on a bender, that Rachel smoked too much weed. I want him to tell me that and that the hours before and after the fall from the horse are hazy because I was ill. I want to be able to disregard all of that and tell myself another story even though I know that story will be a lie.

Marika has been trying to tell me the truth all along. And I haven't been listening.

The sun is low and red. The falcons are out hunting. Soon the last of the day-trippers will drive back along the spit to the mainland and the Mer-Chicken and the Green Man and the Black Dog and the sprites and imps and goblins in the quarries will begin to stir and stretch their limbs. Soon the young offenders in the YOI on the cliff top will be released from lock-down and the refugees locked in the Citadel will be returning from their evening meal to their cells. Will is due to start serving the Sunday evening crowd at The Mermaid and Julie will be going on shift again at the Port Police. Soon the police will come to understand that Dex had nothing to do with the attack last night and let him go.

Now is the time to look forward not back. Behind me come Anna's footsteps and the sound of her breath quickening. For a long time I thought this story was about Marika but I'm now realising how much of it is about Anna. Spoiled, sad, dangerous Anna. The woman who had everything except the one thing she most wanted: for the father of her child to love her as he did when we were young. I have waited too long for Anna but that's over now. It is time to leave Anna behind. Time, finally, to let go.

Doing nothing doesn't mean you're innocent.

As I'm making my way through a narrow thicket to where the road curves away to the south across the cliffs to the quarry, I am checking for a signal. A fold in the land is blocking it here, but a few steps further up the hill behind the tangle of the wood lies the car park from where I picked up my texts and emails and where Gav was parked behind the ice cream van what seems like an age ago now. Back then all I wanted was to forget Marika and have fun. Looking back, whatever fun we had seems beside the point, a smokescreen, a cover, the mist across the water that vanishes with the sun. The bond is broken. Marika broke it. Marika set us free.

The sun is sinking over the sea, casting long, low shadows. To the east, the cliff face burns in its borrowed light. The peregrines are gone and the ravens are heading to their rookeries. I'm rounding the bushes at the entrance to the car park now. There's a rustling in the bin and something wild suddenly scoots away into the undergrowth, setting off a chorus of bird alarms. There are three bars on my phone. The world has shrunk to those three bars. I need to gather my courage. Fifteen years of my life has come to this. It is the time to step out from the noise and be the signal. I have never been surer of anything nor less certain. My heart is jamming in my chest and my heart is saying go. Pulling up my contacts I scroll down until I reach Luke Bowen and for a few wild seconds all the memories come flooding back. The late nights laughing and the soul searching and the growing up together. Then my finger moves across the screen and I tap the phone icon.

At that moment a shout echoes off the cliffs, a raw screech powerful enough to send roosting birds spraying from trees. It's the sound crashing trains would make if they were human, a cry of derangement, of distress so terrible it rips holes through time. For a brief nanosecond I think that shout is coming from me until, looking about, I see Anna standing at the entrance to the car park, one hand pressed over her mouth, the other on her chest, too shocked to move. The shout has died on her lips, replaced by odd keening bleats, like a dog tied up too long. How silly of me to imagine I could outrun Anna or ever leave her behind.

A solitary midnight blue Audi is parked at the far end of the car park where the tarmac gives out to a wooded path leading up to the quarry. The engine is running but at my current vantage no one is visible through the windows. The doors are all closed and from the exhaust pipe a length of green and yellow garden hose runs around and up through the window on the passenger's side. There is a terrible stillness to the scene. Then Anna crumbles, the way a tower block or skyscraper crumbles when dynamited, as if from the inside out and I'm running towards her, shouting her name but before I can reach her she is waving me away, pointing to the car and screaming, 'No, not me, go to Bo.'

I am conscious that I have ceased to be a bystander and become a witness. But everything is happening in such an odd, dreamlike way, as if I am hardly part of the action at all.

What did we do?

We did nothing.

The tarmac is firm beneath the soles of my boots though

and I am tearing across it. I'm nearly there now, part running, part stumbling, my breath spitting and gasping like a cornered cat, a terrible drumbeat in my chest. Reaching the vehicle, my eyes scan the interior, taking in the leather seats, taking in the polished dashboard, taking in the pipe and the gap in the window where it has been forced through, taking in the daypack on the back seat, my heart an engine driven in the wrong gear, my heart a view from a high speed train, my heart the undertow you have to fight to get back to shore. I'm afraid to open the door. I am afraid of suffocating. I'm afraid of what I might see. I am afraid because Bo isn't there.

Breathe.

The sound of my voice carrying across the expanse of tarmac.

'No one in the car.'

Anna's head shoots up. She is reconstructing her body, rebuilding the spine, the muscles and nerves and sinews, gradually coming back to life.

'Check the boot.' The boot is locked. But the engine is on. I'm afraid of whatever might be in there. I'm afraid of finding nothing.

'I'm calling the police.'

Anna is beside me now, panting, her tongue lolling like a greyhound's.

'No.' Her chest is heaving and she's hunched over, one arm resting on her knee, the other patting the air to stall me. She gulps, sets herself upright. Her chest is spasming as if she's about to be sick but she's dancing around the car peering inside, one hand shielding her eyes, nose pressed against the glass as if she doesn't quite believe me or the evidence of her own eyes.

'No, we have . . .' between intakes of breath, '. . . to open the door . . . unlock the boot.'

Calmer now, I am able to see what Anna is not, that, unlike the other doors, the driver's side door is unlocked. But which of us will risk the life-stealing air? Not me. I am already feeling quite suffocated enough.

'I'm going to take the hosepipe out of the exhaust.'

Anna blinks an acknowledgement.

I make my way round to the back of the vehicle. The pipe is resting inside the exhaust but there's no seal. If I hold my breath and lean down keeping my head held high I figure I should be able to pull it out without the fumes overwhelming me. I grasp the hosepipe and give it a yank. As it slides, I whip away my hand and spring back.

'Open the door now.' Even as I'm saying this I can see Anna's in no state to follow instructions. She has moved away and is clutching her hands and rocking. It's up to me. A blast of carbon monoxide in high concentration can cause collapse and death in seconds. I read that somewhere.

No, I am not going to do nothing but I am not going to do this.

'I'm calling the police.' I take out my phone and am plugging in the passcode when there's a sudden rush of cool air and Anna comes bowling towards me, her arms raised like a kick boxer's and with a sideways spin her right leg rises from the tarmac and whips out and smacks into my hand, loosening my grip on the phone, which arcs up and into the air and lands with the shattering sound on the ground. And Anna and I are left staring at one another, speechless with shock.

In a quiet tremble Anna says, 'Just open the door and get the fucking key.' And although I could say no to Anna, it occurs to me that I never have, not once, not directly and I'm not about to now.

Because me.

Because Anna.

So I go in and, holding my breath, reach for the car door handle. It gives surprisingly easily, pops open almost, letting a plume of fumy air billow into the wind. I wait for a moment then dive in, grab the keys and switch off the engine. Anna's head is in her hands and her body is shaking. That's when the dread sets in. Something about seeing her so undone, so absolutely unravelled is paralysing. For a moment neither of us can move. Then, rising to her full height, Anna gulps in a breath and begs me. The key fob is in my hand. All it takes is a press of the button. The contact between thumb and plastic. The tiniest pressure. An electronic peep.

'Unlock the boot.'

A click, a slow swing and a sharp cry. And nothing.

Fuck.

Anna, grim-faced and string-mouthed.

Me calling Bo's name.

Again, nothing. Where is Bo and what has become of him?

Anna will not calm herself until we have found him, so there is nothing for it but to search, first the periphery of the car park then, when that yields nothing, one or other of the paths. But which? The pathway leading back down the hill to Fossil Cottage, the bridleway into the woods I took at Will's advice that first morning, or the rough track running along the cliff up to the quarry.

'What do you think?'

Right now Anna cannot think. For the first time in the fifteen years we've known one another, Anna wants me to do the thinking for both of us. So I set myself to the task, gathering the info, mustering all I know about Luke Bowen.

In all the years we've been friends, what has mattered most to Bo is to win. Bo is good at winning; so good, he's forgotten that winning is not the same as getting everything you want. Winning is not control. This is what the car and the exhaust pipe is all about. It's Bo trying to take control of a situation he cannot win. Where will he be now? I've no idea but wherever he is, he'll be dangerous. The truth about Bo, the hard, shiny truth lurking under the years and years of rocky sediment, is that Bo is afraid. He is afraid of not knowing who he is or what he will turn out to be. He is afraid to discover that the real Bo is just a series of stratifications, a series of sedimentary layers built up over the years. He is afraid to discover himself at the bottom of all of that, to find someone hardened and ossified, someone who is no longer real at all.

'I think he'll have climbed higher. He won't have wanted to descend. It'll feel too much like failure. He'll be up there somewhere.' I point to the path leading up out of the woods onto open terrain. Anna takes a deep breath.

'OK, let's go.'

The path runs between brambles and low wind-torn shrubs up to the lip of the cliff and runs alongside for a while before access is blocked by a gate and a sign.

Danger, erosion, do not pass.

Anna calls Bo's name. The sound bounces off the stone and falls over the rocks to the sea below.

An alternative path turns inland and snakes through the gulley between two bluffs and into the quarry where several pathways push between strewn boulders, rubble heaps, pocked cliffs and man-made caverns.

Anna has recovered her self-possession now and, with it, the need to organise. We should be systematic, she says. She will search the quarry nearest the road if I will comb the area around the cliff edge. She doesn't say but the implication is clear. If Bo has gone over the edge, she doesn't want to be the one to find him. She tells me to text if there's any sign. Which is when I remember that I've forgotten to pick up my phone. It's lying in the car park where Anna propelled it. Well, never mind, we'll just shout.

Though the path across the cliff edge itself is closed, from the quarry there's a track leading to the crumble of smaller rocks and scree at the cliff's edge. Here the wind is punchy and raw. Seabirds rise up like balloons, bank and head inland to their roosteries. From the cliff's edge it's a long drop. All that is visible below is a short curl of pebbly beach battered by waves.

I move back along the path as it snakes between two vertical faces of cut rock, clambering over cracked slabs and rectangular-shaped boulders graffitied with names, dates, hearts, the occasional Green Man, Mer-Chicken or some other mythic beast. A flash of red appears out of the corner of my eye. At first I think it's a bird, but there are no red birds here, nor anywhere around, unless you count robins. And the flash is pillar box or London bus. As I approach, the redness grows in size and resolves into an outdoor jacket. The patch of darkness in its midst becomes human hair. Bo is squatting in the shelter of a cave made of quarried boulders. On the ground around him are strewn old crisp packets, dirty tissues, a fire ring from where someone has lit a barbecue. He's sitting all curled up, his hands clutched around his legs, shaking and biting his lip and, shocking to see, since, in all the years I've known him, this is the first time I've ever witnessed it, Luke Bowen is crying. Nothing like the Bo I know. I shout out to Anna to let her know I've found him.

'Mate.'

He mutters, 'Leave me alone.'

Anna arrives and rushing to him leans in between the rocks, sweeps him up in her arms, strokes his hair and covers his head with kisses. For a moment Bo is still, passive in Anna's embrace. Then very gently, with the palms of his hands, he pushes her away. She hops backwards, stunned.

'What the hell were you thinking?' There's an edge to her voice, some thread of vindictiveness. She's tired and angry and tired of being angry. Exhausted, finally, of his running away. Rage won't help here. Bo has neither the will nor the resources to combat it now. Sensing this, Anna pulls away, defeated, and takes up a position nearby, clenching her hands and forcing herself not to say anything she might regret. What Bo needs now is to be managed. And that, at last, is something I think I can do.

'Mate, you are sitting in a cave. You are literally a caveman right now.'

Bo looks up and stares at me, as if trying to recall who either of us is. I watch his mouth move from a miserabilist curl into a baffled wobble and at last into something approaching a smile. I've amused him. He's never been able to resist a joke.

'Come out of the cave.'

Again the smile. He runs a hand through his hair and rearranges his face. His body stirs and relocates its strength. Falling onto his knees he scrambles to the edge of the rocks and taking a deep breath, stands. Whatever creature he had become has gone.

'If you're so keen to do yourself in, the cliff edge is right there.'

He glances over, shrinks back a little, blinks.

'We need to talk.'

He takes a seat on a partially carved stone at the edge of a large array, his body framed now by the bluff. Anna perches on a stone beside him, looking dazed and defeated, like a stunned animal waiting for the death blow. I am the only one standing now.

'She knows,' says Anna.

In a small voice, Bo says, 'I hate myself.'

'You're not alone.'

He looks up, expecting some kind of redemptive confession. 'I hate you too, mate.'

He's clutching his knees now, the knuckles frosty with tension, gathering strength in the way a snake gathers itself before it strikes.

'It's not like I ever hurt anyone.'

Anna chimes in. 'Really, Cassie, he didn't. Most of those women won't even know anything happened.'

'It'll stop, Casspot. Never again, I swear. I don't even know why it started. It was after Anna's accident. My head got muddled.' He's crying again now, running off at the mouth with excuses and lies.

'There was no violence,' Anna says.

'Christ, Anna, date rape *is* violence.'

'If you make me go to the police station I'll hurt myself,' Bo says. 'I already tried, you saw the car. Next time I'll go through with it.'

'Cassie, it's me, Anna. Your friend. And I'm begging you. Please don't get Bo involved in this. Don't get any of us involved. What good would it do? I'm a mother. Think about Ralphie. We can get through this, all of us, the Group, together.'

'They dragged her body from the Thames.'

'He didn't have anything to do with that woman at the festival, did you, Bo?'

'Absolutely not. That girl delivered a pizza earlier that evening, I always order from the place she works for. Christ, I was the one who recommended them to Dex. But that was all. I never even saw her after that. Except in the alley.'

'You saw Bo, Cass, remember, behind Dex in the church-yard? Bo didn't have anything to do with it. It wasn't him then and it wasn't him last night.'

Swipe right, swipe right. Say yes. Say no one was hurt. Say you understand. Believe. But why is Anna still trying to protect us? What is she still hiding?

Bo is quiet now, shaking his head. 'For chrissakes, just tell her the truth. It's not like she can do anything about it. Tell her. If you won't I will.'

What happens next takes a second, less than a second, a fragment of time that is here and gone but seems to last forever. I don't see it coming. None of us does. It's as if time has stepped over us and turned back on itself. All I see in that second, that everlasting moment, is the hand and the rock inside it and the blurry outline of the figure who has sprung from behind the rubble and then the look of absolute shock on Bo's face as the rock crashes down on his head.

40

Anna

Cassie has her by the hand and is shouting, though it's impossible to hear what she's saying. The noise in the street is bad enough but the racket in Anna's head is so deafening it's threatening to blow her skull into tiny fragments.

Who knew that thoughts could be so uncontainable? They're spilling from her head, entering into her general circulation. She can feel the poison of them trickling through her system, pricking her neck, her palms, the soles of her feet. Is there any rowing back from this? A way to unsee the unwatchable? How can she speak of this, even to herself, most certainly not to Cassie. Squeezing her friend's hand, she turns her head to see, touched by Cassie's desire to rescue her. But Cassie has not seen what she has seen. Cassie does not know.

A single thought coalesces from the stream and rises to the surface, foamy and rank, like the scum on a pot of boiling bones. It takes a moment for it to collect into something approaching language. The instant she hears it she recognises its truth.

Something will have to be done.

In moments it establishes itself as a horrible chorus line in Anna's head. An earworm that needs digging out. This has gone too far now. The other party is out of control so it's going to have to be Anna who takes care of the situation. Anna who sorts it. Anna who makes it right. No, not right. It'll never be that. It falls to Anna to make it go away. She must do it in a hurry. Now. She stops looking ahead and turns her attention to the crowd. The press of people. Cassie is ahead of her, their hands still clasped. All she has to do now is to let go.

Let go.

Her hand springs back. She sees Cassie's head swing round, the alarm in her eyes. Cassie waves but she's helpless, drawn inexorably forward by the human current. This is what Anna has hoped for. She sinks back and allows Cassie's head to blend with the others around her until it melts into the crowd.

Then Anna is being pressed forward too. She puts one foot in front of the other, dodges under an arm, and in an artfully strategic move steps to the side, out of the current, a black Rook edging towards a white Queen. The woman in the alleyway will most likely be gone, her attacker most definitely so, but there is always a chance Anna might catch up with them. With that thought in mind, she edges her way back until she's reached the open gates to the churchyard. It's dark and a couple of the street lights have been smashed but the moon is a polished hubcap. As Anna dives back inside the churchyard, she thinks how easy it would be to do nothing now. To dissolve into the flow of people, cast her lot in with Cassie and claim ignorance. What is it that keeps her focused?

Love? If it's that then it's fucking twisted. If not that, then it's something deeper. Some residual rage from the encounter with Ollie. Some urge to claw back the power, maybe? She doesn't wish to think about what that might say about her. Doesn't want to care. She shakes herself free of all thought. Now is the time for instinct. If there's one thing Anna trusts, the only thing she trusts, it's that.

She's working her way around the back of the church now, to the path between the wheelie bins and the outbuildings, to the scene of the crime.

Because it was a crime. She knows that as firmly as she knows she will never admit as much.

She's standing by the wheelie bins and can see far enough into the path between the outbuildings to spot what looks like a mound or a heap of clothes. Her heart ticks louder. There's a surging at her temples. She approaches cautiously. The mound stirs. She gets the impression that it is unravelling itself, like a plant brought out of the dark. Her breath catches and billows inside her. At the entrance to the path she stops.

Can it be?

It is. Though she's almost unrecognisable, even from a few minutes ago. Her hair is matted and filthy, as though she's been pressed into the dirt. As though she's come from the dirt. She's on her knees, with her hands braced over her head. The knuckles of the right hand are bleeding but the hands too are filthy and she's rocking to try to comfort herself. If this were yoga, you'd say she was in the child's pose and that would be fitting, because she looks tiny and vulnerable.

Anna almost can't bear it. What she's about to do. You are strong, she tells herself. This isn't personal. Except it is. It's very personal. At least to Anna. She scopes around, looking for cameras, sees nothing. Most likely the church can't afford such measures or perhaps thinks it immoral in some way. All God's children. She takes the first steps onto the path between the outbuildings, wishes she could think more clearly, wishes she hadn't had so much to drink. There is no turning back now. A deep breath. The woman hasn't registered her, hasn't looked up. She's still curled over and rocking. In the dark she could almost be some kind of giant beetle. Anna lets out a little gulp of air, or perhaps it's a laugh, though she's not feeling amused. Funny when humour decides to drop by, at the oddest, least appropriate moments. She sinks down on one knee, gingerly reaches out and lays a hand on the woman's back.

'Are you OK? You look like you need help.'

The woman continues to rock. Anna can feel her back vibrating. She may be moaning but if she is, the sound is too faint to hear. The police helicopters are overhead but their lights will not penetrate this far. Anna scoops the fingers of her right hand under the woman's palm and with her left hand continues to stroke her back.

'Let me help you,' she says, though she intends to do quite the opposite. The woman loosens the grip of her hands on her head.

'Are you hurt? Show me where you are hurt.' There is the bloody hand, but Anna suspects that's the least of it.

A smell of piss drifts up. Oh Christ.

Anna is concerned that someone else will see them now, and she'll lose control of the situation.

'Let's get you up,' she says, tucking each hand under the woman's armpits. 'What's your name?'

The woman says something that Anna doesn't quite catch.

'Rita?'

The pile of clothes shifts and her hands loosen their grip of one another. The woman raises herself and sits back onto her legs. This is Anna's first proper look at her face. God, she's young. Her right cheek is covered in dirt. Did he grind her into the ground? How is this in any way explicable? All she knows is that it threatens to expose the Group and that she cannot have it.

'Marika,' the woman says, then adds another name Anna doesn't get. Not that it matters. The less Anna knows about Marika, the easier it will be to betray her.

'It's OK,' Anna says. Marika blinks back at her with haunted eyes. Anna averts her gaze. She doesn't want to think about those eyes.

Another smell rises up, vomit this time. Damn. If there's one thing Anna can't stand it's this. Bad enough when Ralphie spits up his milk.

'Let's get you on your feet,' she says. Marika nods then suddenly gives a huge yawn and shakes her head as if she's trying to rid herself of a wasp. Out of it, Anna figures. Good.

Gradually, bit by bit, Marika rises to a stand. She's not wearing a great deal. A red dress with a flimsy fake leather jacket over the top, that blue scarf. Funny how little of her face Anna recognises, despite the fact that she's seen it before this evening, not only at the cab, but exiting Bo's building. The woman didn't see her, of course, because Anna was sitting in the cab calling up to Bo's apartment, so there's no chance of being recognised. Naturally, she didn't look like this then. She was wearing cycling gear for a start. But she was pretty sure this was the woman Bo had told her he'd hooked up with. His type. Enough like Anna to draw him, the dark hair a point of difference. She didn't seem out of it then. The pills, Anna assumes, must have kicked in later. The back of the dress, though red, is stained with blood and something else, maybe shit. The front of the dress bears speckles of what she suspects is vomit.

Anna thinks about where the nearest ladies' toilets might be at this hour. She needs to get Marika cleaned up before anyone notices her. But where? Isn't the police station nearby? Not there, obviously, but rather somewhere in the opposite direction. The woman is leaning on her arm. Anna slings the other around her back. Better control that way. Now, where to go? An all-night café? Ali's is close. A pub? The Prospect of Whitby? From somewhere deep in the fog of her mind the word no emerges. Why? Then she remembers. Both Ali's and The Prospect have cameras inside. She can't risk that. No, what they really need is access to water.

Marika is standing now, but she's unsteady on her feet. They need to get going before someone sees them and decides to be a hero and call the police. Right now, Marika's out of it and she's in shock, which makes her malleable. But that might not last. Any moment she could become belligerent and demanding. She's not a large woman, just the opposite, but adrenalised people are strong. People off their faces are strong. Where to go to clean her up? A memory surfaces. Visiting her grandmother's grave with her mother, a tap round the back of the church for people to fill their graveside vases. And a wheelie bin for them to dump dead flowers and the wrapping from the fresh ones.

'Come on, let's get you some water,' she says, taking a firmer grip on the woman.

Marika nods and, with some encouragement from Anna, begins to stagger on jelly legs. Progress is excruciatingly slow but Anna is afraid to push her. Just get her to the tap. There are tissues in Anna's bag. Usually there would be wet wipes (Ralphie!) but she left them in the house. The thought crosses her mind to call Isaac, but no, that's a stupid idea. He'd take one look at the broken woman on her arm and be dialling the cops. And he's decent, is Isaac, which is both a reason to love him and to hate him. In any case, decency is not what she needs right now. If the police get hold of

Marika, they'll want to know where she was all evening and that'll put Bo and Anna in the frame. Dex too, since she'd seen Dex talking to Marika briefly by the main stage. Anna can't have that. It's like Cassie said: these people, the Group – they are all the love she has.

They make it as far as the wheelie bins without being seen, Marika leaning on Anna, still moaning, but more softly now. And yes, there is a tap, but the tap head is missing. You'd need a wrench to turn it.

Marika begins to cry.

A flutter, faint as insect wings, transits Anna's face. Christ, this is all she needs. She's never been a woman's woman, finds it hard to know how to react around female distress, unless it is her own.

'Don't worry, we'll get you cleaned up,' she says. It's what she might say to Ralphie at nappy changing time. But Marika is not to be consoled. She's swaying now as if in a trance. Is this a reaction to trauma or the pills Bo must have given her? Her hands are balled up into a single fist which she's holding against her most vulnerable part in some furious gesture of defence. Anna reaches in and gently takes hold in an effort to loosen her grip. That's when Anna notices the rivulets of blood, pale with urine, snaking their way down Marika's legs. Blood setting the skin of her legs into wobbly pin-stripes.

Oh God, this is awful.

She grabs Marika by the arms. She's thinking, there has to be a way to row back from this.

'Is this your period?'

Marika shakes her head.

'Do you know who did this to you?'

Marika issues a sob.

What an animal. Not Bo, obviously, but the other one. That said, though, men were all animals, underneath, even Isaac. Anna takes a deep breath and shakes the thought clear. She can't afford to think like that. Thinking like that will only bring trouble. Questions are spinning through her mind. Where to clean off the evidence without being interrupted or caught on CCTV? She considers giving up and calling the police, then remembers how far she herself is implicated, and not just Bo, not just the third party. Especially now. Too late. That's when she remembers the river.

If she can only get Marika to the water's edge. Wash the evidence out to sea. When Marika wakes from whatever drug-induced stupor she will undoubtedly fall into, her memories of tonight will be fragmentary and hard to pin down. When she looks to her body for corroboration she won't find any. Or none that can serve as evidence anyway. Even if she goes to the police, a young woman who cannot remember why her rectum is torn or why her vagina is bloody and sore, only that they are, is unlikely be taken seriously. And even if she is, there will remain no residue of her assailant. She will live her life in the knowledge that something happened over which she has no dominion. All that will remain of tonight will be a blank.

'Put your arm around me,' she says. Marika has crumpled again and has to be hauled to the upright. She's moaning incoherently but Anna cannot catch her words. Since the police arrived, the churchyard has more or less emptied. They struggle a little but bit by bit manage to wend their way south towards the gates nearest to the river. To anyone witnessing their progress, they will be a couple of friends who've had a skinful at a music festival and are now making a wobbly journey back home. If anyone notices the blood on Marika's legs, Anna will sheepishly mouth the single word 'period'. Women will grimace with recognition, men will run a mile.

They are on Wapping high street when Marika starts saying the word 'police'. She's pretty incoherent and softly spoken, plus she speaks with a strong accent. No one but Anna will be able to make it out. Nevertheless, the thought has clearly entered her mind and it is up to Anna to ensure it leaves.

'Let's get you cleaned up, then we'll go to the police.'

Naturally, Anna has no intention of alerting the cops. Marika whips her arms away and repeats the word 'police.'

Ignoring this and taking hold of the woman more firmly this time, Anna continues to lead her eastwards. She's wondering whether The Prospect of Whitby will have stayed open late to accommodate the festival goers. Perhaps she can station Marika close by then nip in to the ladies' and soak some bog roll for Marika to wipe herself with. She wonders how she's going to persuade her to wipe her intimate parts. Reminds herself that it will be precisely those parts which feel most in need of cleansing.

In her pocket her phone buzzes. That'll be Cassie wondering where she is.

Don't answer.

Christ, this night is turning into a horror show.

'Police,' says Marika, more insistently now.

This is becoming dangerous.

'Let's get you to a safe place, then we'll call the police,' Anna repeats in what she hopes is an emollient tone. Up ahead is a police car. A couple of officers are moving on a few festival goers.

It'll just have to be the river. There's no time to think of anywhere else and no chance of getting Marika there without their movements being caught on CCTV. Thankfully, Wapping Old Stairs are just there. Narrow, lightless and giving direct access to the water. Better still, it's high tide. The river water slops right up the steps.

'Let's just sit down for a bit here,' she says, leading Marika into the alleyway. So close now. If Anna can just persuade her to change out of her skirt and wipe herself, then Anna will wash the skirt and the job is more than half done. For once she's glad that Bo has been up to his old tricks. The woman is infinitely less dangerous this way. Anna leans her charge up against the wall. Marika sways. Anna puts gentle pressure on her shoulders. She's aiming to suggest without being so firm that Marika becomes alarmed. It works. Bit by bit Marika allows her body to slide down the wall until she's sitting on the cobbles. Taking a seat beside her, Anna says, 'Where do you live?' Her phone buzzes again. This time she takes the phone out of her pocket and checks it. Cassie.

Don't answer.

Marika has buried her face in her hands. She's crying, which is good, because as long as she's sobbing she's unlikely to be calling for the police. She repeats the question. If Marika can give her an address, Anna can call an Uber and ride with her. A wash first though. The woman looks alarming, even to an Uber driver used to turning a blind eye. All that blood.

'Now,' says Anna, taking a packet of tissues from her bag. 'Why don't we get you cleaned up?'

Marika nods. She's so out of it Anna can probably do the intimate washing herself without Marika protesting. First, though, the tissues need to be moistened. Leaving Marika where she is Anna places her hand on a thin metal grab handle and edges her way carefully down the steps, using her phone torch to guide her, planting her feet firmly through the coating of river slime, to the waterline.

41

Cassie

In the immediate aftermath of the blow, an absolute stillness falls. The rock, actually a large carved ammonite picked up from the quarry floor, sits in his hand. Gav stares at it for a moment, at the adhesive blur of blood and sprig of dark hair, as if it were someone else who had wielded the weapon, before dropping it from his hand like a discarded sweet wrapper. Beside him the slumped body of Bo, stunned, clasps the back of his head, blood leaking between his fingers.

Anna and I stand back, immobilised, our hands over our faces.

'Oh fuck!' says Gav.

Anna dives over to where Bo is crouched on the ground, but he keeps her at bay with an outstretched arm.

'Fuck!' repeats Gav, startled by his own strength.

If Anna had a weapon she would use it. But all Anna has are the rocks and the hard surfaces of her mind. Rushing at Gav, she slams into his chest. He staggers back a couple of steps before recovering himself. Anna rushes him again, pumping her fists at him, aiming for the head but because of their relative sizes, only making any real contact with his neck.

Anna's shriek boils up from a terrible deep. If it weren't for that sound I might intervene.

'Whaddafuck?' Bo says. His hand is on his head and he's struggling to stand. It's like watching a newborn calf who has already felt the slaughterman's bolt.

Gav moves forward a few paces, squats beside Bo and screams into his hair, 'You fucking fuck. Dex told me what a sick fuck you were, he said Anna had made you promise to stop.' His arms are in silverback stance, and he is spitting and shaking, an adrenalised mess, an ageing not-so Incredible Hulk. If it weren't so frightening it might be comical. 'But I'm not letting him go down for you, you bastard.' A gob of spittle sails upwards then lands splat on Bo's T-shirt.

Anna sidesteps in between Gav and Bo. Her hands are raised, palms up, in a gesture of surrender. She's doing her sheepdog act, herding us all together, but it's far too late for that.

Gav is upright now and clutching his chest. He's having trouble catching his breath.

'What's happening?' I'm hardly conscious of saying the words, though the sound is of my voice.

Between gulps of air, Gav says, 'I was driving back from my sister's when I got the message from Dex that he was at the police station, but I didn't actually speak to him, so I decided to come to the cottage first to find out exactly what was going on. I saw you both running up the hill so I followed you but I couldn't keep up . . .' His eyes sweep about, taking in me and Anna. '. . . I've been behind that rock. I overheard everything.' He's staring at Bo now. 'You're the real reason Dex is in the hole he's in, you piece of shit.'

Bo is on his feet. There are tears in his eyes now. A simper of self-pity. He's still clutching and unclutching his head. There is blood on the palm of his hand where it is in contact with the wound.

'I didn't attack anyone. I had a few tokes with a woman on Friday. Maybe we had a few pills. That's it.'

Gav doesn't answer. He seems as stunned by his sudden, unexpected show of strength as Bo is. No one knows what to do, how to react. This is the first time for all of us.

'You stupid, shrivelled old queen. Dex was right, the chemo has turned you into a mentalist.' His eyes are on the ammonite carving, with its slick of Bo blood and Bo hair. 'You fucking animal.' For a moment Gav looks like he might just go and have done with us and with Dex. Kick out and leave. Decide that he doesn't need this shit, not the way he is right now, but some remnant of dignity rises up in him, or maybe it's recklessness, the last stand of a dying man and, planting his feet firmly into the stone and with his hands balling into fists at his side, he says, 'This isn't your fight, Anna.' Dex came across the pills in Bo's bathroom one time, he says, Bo told him things, stuff that men only ever tell other men.

'If you were so bloody sure of it, why didn't you report it?' Anna says.

Gav lets out a bitter sound and shakes his head. 'A gay man with a long hook-up history, accusing a straight man of roofying women he's never even met? How do you think that would go down with the Met Police?'

'This is your fault then,' Anna says. 'For not doing anything.'

'Well, I'm doing something now, aren't I?'

'Get out of here, Gav,' says Anna stiffly. 'You're despicable. You know who it was who took care of what happened in the alleyway in Wapping? It was me. Not for your sake, for Dex's.'

Gav smiles, though there's no warmth behind it. He's only pretending to be amused. 'Do you have any idea how much money Dex stands to inherit when I die? If I started divorce proceedings today I could disinherit him in three, four months. My husband isn't stupid. And he's not spending the last few months I have in this world in a fucking prison because his friend is a pervert.'

'You just assaulted me. I could get you arrested,' Bo says, limply.

'I wish I'd killed you. I would have, if I didn't need you to come with me to the police. Dying focuses the mind. You'll find that out some day.'

Bo just shakes his head, slowly, sadly, as if standing on

346

the moral high ground. To no one in particular, Bo says, 'I'm not fucking staying in this place.' He takes a step, wobbles, rights himself then takes another, heading back towards the car park, along the path through the bluff at the edge of the quarry to where it joins the track which runs along the cliff's edge, muttering to himself, walking towards the thermals where the falcons are hunting, towards the sunset. On a direct line to the cliff's edge, towards the huge, rosying sea.

It's almost funny to hear Gav shouting after him. Like a father chastising an errant child. Anna is calling him too, but he's not responding. Bo carries on walking, doesn't even turn his head. It's a display of resoluteness, a dramatic turn. Even I know that. This is what he has always wanted, a complete hold over Anna. But he won't die for it. In Bo's mind he's immortal but he's too much of a coward to put his theory to the test. Anna and I both know that. We saw the car. Bo knows it too.

All Gav sees is Dex's get out of jail card disappearing. And that he cannot tolerate. With a great roar, he launches himself forward, pounding the stone path towards the cliff Hearing Gav approach, Bo turns. Behind him is an orange sun and the darkening expanse of the sea. Gav is like a wounded bull in the ring, an outrageous fury-bomb. He's charging at Bo, who is standing his ground, with a shocked expression and something else, the stance already of a victor. Bo thinks he's going to win. Bo always thinks he's going to win. But Gav's got nothing to lose. Thundering towards Bo, he hits him straight on in a rugby tackle, clasping the younger man's waist in an attempt to force him over the edge. There's a moment of confusion in Bo's eyes before he goes down. He wasn't expecting the older man to be this strong. He's on the ground, taking Gav with him. Bo is first up on his feet and kicking out. His right foot catches Gav under the chin, snapping his head up. Gav lets out a cry but he manages to right himself and with a monumental push against his thigh, rises to standing. He comes at Bo once more, but the younger man is wised up now and braced, and the rush ends in a clinch. The two men tussle, Bo breaks away first, lands a punch at Gav's head, which bounces off his jaw. Gav counters with a punch of his own, makes contact with Bo's shoulder.

A yelp rips through the air. The men are too busy fighting to notice that the shout isn't one of fear but one of rage. Anna is suddenly flying towards them, her arms windmilling. With every muscle in her body taut and to the point, she launches herself at Gav. Caught off balance, he staggers back and in that moment she throws out her leg and makes contact with the back of his knees. He slides, begins to crumple. Anna pulls back her arms and braces herself and lands Gav an almighty push. His body gives a shudder, his feet slide then fail to find a purchase. He is paddling now, arms and legs trying to catch something other than the air, he staggers back, teetering on the edge, shock registering on his face. Then in an instant, he recovers his balance.

Bo is standing a couple of feet away, watching on without

intervening. For a few moments he and Anna lock eyes as if seeing one another for the first time. A moment of complete human stillness falls over us, a holding of breath.

Only the earth continues to move and the sun sinks a tiny bit lower. Then, as if from nowhere, a blur of feathers bombs out of the sky, a landing gear of talons descending from the body, aimed directly at the bloodied wound on Bo's head. The falcon makes contact and Bo, shouting, reflexively waves his arms above his head, trying to bat the thing off and the creature, suddenly realising its mistake in taking on so large a target, releases its grip, the long, powerful wing on its left side just clipping Bo's hand as it attempts to rise but its body is within Bo's range. His arm flails, makes direct contact. The falcon is flustered and flapping, its body part propelled by Dex's arm, a whorl of wings and talons trying gain enough momentum, a great whirring of wings hurtling directly towards Gav. I watch him tense as the bird, unable to right itself, flaps and grabs at the air, half-flying, half-tumbling towards him, his arms reaching up to protect his face and in that instant, the momentum of his weight which only a few seconds ago he relied upon to charge Bo, sends him backwards, stumbling and shouting, arms akimbo, over the edge of the cliff and out of view.

All three of us stand stricken and immobile. Gav's screams are a terrible thing. A spray of seagulls jets up over the cliff edge, disturbed by the falling body. I am first to the edge, one eye on Bo and Anna. The wind is buffeting and the salt spray makes everything filmy. The man that was Gav – perhaps still is him – is reduced to a dark smear lying across rocks licked by the sea. Something moves. An arm perhaps, or a leg. A sign of life or the push and pull of the waves?

My eyes sweep along the cliff face until they reach a path carved by feral goats, inhumanly steep, but possible, just. I back away from the cliff edge. Anna and Bo remain where they were, their eyes alive with fear and the horror of what has just occurred. What we have come to.

I am very vulnerable here. Seeking out an escape route I step sideways, never once taking my eyes from Bo or Anna. Would they dare? Right now, anything seems possible. Bo is staring at me now but Anna is looking away, her body language impossible to read. This is what it is about now. A twisted, toxic obsession, Anna and Bo trapped in each other's orbit, each powerless to escape even if they wanted. I scope the ground for a rock with a sharp edge. If they come for me, I will be ready to defend myself.

Marika, I'm going to sort this. This time I'm not running away. I'm done with that, I'm done with the Group. I am done.

All of a sudden, Bo turns. He has made a calculation and I am not a part of the formula. I see his body prepare to propel him forward, the shoulders tense, the legs sprung, a mist of evaporating sweat rising from him. From his pocket he pulls out the keys to the Audi and in an instant he's turned on his heels and he's running.

In five minutes from now he'll be off the island.

It's just me and Anna. Until now I've always assumed I need Anna more than she needs me, but it's the other way round. Every beautiful girl needs a homelier girl to anchor her. I am Anna's lighthouse, her marker, her navigation through choppy waters. Without me, Anna will run into the rocks.

She watches me as I take off towards the path heading for the goat track. 'What are you going to do?'

'What do you think I'm going to do? He's moving.' Of course it's a stupid question. What would any person do? Any person with a moral compass. Any person with an overwhelming need to redeem themselves.

What did we do?

We did nothing.

'Call for help, Anna, do it now.'

Then I'm over the edge, keeping my centre of gravity low, using the branches of wind-torn bushes to keep my balance, and Anna has disappeared from view.

Gav is still alive when I reach him, but only just. He's taken a knocking on the way down. His clothes are torn and there are a number of bloody openings in his face. His torso is twisted and both his legs and one arm are set at a frightful angle. From his lips, a pinkish foam oozes. He's too heavy to lift up onto the track and in any case moving him would do no good. His breathing is shallow and patchy. The tide is coming in and I can already see that unless help comes fast, there'll be no saving him from the sea. The waves are cold and relentless. I take his hand in mine, though I think he is beyond feeling now. In comes the water. Each time it goes out it takes a piece more of Gav's life with it. There is nothing for it but to wait and hope for help. In my mind Anna appears. The last time we had fun together, in the VIP tent, having our shoulders massaged, Anna pointing to the make-up station, telling me how good I'd look if I sparkled. The waves are up around Gav's arms now, washing them to and fro like kelp. The brine has crept over my feet and seeped into my shoes. I will have to leave him and try to find my way back up the goat track. I will not make it all the way up because the track is too steep and there are no handholds. The branches of the wind-torn bushes will not hold my weight. Soon, the sea will take Gav and then, unless I am very, very lucky, it will take me.

The proximity of death clarifies the mind. I recall that night in the churchyard as if it were happening right in front of me. Dex's face in the moonlight, the shadow of a man behind him. Anna saying, *Look they're coming*. Dex's phone torch, the twist of horror on his face.

But here in my mind is Marika, waiting, as she always is, for me to say something or do something. You were easy prey, small and alone and out of it and powerless. I am sorry I led you to that, Marika. I will always regret it. I will try to survive this so that it can be put right. And if I don't, I will share your fate. That seems fair, Marika, doesn't it? I can make my peace with that.

42

Anna

3 a.m., Sunday 14 August, Wapping

Everything in Anna's life up to this moment appears hazy and off-kilter, as if none of it is part of her world at all. Her only reality is here, on these steps, with Marika and her torn clothes and her soiled legs.

'I'm calling the police.' Control the narrative, Anna. That's what her father used to say, man to girl, when he was still under the illusion that she'd follow in Daddy's footsteps. Making a big play of checking her phone, Anna swipes at nothing, looks up, shakes out her hair, trying to seem casual.

It's not over. Marika has picked herself up. Anna steps directly in front of her to prevent her from staggering out into the street.

'Come on,' she says, all action now, grasping the woman by the elbow in an effort to spin her back around, but Marika isn't going. She's steadying herself on the downpipe and using it to swing a little to the left, to give her a direct view out into Wapping Wall. An arm comes up and points.

Something indistinct comes out of her mouth. Anna reaches for her hand and pushes it back into her side.

'Shh.' Anna puts her finger to her lips but Marika repeats whatever she said before, only this time louder.

The sound of shouting comes from the street.

Shit, thinks Anna. This is dangerous. Blinking away the first flutter of panic, she tells herself to keep calm. Stay focused. You can still make this go away.

The river water slops up the steps. The alleyway stinks. The water stinks. Why did Anna ever think this was a good idea? She takes a breath. A picture rises in her mind of a police interrogation room, the kind she's seen a hundred times on the TV but never in real life, and of her, sitting opposite some sly detective, trying to explain away her midnight flit to Ollie's apartment. No, this is no good. She blinks the picture away. She's started this now and she has to finish it. The woman is swaying, zoning out, incapable of calling the police herself. Anna notices the graze on Marika's forehead, the bald patch, partially covered with blood-matted hair where her attacker pushed her head against the wall.

A seed of hope germinates in Anna's mind. Maybe there's an angle on this, a way to wrest back control. She needs to get the woman away from the scene.

'Tell you what, we'll call an Uber,' she says, breezily, as if there's really nothing wrong here, nothing to see.

The woman begins sniffling. Her eyes burst their banks and she's weeping and sobbing, her hands in her face. Look at her, Jesus. She probably needs to go to hospital.

Something rises up in Anna. A burning feeling and an itching. She feels sick. She wishes she could just step out of her skin and walk naked into the filthy water. How cool it would feel. I have to contain this, she thinks, so that it doesn't get out of hand. The sick feeling falls away. Her focus is suddenly absolute, knowing as she does that if she is not careful this whole thing is going to slip from her grasp.

'Listen, the Uber is five minutes away. Let's just stay here and wait.'

Taking the injured woman's arm, Anna leads Marika further into the gloom of the alleyway. Time for calm. This is good. The woman makes a grunting sound, which could mean anything.

'All we need to do now,' says Anna, remembering the scarf around the woman's neck and trying to slip it off, 'Is to get you cleaned up for the cab.' As she turns to step down to where the water is sliding against the steps, the woman grabs at her scarf, and the blue pom-poms slip from Anna's grasp. The woman is a rag doll, almost like a macabre kind of toy. She's leaning against the wall now, close to collapse, very evidently not fine but there's fight in her still.

'Police,' she repeats. Her voice is angry now.

This is exactly what Anna is trying to avoid. Anger is cheap and dangerous. Righteous anger is the most danger-ous of all.

Something is happening out on Wapping Wall. A fight

breaking out. The sound of bottles smashing and men yelling. Anna grabs the woman by the shoulders and staring deeply into her face, says, 'You want to go home, don't you?' The woman nods. Anna is on her toes. Perhaps it's the adrenaline but she's feeling completely sober now, utterly focused on this one thing. She watches the woman's body slump once more, sees an opportunity to step over her conscience and out to the other side. 'Let's just get you home, and into bed. Can you remember your address for the taxi driver?'

The woman nods then lets out a low moan. Her head is floppy and she's murmuring incoherently. It occurs to Anna then that she might die, right there.

'Let's all just sit on the steps and think about this for a moment,' Anna says.

At this point in the game, Anna thinks, she's strayed so far from anything resembling the truth that she's no longer sure she'd recognise it if it came bowling down the road. The thought amuses her, despite herself.

Enough of this, she thinks, it's time to take action. Quickly, before the woman has a chance to protest, Anna removes the scarf around her own neck, goes over to the steps and dips the silk into the river water. She bustles over, wrings out the scarf, crouches low and begins to wipe the woman's face.

'There, I bet that makes you feel better, doesn't it?'

Brought back by the cold water, Marika groans and lifts up her head. Very slowly, doing her best to make no big deal of it, Anna moves to the woman's legs and begins softly to wipe away the bloody evidence. She's cleaned the woman's right leg below the knee.

A police siren wails from somewhere nearby.

Anna wheels about. Her chest is full of starbursts and the back of her skull feels like it might split open. Anna can feel herself losing it. But she mustn't.

She must keep her cool now. Everything depends on it.

'Listen: you don't remember what happened tonight. Not in any detail. You wouldn't be able to identify anyone. Would you?'

Marika closes her eyes and sobs. Anna feels herself rising up out of her body, growing taller. From the corner of her eye Anna becomes conscious of movement. She turns just in time to see Marika lunge forward and run past her towards Wapping Wall, arms flailing. As she lurches past, a ring on her finger catches Anna on the side of her neck.

Anna turns on her heel. She has to get Marika back. As she surges forward she feels her ankles giving way and suddenly she's arcing through the air, her hands grasping for anything and finding Marika's hair. With a hard smack the two women come down together. For a moment nothing moves, not her hands or her body or her brain. Then a terrible hot burning starts up in her palms and with it her brain kicks in. She pulls herself upright, spins about and jumps to her feet. Marika is lying on the ground inside the alleyway, out for the count.

Turning, Anna storms back into the alleyway. What the

fuck was that? She's trying to help the woman and this is how she reacts? An overwhelming rage comes over her. Moving over to the form beside her she grabs Marika's ankles and, mustering her strength, drags the woman inch by inch towards the Old Stairs where the murky, evil smelling water is waiting to receive her.

43

Cassie

Morning, Monday 10 October, Royal London Hospital

You don't know you're dying until the process is already underway. It can take a while to catch up with yourself. The first time it happened to me all I sensed was a feeling of drifting towards the horizon. Only as an afterthought did it occur to me that I had began to die – before the more startling realisation that the process would be complete only in the moment I ceased to be able to think about it. An odd calm set in. There was no pain or panic, only an overwhelming feeling of sadness. If it hadn't been for Marika, I would have given myself up to it.

I've quite a bit of time on my hands to think about this question and I haven't come up with an answer. Being in a coma isn't what people think it is. I am dead to the world and yet I am not dead. I have heard voices talking about all kinds of things. Voices spilling their secrets, secrets told only because the bearer thinks you cannot hear and will not tell. It is powerful, living on the seabed like this. Why am I down here in the murk and mud with the flatfish and the stones? If I am dead, would I still hear the voices? Would I have heard the story of my rescue? Would I know that a passing fishing boat plucked me from the sea, shortly before pulling Gav's lifeless body onto deck? What if I am hovering in the gap between life and death? Will someone find me down here? Will they pluck me from my silence and give me voice?

Speaking out is hard when you cannot speak. Being a messenger is hard when you do not know how to reveal your message. This is how fossils begin their journey from life to death, isn't it? As shells and bones lying in the mud. Time turns them to stone. It turns them into forgotten things, objects that cannot move or speak or hear, that can do nothing but wait for the storm to wash them up onto the beach, among the pebbles. Perhaps someone will pick them up and turn them over in their hands and say, *Look, here is a messenger, I wonder what the message could be?* Perhaps the tide will suck them back onto the sea floor.

The first time I died, after going into the water, I came back and these days I'm more immune to the seductions of the process. I am also more familiar with it, which is how I know it is happening again. I have the same feeling of pressure, the burning in the lungs, the sense of there being no air. Is this another kind of drowning, a different path to death, or something else? Is this, I wonder, what being murdered feels like? The hand pressing the pillow into my face wants to push me into the murk from where I can never return. That is why they are trying to kill me.

Should I stay down here on the seabed or rise up and speak? Should I fight to stay alive? What exactly am I fighting for? Do I remember?

Yes, I think I do.

How can I create a storm when I cannot move? The person trying to kill me knows this. They are afraid of me moving, they are scared of me creating a tumult. But if I am to rise from the sea, if I am to come out of the water I must find a way to struggle to the surface.

This time I am not floating towards a horizon. I am kicking and screaming but nothing is moving and my screams are silent. This time dying hurts because I am not going to go down without a fight. Not again. There is no wave of sadness. This time there is only rage and rage is powerful. This is, after all, what has been keeping me alive. I have things to say and I will say them. But the pressure on my lungs is a terrible thing and there is no air in my throat and my life feels as if it no longer belongs to me and right now I don't know what I can do to reclaim it.

If I could shout I would. If I could thrash and punch and claw my way out of this I would. But I cannot make my body move.

Time is running out. I sense that. My thoughts are becoming incoherent. I need oxygen.

What did you do?

I did nothing.

I need to act while I can still think. Before the process

of dying is complete. I will not be killed. I want to live. I will live.

I have things to say.

If I can move something, anything, then I stand a chance.

What can I move? Let me try.

Time is running out.

If I could release the pressure on my lungs. If I could move. Let me try. What can I move?

Oh yes! My jaw! If I can move my jaw then perhaps I can bite or scream. I must move upwards, up through the water. I must surface. What a long way it is, from the sea bed to the place where water meets air. What a steep climb. I must rise, though, I must surface into consciousness before all the air is gone from me.

My lungs hurt, my throat hurts, my face hurts, my heart is kicking like an antelope as the lions bring it down. All I have to do is to open my jaw and use my throat and shout out. I am confused. I am on the sea shore, I am at the top of the cliff, I am on the surface of the water.

A siren goes off, no, a shriek. A scream of sorts. That is me. I am shouting and thrashing against the pillow. And suddenly the pressure stops and I can feel my lungs heaving for air and my chest expanding and my throat coughing and I am free. I am on top of the cliff, I am at the surface of the water. When I open my eyes now what will I see?

'Cassie? Cassie!'

My eyes fix on a blur of human skin. Oh, it's so bright! There is too much light.

But that's it! I have done it. I've come back from the almost-dead. I am here. I am in the world.

You did nothing.

But I did, I did. I saved myself. And now I can tell my story.

'Nod if you understand what I'm saying to you,' a voice says.

I know this voice but not its owner. I nod because I am beginning to understand all sorts of things.

'My name is Frank. I've been looking after you since you were transferred up here. You were shouting just now, do you know that?'

I am saying something but I don't know if Frank can hear me. I think what I am saying is 'Bo.'

Someone enters the room and shines a light in my eyes and tests my reflexes and pats me on the hand and says some things, but the words fly by before I can catch them.

'This is Dr Hale,' Frank says, in a voice that suggests he is repeating something. 'She's the neurologist.'

Dr Hale says I have been in a coma. She says I've been coming out of it for the last few hours.

'We've been expecting you to wake up.'

I have woken. I have swum from the seabed towards the light. But now the light is blinding. Give me time and I will adjust to this new world which is not new but the old world into which I have been reborn.

'Oh, your pillow must have fallen on the floor,' Frank says. He'll fetch me a clean one when he gets a moment.

Dr Hale says not to try to say anything yet. She says I will feel confused. I do, though not about some things. I do not feel confused about the fact that Luke Bowen put a pillow over my face and tried to kill me. He would have succeeded if I hadn't come up to the surface, if I hadn't decided to live.

The pillow will have Luke Bowen's DNA on it. There will be CCTV footage of him leaving the hospital. When I can I will tell them that. And I will tell them about Gav and Marika and about Rachel and all the events at the Wapping Festival and then, later, on the Isle of Portland. I'll tell them everything they need to know about Anna.

'Don't worry if you can't speak. It'll come,' Frank says. Dr Hale has gone but someone else is in the cubicle with him. There's murmuring and the fragments of some conversation. Someone is touching my face, but ever so softly now. There's a sound coming from me. It's meant to convey meaning but I'm not sure it does.

I cannot see yet. My eyes are open but I cannot see.

Frank says, 'When you're more awake the police would like to speak to you. Someone called Julie is here from the Port of Portland Police, but there's no hurry.'

I would like to speak to you too, Julie. I should have spoken to you before. But now I have more to say. The confessions I've been hearing. The secrets people will tell you when they think you will never be able to tell.

The sound of people talking.

There is an ammonite on my wrist, on the delicate skin

under which the blood vessels run like seaweed. I may be looking at it or I may simply be remembering it.

I am drinking something sweet through a straw.

If my eyes are open they may be blinking at a postcard of an old cottage with tiny windows and a forlorn air, sellotaped to the cot sides of the bed. It could be a warning or it may be in my head.

There is a lot in my head and even more in my heart.

'Your friends left that,' Frank says. So this means my eyes are open. Yes, I can see Frank's face now. Eyes as deep as wells. Brown, beautiful, expressive eyes. 'They've been here every day,' Frank says. 'The couple come together and the other one – Dex is it? – always on his own.'

The voice changes tone. Maybe Frank and Julie are speaking to each other but I only pick up the tail end of the conversation, Frank saying, 'Since then I haven't seen the couple at all.'

Julie's voice now, her hand on mine, her body warmth like a small sudden sunburst on the skin of my cheek.

'Cassie, you might not be able to answer this right away. Can you tell us what happened at the cliff, before you went into the water?'

I can hear this now, I can understand it all. But it is too complicated to say right now. This is more than me and Bo. This is Dex and Gav and Marika. Most of all, this is Anna.

'She's getting tired,' Frank says.

My eyes are shut because everything is blurry. Because

the world has not yet come into focus in my head. But I want to say, I need to speak.

I am saying no. I have risen to the surface of myself to say no. Because if we don't say no, the ones who bear witness, then who will?

44

Cassie

Afternoon, Tuesday 25 October, Royal London Hospital

Waking from a coma isn't as simple as stirring from sleep. Days slide by and still I have one foot on the seabed and another on dry land. Bit by bit, taking my time about it, I move into consciousness, first for a few minutes, then for an hour, for two, three, until I am awake more often than not. Dr Hale tells me that for someone who was in the water as long as I was, I am lucky to be waking at all.

I told you at the start that I would spill all the secrets and that everything would be explained. But every story contains more secrets than you can know and there are always fewer explanations than you imagine.

Anna never called for help, as I asked her to. She knew it was safer to let me drown. When I did not, she and Luke (I prefer to call him by his real name these days) visited me from time to time here at the Royal London. They wanted to keep an eye on my progress and put on a show. Perhaps they felt sorry for me, though I doubt it. Dex came too, though only ever when he thought Anna and Bo wouldn't be there. When they were together, neither Anna nor Luke ever said anything, but the moment one of them left the room the other would confess. The burden of their secrets was too heavy for them. They did not know then that I had already begun to rise through the layers of consciousness, and was listening and took in everything I heard. But stories aren't evidence. And perhaps Anna and Luke knew that too.

It was Portland, not me, that did for Luke. Hours after the incident at the cliff, a local man confessed to attacking his ex-girlfriend and the Port Police released Dex. He remained a person of interest in Marika Lapska's death. The police knew all along that Marika delivered pizzas to Dex and Gav's house, because they checked her employer's records. The fact that Dex hadn't shared that information when he'd first spoken to them had made them suspicious then so they took him back in for questioning. That led to a search of Fossil Cottage which led in turn to the discovery of Luke's pills – street Rohypnol, the kind which does not colour liquids, only ever bought for one purpose and the same drug as found in Marika's blood – where I'd left them, behind the sofa, only my and Luke's fingerprints on the foil. They also found traces of the drug on a coffee mug in the room at the top with a view out across Chesil Beach. They took Luke in for questioning in London and, of course, he denied everything but they'd gone to his apartment building, checked out the CCTV, and seen Marika arriving at the building on the night of her death then leaving again not long afterwards.

Luke realised the noose was tightening that weekend on Portland. It was why he'd slipped roofies into my coffee. He was hoping I'd forget about Marika. Perhaps he was counting on me falling from my horse. Then he was hoping I would drown. Finally he was banking on my remaining in a coma. But I proved remarkably resilient. It was only when I began to show signs of emerging back into consciousness he decided he would have to kill me, but by then he was a desperate man. A few hours after he put a pillow over my head, the concierge in his block of flats saw him on CCTV in his car in the underground car park of his building, with the engine on and a length of garden hose leading from the exhaust. The concierge pulled him from the car. He went back to Dorset, to his old fossiling haunts on the Jurassic Coast. He must have grown tired of running away because he turned himself in. Perhaps he knew the police would catch up with him eventually. When he was charged with the sexual assault on Marika, police sent their digital forensic specialists in search of the Big Black Book to use as evidence, but Luke was skilled enough at the technical stuff to ensure all digital traces of it were gone. There are women out there still who might never know what happened to them when they made the fateful decision to swipe right on the profile of a cool-looking tech entrepreneur with a charming manner and a taste for expensive wine.

Julie told me that if the Group hadn't gone to Portland, the police may never have discovered the truth. They still haven't, not quite, but it is easier this way. Luke Bowen has taken the rap for Marika's death. Friends should do their best to get each other's backs. Luke himself would say that, I think. It's the least he can do.

As soon as I was able, I told the police all I knew about the events in the alleyway in the churchyard. By then they knew that Marika had gone in the water somewhere near there. They had a forensic hydrologist on it and they were sure that what happened to Marika was unlikely to be a suicide. A body is found in the Thames every week. The police know how river suicides work. People wanting to die launch themselves from bridges or buildings into the middle of the body of water, from where they know they will have less of a chance of dragging themselves out. They do not simply step off into the water, because it is too easy to get back to land. After the article appeared in the *Standard*, a passer-by came forward to say that he had seen two women fighting in the alley at Wapping Old Stairs. He had given a description of a dark-haired woman in a red dress. Police checked a newsagent's CCTV on Wapping Wall and saw Anna leading Marika towards the river. When they questioned Anna, she claimed she'd put a drunk woman into a passing cab, but searching the alleyway they found drag marks and traces of Marika's blood.

On the night of the festival police had also questioned a man named Oliver Seton who appeared at A&E with a head wound, claiming a woman called Anna had thrown a vase at him. He said he didn't know her last name, only that she was married and had a son called Ralph. The case was hardly the most urgent that night and so it languished in the police records until an officer found the time to check the apartment building's CCTV and identified Anna as the woman who had thrown the vase. It was this which spurred them to return to Wapping Old Stairs and this time, caught on an old nail at the edge of the steps, they found Anna's silk scarf and on one corner, inside the hand-rolled selvedge, preserved from the water by the fabric, a single pubic hair. It belonged to Marika.

It was Julie, the Port of Portland policewoman, who told the detectives in London that Anna hadn't called for help on Portland for more than two hours after Gav fell from the cliff. And it was Frank, the nurse, who told Anna I was waking up and noticed a flicker of panic on her face.

It must have been then that Anna and Luke hatched the plan to kill me. I became the final piece of the puzzle. The one who knew for certain what they had done. They did their research, Dr Hale said. Coming to the surface can be dangerous. The brain flips out and shuts the organs down or else sends out panicky signals to the heart. People in comas don't always make it. Sometimes they have seizures. Sometimes their hearts give out.

Not long after Luke gave himself in, the police picked up Anna. She cried and begged, and tried to play the mum card, but for once in her life, Anna's luck had run out.

There are real ravens and peregrine falcons on Portland, but Julie's laugh is a raven's cackle and when I think of her, I think of the way a falcon singles out its prey and with outstretched talons, swoops in for the kill. Fossil Cottage exists, you can find it on the internet. If you like you can rent it for holidays and weekends, though now I've told you what happened there, you might think twice. But there is a Fossil Cottage in my mind now too, one that listens and watches and sometimes groans at night and other times has conversations with owls. When I sit there in my imaginary Fossil Cottage, Marika comes to me and we talk.

I'm due to be discharged soon. Dr Hale thinks it could be tomorrow. I'll be returning to my room in the shabby flat share in Tottenham and to pizza night and rubbish telly and to the uncomplicated company of my flatmates. And it will be all the aces. Will said he'll come up and visit some time and if he does, I'll show him the view across the bus station and I'll tell him everything I've seen.

It is impossible, I have discovered, to be a bystander without becoming a witness, and to witness an act of violence is to have its dark energy work deep inside you. What we saw in the alleyway could not be unseen and in some unspoken way we understood the risk we were taking by pretending it could. Perhaps we can never really know how even our most intimate friendships will fare until they are put to the test. The centre did not hold for me and Anna and Bo and Dex, not so much because we witnessed an act of violence on a late summer evening, though that was certainly the catalyst, but because the friendship we shared had no heart.

Though I never knew Marika, she is a livelier presence

in my heart than Anna, Bo and Dex were or will be again. But Marika did not die so I could be saved. This is not one of those narratives. Her death was brutal and senseless in the way that the deaths of women at the hands of the men who feel entitled to hate them and the women who collude with their hatred always are. Marika counted not because she redeemed me, but because she was Marika. Her life has a value her death can never begin to match.

A while ago now I told you that when I was done with telling my story, when everything had been explained and the secrets were finally out, I would ask you a question. And in a while I will. Before I do, let me say I know this is the part of the story where you might expect to find out who raped Marika in that alleyway on a late summer's night – but life is sometimes more complicated than that. The statistics tell us that most rapists are repeat offenders, and that means Marika was probably not her rapist's first victim and almost certainly not the last. Rape is usually a serial crime and rapists get away with it all the time. I can only hope that the man who rammed Marika Lapska against a wall and left her like a dropped tissue in the alleyway of a churchyard is caught before he can destroy other lives but, the truth is, he is most likely still out there. Although he remains the chief culprit, in one sense, all four of us are guilty too. We saw it happening and for all our separate, dishonourable reasons, we did nothing to stop it. We are all implicated not only in Marika's rape but in her death, too. Because when a crime is committed there are no bystanders or onlookers. There are only witnesses.

And so, to that question. In fact I'm going to ask you two.

If you had been in the churchyard that night, what would you have done?

And are you sure?

ACKNOWLEDGEMENTS

A book is a team effort. Among those on my team for this one are: Jon Appleton, Claire Brett, Clio Cornish, Liz Hatherell, Louise McGrory, Lisa Milton, Kate Oakley, Joe Thomas, Darren Shoffren and the teams at HQ and HarperCollins. Matthew Marland, Peter Robinson and all at Rogers, Coleridge, White Literary Agency.

Big thanks to all.

Also to Ian Goldup for advice on the workings of the Coroner. Any errors are of course mine. Gratitude as always to Simon Booker who helps me keep it together and to the Killer Women who keep it real.

ONE PLACE. MANY STORIES

Bold, innovative and
empowering publishing.

FOLLOW US ON:

@HQStories